Melting

Tegan Phillips was diagnosed with Fibromyalgia at 16-years-old, and has used her lived experiences to convey character's struggles in fiction. After a school trip to the States, she discovered her love for ice hockey and wrote her debut novel, *Melting For You*, in the years following.

Melting for You

TEGAN PHILLIPS

hera

DK Penguin Random House

First published in the United Kingdom in 2025 by

Hera Books, an imprint of
Canelo Digital Publishing Limited,
20 Vauxhall Bridge Road,
London SW1V 2SA
United Kingdom

A Penguin Random House Company
The authorised representative in the EEA is Dorling Kindersley Verlag GmbH.
Arnulfstr. 124, 80636 Munich, Germany

A CIP catalogue record for this book is available from the British Library.

Print ISBN 978 1 83598 110 8
Ebook ISBN 978 1 83598 112 2

Printed and bound in Great Britain by Clays Ltd, Elcograf S.p.A.

Look for more great books at
www.herabooks.com | www.dk.com

1

To anyone with a chronic illness who feels like they are lesser. You deserve that big movie kind of love. Until you are ready to have your own, find it in these pages.

Prologue

Ellis

The door of the dorm clicking behind me should bring relief, but it doesn't. My muscles revolt at my movements; just a few more steps and I'll be in my room. I can be alone and suffer through the night until I can force myself to move. With each step my body screams to stop: my bones feel as though they are pushing against my skin, they want out and will do anything to get it. My back feels bruised and raw but there would be nothing to see if I looked in the mirror. All that internal pain and nothing to show for it. When I do make it to my room my feet falter.

"Hey, Sunshine." My boyfriend is lounging on my bed reading a textbook.

Liam Ruinsky, star offensive player for our university ice hockey team, is shirtless on my bed and I can't even enjoy it. Just the sight of him relaxing in my space is what pushes me off a cliff. Dropping my bag at my feet I burst into sobs. I'm not a crier. I'm a push-through kind of girl. But it's too much. I want to cry, to have someone to cry to. And now that's Liam.

"Whoa! Hey Ellis, what's wrong? Talk to me." In a flash he is off my bed pulling my body into his arms. His voice low and caring, I know him well enough to hear the panic there. I wish I could answer him, wish I had the words, but all I have is hiccups and tear-streaked cheeks. Taking my elbows gently in his hands, Liam guides me over to my bed pulling me onto his lap. He doesn't hold me tightly, too scared. Scared he might hurt me.

It just makes me cry harder. I want him to be able to squeeze me, to hold my broken pieces together, but we both know he can't. When I was diagnosed with fibromyalgia I thought everything would get better. Delusional, I assumed that when I finally had a diagnosis it would mean I could start treatment and I would be normal. What happened instead was, I'm still in constant pain. Medication can do a lot but it isn't a magic wand.

Every day I push through pain and fatigue just to try and make my life better. I wanted to make something with my life, but my body is working against me.

I was six when my dad died suddenly of a heart attack. It was a painful and unexpected loss, but I focused on my future as I grew up, he didn't get a full long life so I want to live mine fully in his honour. I thought I could use my inheritance to get myself ahead somehow. He spent so much time investing and working his way up in the real estate firm to build a solid pot for us to live with. He wanted us to be able to keep up with his peers, as well as getting an education for me. But my mother, Eleanor, had something to say about that. She lost her husband, and because of that, she thought she was entitled to all of his money. That was the first time she told me she wished I was never born. I've seen pictures of my parents when they were younger, so in love and happy. But the woman in those pictures at fancy galas is not the one that raised me. I don't think she every really wanted to be a mum. It was just the thing everyone around her was doing so she felt like she would have been an outsider if she didn't and she couldn't stand that. She was a perfect wife and for her, that meant she had to be a mother, too. Even with her lack of maternal instinct, Eleanor was hardened further by my dad's death, and I was all that was left of him. She planned to make me great, someone who, in her eyes, would be a good wife and marry rich so I wouldn't need my father's money.

But I haven't married rich, and she didn't get her money. In his will, I was his main beneficiary. I thought about giving it to her, thought that if I did she might let me be free. But it was too big of a risk. Instead, when I turned eighteen, I left her a note telling her why I was leaving and jumped on the first flight from London to Seattle. I wanted to be out of her clutches and using Dad's money was the only way I could do that. I may have gotten out from under my mum's thumb, but I'm not free. Now, instead of being ruled by her, my own body rules me instead.

Liam holds me, stroking a gentle hand through my hair in what I think is an attempt to slow my heaving breaths. He murmurs against my hair to follow his breathing.

"Ellis, please. I need you to breathe in for four," he says, worried. I try my hardest to follow along with his commands. In for four. Hold for four. Out for four. Hold for four.

"I was sat in the back row." My voice cuts between us, scratchy and strained, but Liam will hear me. He always hears me. "I couldn't get comfortable in the chair, but that isn't new. I just didn't pay any attention. I was so wrapped up in the lecture that I ignored all the signs, my leg kept twitching and my spine was on fire, but I just wanted to *push through it*, you know?"

"What happened El?" Liam's fingers keep running through my hair, grounding me.

"When the lecture ended I tried to stand up… my hips locked. I nearly screamed. For a second I forgot about my pain, just for my body to remind me that I don't get to forget." Tears fall over my cheeks as I relive it for him. "The moment my hips clicked, pain burst out of me. I must have made some sound because eyes flew to me, rows of people watching me try to walk. I had to walk down all the stairs, but my joints just wouldn't bend. I had to waddle with everyone watching me. I could feel them looking, they thought it was funny. I could hear them laughing."

"I'm so sorry El, nobody will remember by next week. It will pass." His eyes are sympathetic, but his words don't have their desired effect.

"It won't pass! Not to me. I am going to be a weirdo forever. You are too scared to even hug me properly because you think it will hurt. None of this is going to pass."

"Ellis, listen to me." Liam's voice is suddenly commanding as he tugs my hair gently to pull me away from his chest so he can meet my eyes. "You are exactly who you are meant to be. Kind, loving and so damn smart. You have been through so much and you show up every day. Even when you should rest. I know athletes that couldn't take an ounce of what you feel, but you never use it to get special treatment." He barely breathes as he rants on, "You work hard, study and smile even when you could be curled in a ball on the floor from the pain. Hell, you deal with me upset when I lose a game even though it probably seems silly. I am in awe of you. You have so much good, don't let some people who have no idea who

4

you really are make you feel like you are not everything. You *are* everything El."

By the end of his crusade I'm stunned. My tears dry and I am speechless. If I speak I will utter those three little words. Ones that are too big for Liam and I. When Liam and I started this tryst, I was clear it could never be love. In three weeks' time, Liam will enter the NHL draft and I won't follow him.

At the start he was okay with that. I don't know if it was because he thought we wouldn't get serious or if he thought I would change my mind. Now, as the draft gets closer I can see the wariness in him. A New York scout has all but told him they are picking him and he'll be taking their offer. He is moving to the other side of the country and he deserves it. Truly, he is special. He might think I'm everything, but Liam has more potential than most. He is a master on ice and he should share that with the world, even if it's going to wreck me when he walks away.

"Come with me," he whispers, as though he knows what I'm thinking. It's not the first time he has asked, but I always give him the same answer.

"I can't, you know I can't." My words are resigned.

"Ellis, I—" My hands cover his mouth. I can't hear those words. My heart is already half broken, I can't have it shatter.

"Please. Don't say it," I beg, but Liam's fingers circle my wrist pulling them away.

"I have to, I love you. I want you with me. You and hockey mean everything to me and I don't want to let you go." I can see the battle in his eyes.

"I want to build my life here, I have plans of my own. I can't throw them away." *It would just prove Eleanor right*, I think.

"Ellis, please." Now it's his turn to beg, and it slices at my weakened defences to hear him plead for me. For *us*.

"Your life is going to be amazing Liam, I know it. You will be the best player in the league. Women will want to be with you, men will want to be you. I can't stand in the way." The truth in my words hurts me more. Having fibromyalgia means I need more than most. More care, more time, there are things he won't be able to give me. He will be travelling for games, he will have to train like hell – especially when he first starts. I couldn't bear to make him feel like he isn't enough, doing enough.

"You won't be in the way, you'll be by my side."

"Being judged by millions of women who think I'm not good enough," I say, my voice shaking. "Never able to go about my day because sports reporters will be all over us, whether you win or lose." If all goes to plan, Liam will be a famous athlete, and everyone in the world will have a say in what woman he deserves. I can't listen to hundreds of people tell him how much better he could do.

"I will protect you, with everything I have. Don't make me choose." I see tears filling his eyes, I press a light kiss to his lips to distract him.

"I don't want you to choose, Liam, I want you to go to New York. I want you to win the Stanley Cup and celebrate with your team. I want you to get everything you have worked so hard for."

"I want you, too." He sighs, knowing I won't change my mind. Knowing a goodbye is near.

"I know. I wish we had more time," I admit.

"We could have forever." His voice is pained and I have to bite the inside of my cheek to keep a whimper at bay. Tears burn my eyes but I do what I can to stop them.

"It's just the wrong time," I say, with a hopeful tone; convincing myself that if we cross each other's path again one day, we might be in different places. I might be stronger, more suited to him. He will have found all of his happiness in hockey and might be ready to come back home.

There are so many things that could change, but I hope he stays the same. Kind-hearted and fiercely protective. The man I wish I was ready to love. As much as I want things to change, so much of me wishes I could freeze time in this dorm room. Despite the emotional pain knowing my heart is going to break in a few short weeks, I am happy in his arms. I will hold on to the hope that when the time is right, when we need each other the most, we will find our way back.

I will find my way back.

Chapter One

December, 10 years later

Liam

Drinking in a packed club is not my idea of a good night. Not any more. During my rookie NHL season I drank, partied a lot, and fucked even more. That got old fast. Now I'm thirty, packed bars are hell, but I don't have a choice. The team demanded my presence, so here I am.

Actually, Cassie, the Seattle Spears PR manager, demanded my presence. Told me if I want a renewed contract when mine is up at the end of next season I have to be an "active part of the team".

Outside is freezing and wet, a normal Seattle winter. I didn't miss those when I was in New York because I got to enjoy the snow. I did miss them in Vancouver, that place takes cold to another level. I'm aware of the irony: a hockey player complaining about the cold, but as I'm brutally reminded again, I'm getting older. Inside the bar is at least 90 degrees and packed to the rafters, it feels so much worse when you take up as much room as I do. Each step I take out of the bathroom bumps me into the path of another person, I give up apologising, it's too loud for them to hear my apologies anyway. Still I try to slither my 6'4 frame through gaps in the crowd to minimise collisions.

After a few more hits, I spot the table with my fellow Spears players surrounded by women. Jay Brink or "Edge", the team enforcer and my closest friend who traded with me from Vancouver two seasons ago, is sat on the outside of the fray next to the Seattle Spears captain Aiden Anders, who goes by Anders (great nickname, I'm aware), and I can see they are far from interested in the women surrounding them.

"I give it five minutes before she slaps him." Anders laughs, his southern twang stronger due to the alcohol. I don't need to follow his eyes to know they are talking about Finn Jonas, the Spears rookie sign. Rook was the number one draft pick this season and he is soaking in the fame like the kid he is. Floppy hair and a butter wouldn't melt Canadian accent help him seem innocent, but he is a wannabe ladies' man through and through.

"What d'ya think Ruin? She gonna slap him or kiss him? Fifty bucks if you're right." Edge nods in the direction of the bar and I am down to win money from my team. Despite his young age, Rook gets almost any woman he wants with his heartthrob charms. Before I pick my side I swing around to see the woman he has chosen as his prey. Long legs coming from sky-high heels, and a skin-tight red dress hugs her frame. Her body seems to go on for miles, and it's rare to see a woman so tall enhance that height with shoes that high. Then I see her beautiful face.

A rock sinks in my stomach, the room spins. I haven't seen that face in ten years and memories flood my mind. The last time I saw her my heart splintered in my chest. Now here she is again. My heart thunders in my chest when Rook steps even closer so she can hear him over the boisterous crowd.

"I'm going to kill him." I sound hoarse against the sudden dryness as I begin to move across the bar. I can hear the boys shouting after me as I go.

"Rook, get lost." I pull at Rook's shoulder. He stumbles before he looks at me as if I'm crazy.

"Oh Ruin, joining the party, eh? I didn't know you liked to share." He has the audacity to wink and it elevates my rage. Not that she notices of course. Her eyes are on me, widened with shock.

"Go find the others." I turn to face him fully so he can read the sincerity in my eyes.

"No need for the dramatics." He brushes me off with a laugh, stalking away with a false swagger. As I turn away from Rook, there she is.

Ellis Ainsley. My one that got away. Her dirty blonde hair is a lot shorter than it was a decade ago, but I already knew that. Following her on social media is an addiction; at least once a month I check to see how she is. I do it from an anonymous account, of course. Can't have my ex knowing she still owns me when I shouldn't be thinking about her at all. I do it to see if she is still as beautiful as I remember, but the camera hasn't done her justice. Her hair is not the only thing that's different. The woman before me now is a mother to a beautiful son; a business woman who owns her own florist, Bloom and Blossom, right in the city just like she dreamed. She's older, too. Not that age hasn't been kind to her, but I see the maturity in her. The small laugh lines that frame her eyes. Every little change makes her more beautiful than my fantasies remember.

"You're a caveman, you know that?" Her British accent is still strong as she interrupts my perusal. She hides her surprise of seeing me behind a teasing smile.

"You're beautiful, you know that right?" I push the conversation back to her. I *am* acting like a caveman but I want to know about her. How she has been.

"I do. Your *friend* was just telling me how beautiful I am, too." She smiles.

"How've you been?" I ask. This isn't the best place for this conversation, the music is loud and we have to lean in close to hear each other, but I revel in her proximity.

"I'm as okay as I can be. You know how it goes." She takes a sip of her drink before meeting my eyes again. "I'll never be normal but I'm okay with that." Silence falls between us. I wish her answer was different, that she could stand here and tell me that she is the strongest she has ever been, that some magical drug has stripped away her pain. It isn't realistic, but Ellis deserves one day without pain, without having to suffer so much.

"So… You're a mom?" I lean in to ask her after a moment of charged silence. I know the answer but I want to ask her about her son. Maybe ask about his dad.

"I am. He is the best thing I've done. Even if I hardly ever get a night off, he's worth it." Her face splits into a breath-taking grin. She has always been beautiful, but in the low light of the bar her smile shines all the way to her eyes. I'm speechless as I look at her glow.

"Fuck Sunshine, how do you still do that?"

"Do what?" She rolls her eyes. It reminds me of all the times she rolled her eyes at me years ago. My heart lurches and my blood heats thinking about what that sassy attitude lead to when we were younger.

"Make the world stop spinning." I shake my head. How after all these years apart she still manages to break me into pieces is lost on me, but I don't care. I also don't care that I can feel the eyes of my teammates on us. In the two years I have been back in Seattle I haven't dated anyone. I haven't even flirted and now they see me call dibs like a teenager. It's because of her. Nothing felt right about trying to date in this city if it wasn't Ellis.

"How do *you* still do that?" she asks stepping closer to me so I can hear her over the crowd, we are toe to toe and eye to eye in her heels. Her lips are painted a similar red to her dress and it is taking everything in me to tear my eyes from the way they form her words. Lips I used to know so intimately bring back memories of every time I kissed them, every time they trailed over my body.

"Do what?" My hands fall to her hips and over the noise of the crowd I can hear her breath hitch at my hands encompassing her waist.

"Make me want to kiss you," she whispers and licks her lips.

Wrapping my fingers around her wrist, I lead her towards an exit I saw earlier. I don't want to kiss her in a dirty alley but it is better than here. Here it's too loud to hear her whimpers, too crowded to feel intimate. There is also the worry that a fan might snap a picture. I wouldn't be able to forgive myself if Ellis found herself on gossip sites because I couldn't get a grip of myself.

Not paying any attention to the Staff Only sign on the door, I swing it open to see an alley filled with trash and cigarette butts. But if it means I can get Ellis's lips against mine, I can make do. I wish I could get her to a bedroom or somewhere that smells a little better. Maybe next time.

My lips are on hers with a complete fever, making up for lost time. One of my hands stays on her waist, the other buries itself in her curls. Ellis kisses me back with everything she has. The pressure of her body against mine, the sting as she nips at my lip wanting more. Once my tongue meets hers all bets are off. We wipe away the last decade as my body remembers the feeling of her body under my hands, commanding her.

I pull back, but Ellis's whines turn to moans as my lips travel over her jaw and down her throat just the way she used to like it. Based on the way her fingers tighten against my shirt I would hedge she still does. My brain says that we should stop before anyone takes pictures but my body doesn't listen. Instead I push myself tighter against her knowing she will feel my bulge trying to push against my zipper.

"Sunshine, come home with me." It isn't a question, a demand that I whisper against her jaw. There is only one way I want this night to end: Ellis laid out on my bed until the sun rises.

"Just tonight. I can only give you tonight," she pants. I thought a year was going to be enough in college, but it wasn't. I'm not sure if one more night will satiate my fire. But I'm willing to find out.

Chapter Two

Ellis

This is a terrible idea.

But how can I say no? I told myself I was imagining Liam when I saw him across the room, it was a flash of him in the crowd and I convinced myself I was imagining him. Why would he be interested in approaching me? We were in a bar full of other beautiful women who *weren't* his ex, so he had no reason to notice me. But there was no mistaking it: the way he walked, the sound of his voice. It was Liam.

He is looking at me like he craves me after all these years, but that's how he must look at all the girls. With his following, he can't be short of options. But to feel this desired one more time, I can't pass that up. Not many people want to commit to the woman with no spare time and bucket-loads of emotional baggage. But as Liam slides into a taxi besides me I can feel the waves of desire coming off him.

"Fuck, I've missed the sounds you make," he murmurs against my jaw, goose bumps cover my arms.

"One night Liam," I say again. I don't know who I am trying to convince. Mister Big Shot NHL isn't going to want more than one night with me. For him, this is just convenience, or nostalgia, but for me it's a night of freedom from all my responsibilities. Lyndsey, my best friend and only employee, is opening the shop tomorrow and was more than happy to take care of my son, Jack, overnight. Plus, one more night with Liam… It's too hard to resist.

"I want your number El." His voice is low and his eyes intense, his gaze makes me squirm in my seat.

"There's no need," I remind him. This can only be tonight.

"Ten, nine, eight…" He starts to count down, smirking at me as though he has won. But I'm not the same girl he once knew. His threat of an impending spanking just excites me.

"You can't just count down to get what you want any more," I laugh, but the sound is uneasy. My mind feels empty from having his lips on mine.

"Seven, six, five…"

"What? You get to one and I get a spanking, I'll just enjoy it." I keep my voice low to avoid allowing the taxi driver to hear every part of our sordid conversation. I kiss Liam again, hoping it will distract him enough to drop it.

He pulls his lips from mine, throwing his head back against the seat of the taxi. "Jesus Ellis, you drive me crazy. I want your number before we get out of this car."

"Just kiss me instead," I whine.

"Nope." His voice is light. The opposite to mine. "Not until I have your new number." His eyes shine with satisfaction. I want him, he knows it. And if giving him my number is what it takes, then fine. I guess he can have it.

"Jesus Liam, fine!" I snatch his phone from his hand, I think for a split second about putting in a fake number, but knowing my luck he will call it now to make sure it works. Needing his hands and lips on me again, I jab my

15

number in and toss it back at him. "Now kiss me. *Just* for tonight."

"If that's what you'll give me." He kisses me again as the car stops.

Scrambling out of the door in the dark, I can't make out much of the house. I know I'm not going to be spending a lot of time here. One thing I do see is the white rendered concrete wall beside his front door as Liam pins me against it while he gets out his keys. He fumbles with the lock, finally opening the door and ushering me inside. I am barely through the doorway before my dress is bunched around my waist and his hands are palming my ass cheeks.

"I'm going to count down and if you don't get upstairs and in my bed before I get to one, I'll turn this ass as red as your dress." He spanks me lightly to get the point across, but I know he isn't bluffing.

"We're playing games again now? I told you, I'll like it." I raise an eyebrow, my heart thumping.

"Let's see who wins." He winks at me.

I hesitate. "Wait I don't know where your room is?" I glance behind me at the staircase.

"Then you better run quick Sunshine. Ten, nine…"

A part of me was looking forward to a slower look around Liam's home. There are only a few lights on so I can't see the details of the rooms. I can see trophies on shelves and a large brown sectional, but the little parts that would make it his are a blur to me. After all this time apart, I want to see who he has become. How much he has changed. Or is he the same boy I've always known? The same one I fell so hard for once upon a time.

I want to pretend that he is, just for now; I want to pretend we're both the people we were. Teenage puppy love, no worries except our finals and each other to lean on no matter what we had to face. But there's no time to snoop around as I kick my heels off and take for the stairs even though it is a win—win for me, either way I get great sex just with or without a spanking. Tonight, I would choose without, I'm too desperate to wait. It has been a few months since I last had sex and a few more still since I had *good* sex.

From downstairs I hear Liam getting closer to zero, and I know if he finds me before I find his bedroom he will live up to his name. Liam "Ruin" Ruinsky is going to ruin me, if he hasn't already. That damn nickname always seemed so childish to me but seeing him now as a man with more muscles than I could count it suits him more. I can imagine the fear in opposing players' eyes when they have to come stick to stick with him.

Salvation comes to me in the form of the third closed door I peer into as he shouts "One" from the base of the stairs, his footsteps thunder around the house but I've found it. The first room was a towel closet and the one next to that was a large marble-covered bathroom but this is his room, I know it as soon as I step in. Dark grey walls and floor-to-ceiling windows frame the four-poster bed. I know it isn't a guest room because of the broken hockey stick from his final college game pinned to the wall.

Out of the corner of my eye I see him run from around the corner. I launch myself onto his bed, kicking my dress off as I go. I silently praise myself for having worn a matching underwear set. Though I originally went out with no real intentions of anyone seeing it, Liam changed that mindset quite quickly. He always had that ability. By the time he makes it to his room I'm in nothing but the black lace set. Both of us are breathing hard, but the slow smirk that flashes over his face when he finds me makes me breathe harder still.

"Now that is a beautiful sight," he says, leaning his hands on the crossbar of the door frame scanning me from head to toe, not rushing himself. "Shame I'm going to have to mess it all up." His strides are slow as he walks to the edge of the bed but my heart is still racing, my eyes are bouncing all over his body. It doesn't matter that I am near naked and he is fully clothed, because I know what's underneath is going to be worth it. Before I manage to get in my own head about how much my body has changed over the years, Liam grabs me by the ankles and tugs me down the bed.

The thud of his knees hitting the plush carpet wipes every thought out of my head except for anticipation. Mr Ruinsky loved to eat me out. It was like he could never get enough, he would say that he played better if he could still taste me when he stepped out onto the ice. And who was I to fight that? I was a twenty-year-old who had never gotten head before. Now he looks up at me once again from between my thighs, his eyes half lidded as he nuzzles against my thigh inhaling as though he's found the sweetest aroma. Always a tease, he pulls my underwear down my legs slowly. He has all the time in the world apparently, not the one night I have promised.

"Liam, do something. God, please I need it," I beg aimlessly into the otherwise silent room.

"So sweet when you beg Sunshine." He smirks, finally pulling my underwear off completely, tucking them into his jeans pocket.

With his eyes still locked onto mine he dives in, licking me from bottom to top. Once he has a taste it unleashes something. I don't know if it is from years apart or if he has developed even more love for eating pussy, but he lets out a growl before burying his head between my thighs. He makes a mess of me, his tongue fucking into me for a few seconds before switching to licking and sucking at my clit. The sounds of him lapping at me mix with the moans I fail to hold back. One of my hands threads into his hair, he moans against me as I tug on his longer locks and the vibration of the sound triggers the first wave of my orgasm. I am on the cusp and he can tell because he slides two of his long fingers into me as my thighs begin to shake around him.

While I recover I enjoy the view as Liam pulls his shirt over his head and finally unbuttons his jeans. He must be uncomfortable, his dick is big and those jeans are so tight I'm surprised he even has enough blood in his brain to stand, never mind anything else. I gather enough sense to unhook my bra. I might come again just from the way his eyes drop to my chest and he licks his lips. *Why* does he have to be so sexy? How does he still have this effect on me after all this time?

Liam drops his boxers and my heart starts to thump again. I had convinced myself that I was exaggerating when I thought about his dick over the years, that I was tricking myself with blind nostalgia. But I was right. The man is as hung as I remember. As he starts to crawl over me, I back myself up the bed until I hit the plush pillows, throwing myself down amongst them. The warmth of his skin sends shivers over me as he gets closer.

"Do I need a condom?" he asks, his voice a whisper against my heated skin.

"No, I'm on the pill," I tell him. Perhaps a reckless decision, but I still trust Liam – I know that if he thought for a second he has an STI he wouldn't suggest this, so I give him the go-ahead. I can't wait a moment longer.

Once his weight settles between my thighs I have a sudden moment of clarity. *This is probably a very stupid idea*, I think to myself, *he's still your ex.* But before I can give it enough thought, Liam lifts my thigh over his hip and notches his cock into me. There are no thoughts in my mind other than Liam. His dark eyes are my only warning as he thrusts, stealing the air out of me.

"Fuck Ellis, you're so wet for me," he says, his arms shaking beside my head from the force of staying still until I am used to his size. I squirm beneath him, adjusting myself until I find my hips moving naturally against him.

I can feel all of my muscles starting to relax while he starts to rock his hips in time with mine before he starts to fuck me harder. Faster. Deeper. He is fucking me as though my body has always been his. I wonder if a part of that is true. Nobody has been able to reach as deep in me as Liam.

"Liam, don't stop. You feel so good. Ah fuck." I babble as I bring my other leg to wrap around his waist digging my feet into the base of his spine.

He groans against the heated skin of my neck between his kisses and bites. I'm way too old to have a hickey, but it feels way too good to tell him to stop.

He pounds into me from above, but I tug on his hair to pull him from my neck just to see his face. Without slowing his hips, he snakes one of his hands down my body, circling his fingers around my clit. I wanted to watch his face but the power in his eyes is more than I was expecting, than I can take. There is something in them that I don't have the capacity to place, but it seems dangerously close to longing. His cock hitting my G spot and his fingers on my clit throw me over the cliff into my second orgasm. There is a telltale feeling of him throbbing inside of me before he slams himself as close as possible before coming inside of me.

He regains some strength, breathing deeply on top of me. With a final, guttural sigh, Liam rolls us both over so that we are lying facing each other, my thigh still hitched over his hip, still buried inside me. I can see Liam is trying to find some words to say, but I have forgotten every word I have ever known.

"I know it's just one night El, but at least stay until the morning?" His words break the silence. I couldn't turn him down if I tried, so I nod.

I know if it's going to be one night, I'm going to make it count. I don't know when I will get another night like this. After three more rounds: one in the shower, one against the bathroom wall and another in the bed, Liam falls asleep while I lay on his chest. I know I said I would give him until morning, but if I don't leave now I'm not sure I ever will.

Just like I did ten years ago, I leave him again. Quietly, I tap away at the Uber app on my phone, patiently, nervously tracking the driver. Years ago, I left him with the shreds of my heart and a bright future ahead of him. Back then, I wanted to see him succeed and I know he couldn't have done that with me hanging around. I told myself that if anything is truly meant to be, then we would find each other. But this doesn't feel like how I imagined. I thought our lives would be simpler. He would have retired and be ready to settle down, I would have my pain in order. We would finally be perfect and we could ride off into the sunset. I don't want to be here when he realises that this one night of fun was all he wanted. I don't think

I would survive the "it's been fun, I'll call you sometime" conversation.

Even as my mind screams at me to go back upstairs, to stay at his side for just a few more hours, my heart knows it would hurt too badly. I pause downstairs, opening a couple kitchen drawers quietly until I come across a notepad and a handful of pens. I scribble quickly as I notice headlights approaching outside, my hand shaking slightly with indecision:

> *It was good to see you.*
> *I'll miss you.*
> *Sorry for sneaking out, but I guess I've got to*
> *go back to real life.*
> *Your Sunshine x*

Chapter Three

January

Ellis

Every morning when I wake up there is a second of peace. Where I am not in pain, where I don't have to make decisions. There's a split second where my only problem is getting out of my toasty bed when I know it is going to be cold. That's when I remember everything else. The hundred things I have to do, for my business, for my son. The list is never-ending. Then I have to assess my pain: will I be able to go about my life with my baseline problems, or will I have to dose up on painkillers and hand over a bunch of responsibilities to my employee and friend Lyndsey?

This morning I am pleasantly surprised. My bones click as I stretch but there is no thundering pain in my joints or blinding burning in my muscles. Well, no more than usual. Still, just like every day for the past few weeks my full night's sleep hasn't been enough.

Pushing myself out of the bed, sliding my feet into the nearest pair of socks to warm them up, I trudge to the bathroom. Dodging kids' toys and a selection of rubber ducks, I flip on the shower head. I have a little bit of time before I have to wake Jack up; my kid can sleep like the dead. It's handy when there are things I want to get on with in the morning, but a nightmare when I need him to be up for kindergarten. I started setting my own alarm even earlier to accommodate his tossing and turning and refusal to wake up into my routine.

As the warm water falls over my skin, washing away the cold of the early morning, I feel my body unclench. My head drops down so my chin rests against my chest, stretching my muscles as the warm water makes them more pliable. It's instant relief, but I know once the shower turns off the lack of pain won't last for long. Every bit of my skin pinks under the steaming water and I tip my blonde hair into the stream, washing it hastily, knowing that if I stay here much longer I won't want to leave the comfort. As soon as I am towelled off I wrap myself in a dressing gown to go for the first attempt at waking my son.

"Jack bub, it's time to wake up." My voice is sweet but it doesn't rouse a flicker from him. He hums back at me in affirmation but I know him well enough to know he didn't hear me. I walk into his room and push the curtains back to bring some of the morning light into the pale blue space, but apart from a small whine Jack doesn't make any moves to wake up.

Leaving him for a few more minutes, I wander back into my bedroom, throwing on my clothes for the day. Being the owner of my own florist means I can wear pretty much anything. I'm never going to turn up in a mini dress and heels, but as long as I can stretch to high shelves and bend down to low ones without flashing my underwear, anything is acceptable. I settle on a pair of black leggings and a large jumper that gives me room to move but will keep me warm in the wintery Seattle weather. Lyndsey always looks so put together. Her ginger hair is always perfectly curled and her clothes look so classy even on a budget; even if she were wearing leggings and a jumper I am sure she would find a way to make it look elevated in a way I can't.

When I first interviewed her, I thought we wouldn't click. She looked so well-established, all while being four years younger than me. But she proved me wrong pretty quick. To be frank, behind the perfect clothes she is just as much of a mess as me, hence why we clicked. It brings some levity to a workday to share stories of her crazy dating life and my life being a single mum. She has never judged me on my limitations and I don't think my life would run as smoothly as it does if I hadn't found her.

"Jack! I'm making breakfast!" I shout in a singsong voice as I walk down the corridor back past his room and into the open kitchen living space of our flat. I am not exactly a master chef, but there are a few things I have perfected; waffles are one of them. I add eggs to the powder mix, as Jack yells after me, "Five more minutes!" his voice muffled where I know he is burying it into his pillow. He acts more like a teenager than a five-year-old most days. I don't like thinking about how much he is growing, but it is glaringly obvious when I pack the lunch I made last night. My baby is in school and it almost kills me.

The smell of the waffles on the griddle rouses Jack finally as he comes trudging down the hallway with his little blue train blanket clutched in his hand. Maybe there is still some of my little boy there.

After clambering up onto one of the bar stools at the breakfast nook, Jack bundles the blanket up into a makeshift pillow and plonks his head on top. His lack of early bird traits reminds me of his dad, my ex-boyfriend, Michael. He too was a nightmare in the morning. God forbid you wanted to ask him something before his coffee. As long as Jack is where he needs to be on time, and he continues to be the kind kid I know he is, I will let him have his power naps.

When you have kids, you have to pick your battles. Recently, I have been too exhausted to fight any that I won't win. Having fibromyalgia comes with chronic fatigue and I'm just too drained to argue with him when it isn't causing any harm. Lately, my fatigue has reached a peak, my mind has been under so much stress that it is punishing me in a physical way. Giving Jack his plate of two waffles with pre-chopped fruit and some apple juice, I think back to when this stress started.

I don't have to think for long. December. Ever since that night, my mind has moved a mile a minute running through everything. He tried calling me for a few days, but I never picked up. Just because I gave in to giving him my number doesn't mean I was ever willing to reply. I think it was just the fact that I slipped out hurt his ego. He isn't used to hearing no. A small part of my brain wanted to answer. That bit of me that still believes in fairy-tales wanted to run into his arms and believe that we are meant to be together, that seeing him that night was fate. I don't believe in fairy-tales any more.

I'm a mum. I can't go around throwing myself at men hoping for a relationship, I have too much to think about. Jack has to be my priority, not getting my rocks off. That night was amazing but it was just that: one night. Though the stress relief of a few good strong orgasms was amazing. I was all but walking on clouds for days after-wards. Lyndsey pushed and pushed wanting every detail, but I just told her half-truths. I told her I met a hockey player and he brought me to his place. I just left out our history. I wouldn't be able to deal with the judgment in her eyes, sleeping with an ex is never a good idea. He is an ex for a reason and I don't need her to remind me of that.

Liam and I are different people in different places in our lives. He is at the top of his game, women screaming his name, throwing their panties at him in the street. That just isn't something I could expose Jack to. That is, if Liam would even want to see me again. It was one great night, he has probably had a bunch of one-night stands in his life. Hell, he's probably had some since ours. Not that I blame him, he doesn't owe me anything, but that is just the truth. He doesn't want to be shackled to a single mum. I let him go ten years ago because I didn't want to hold him back and that still stands.

I just have to get my heart to remember that. I knew I was fooling myself when I said one night would be enough. A little bit of Liam would never be enough, the chemistry between us is wild. I thought there would be a learning curve when we got into bed but it all clicked into place. Even with all the years apart, with all the other people we have had in our lives, we still just worked. The minute he had his hands on me, my body was flashed back to ten years ago. As though there hadn't been any time away, our bodies recognised each other. It was fireworks. But just like fireworks, they are good for a bright beautiful display but they fizzle out. They aren't meant to last.

Jack scrapes his chair backwards and wanders off to get dressed, leaving me in the kitchen, my own breakfast untouched. I shovel some waffle into my mouth as I clean up the mess.

As I grab his bag, I swing by the calendar on the side of the fridge to check if he has everything he needs for today. Last time I forgot to check, he was the only kid without a show-and-tell. Mum guilt was strong that day, seeing his sad little face come out of the gates wrecked me. I won't make that mistake again, so I check down the list. But it's something else that catches my eye.

My period is three days late.

My period is like clockwork.

Fuck.

My mind reels thinking about when my last period ended. I never forget to take my pill, I know I haven't missed a day. I take it at the same time as my last round of painkillers every day and I sure as hell never forget them.

Then it comes back in flashes. Me laying on the bathroom floor heaving into the toilet. Jack had picked up a bug in school and I caught it. The burden of comforting your sick kid is that the germs are in your face too. I wasn't sick for as long as him, maybe a day and a half but that's enough isn't it? I pull out my phone to google. Maybe vomiting only affects the effectiveness of your contraceptive if you're ill for a week? God, let me be wrong. I can't be pregnant. But Google proves my fears, vomiting can make your pill ineffective, and that damn illness ended days before my one-night stand.

I was on the pill. The pill just wasn't on me.

"Mum, we have to gooooooo." Jack tugs on the hem of my jumper and my eyes snap to him. I have to take my kid to school and open Bloom and Blossom, I don't have time to think about the high possibility that I'm with child. That will have to be a nightmare for later.

But as I throw my jacket on, I have a gut feeling. I'm going to be a mum to two and I'm going to have to use Liam's number after all.

Chapter Four

Ellis

This isn't the first time I have sat on the blue tiled floor of my bathroom. It won't be the last time either, but this time, my world is shifting. The many other times I've sat on this floor since I moved into this two-bedroom flat I haven't taken the time to notice my surroundings; I am usually too busy overthinking and spiralling to notice the state of the room. I locked myself in a different bathroom before Jack was born, that's how I found out I was going to be a mum for the first time.

I held that pregnancy test in my hand and the stark white of the freshly painted walls hurt more than the burning of tears of when I learned I was going to be a mum. Today, Jack's tiny five-year-old fists are banging against the door, a constant little reminder of the bomb that is about to detonate.

When I don't feel like I'm winning at life or at the single mum game, this little room has become my tiled sanctuary. Today I am definitely not winning. Reality is that I have to face the music at some point; being a single mum is hard, but a disabled single mum of two feels like a different story altogether.

The little white stick in the sink waits for me. I sit on the floor where my long legs can't stretch out fully without hitting something. I've tried to distract myself but I can't help but look at all the ways this room has aged since I moved here. It's a lot less white now and the bathtub is rimmed with toys. Frankly, it could do with scrubbing in here, but there isn't time left in my day.

The steady banging on the door synchronises with the hammering of my incoming headache as I finally reach for the pregnancy test. My heart skips a beat.

Those two lines can't be denied: I'm pregnant. With Liam's baby. *Shit*.

"Mummy, I need to gooooooo!" Jack's little voice sings from under the door.

"Damn, you must really need to pee with all that banging," I say with sarcasm that rolls right over his little dark brown waves, leaning to open the door.

"Yup, and I didn't think you were gonna open the door. You need to be quicker, Mum," he says as he hustles to use the toilet; I can see so much of myself in him. The way he rolls his eyes, the way his tongue sticks out when he is concentrating. My little shadow.

When Jack was first born and his hair started to grow darker, it hurt my soul a little bit. I was the parent that had carried him and the only parent that was going to be raising him, and yet he is the perfect carbon copy of his dad. How dare his absent parent get the honour to have my son look just like him.

I have approximately thirty seconds before he wants to wash his hands and sees the little problem I am hiding in the basin. I stuff it up the sleeve of my oversized hoodie and turn to get his stepping stool so he can reach the taps.

In the mirror above the sink, the woman looking back at me is distorted by smudges and water marks. My short blonde hair is flat and unwashed and the blue rings under

31

my eyes look more akin to a Tim Burton cartoon than a real human. The closer I look, the more haggard I seem. The lines in my forehead seem more pronounced and my lips are cracked beyond belief. Just last month at the bar I had felt beautiful, but now I can't remember if I actually looked it or just felt it under Liam's gaze. He always had this knack for making me feel just *more*.

Prettier. Smarter. Stronger.

Unbeknownst to me, while I have been cataloguing my flaws, Jack has left me to my own devices and has gone back to his remaining moments of screen time before dinner. Dinner that I have yet to start cooking. Dinner that I don't think I'm going to start cooking anytime soon. Pizza it is, I guess.

With dinner confirmed, my thoughts turn back to Liam. I know I have to tell him. But I can't help but remember how this ordeal went last time.

In short, Jack's dad Michael was a dick. He was always a dick. Frankly, I'm not sure why I thought he would act any less *dick*-ish when I told him I was pregnant. My young heart wanted to believe he would take me in his arms and spin me around like in the movies and shout the news from the rooftops. Instead it was a lot of yelling, swearing, and him demanding a paternity test even though we had been exclusively dating for a year and a half. Apparently when he said we were exclusive, to him that meant coming home to my bed every night but had no jurisdiction on what he did during the day. Or should I say *who* he did during the day.

In the end, he was unwilling to be in Jack's life and I couldn't argue that I wanted him there. Five years later and there has not been a dime of child support or a birthday card. I don't even know where the man lives any more. Which is probably a good thing.

Still, I know I'm one of the lucky ones, getting my business degree and opening my own flower shop with what was left of my savings has not been a yellow brick road, but it was *my* road and I thank my stars every day that it has been enough to support Jack and I.

When I started renting my little shop front, I never could have thought that it would be able to support me and my son: but it turns out everyone needs flowers. A bouquet to say sorry. A bouquet to say I love you. A bouquet to throw to your bridesmaids. In a way, I get to be a small part of all those things, I get to see the smiles my flowers give to people and it makes each second of pain worth it.

That little shop was the reason I was out at all the night I bumped into Liam. A regular customer had been flirting for a while but he was not my type, seemed quite full of himself really, but after a few weeks of him coming in to ask about me and flowers, he asked me out again. Lyndsey said I had to go. That five years is enough time to be single and even if this man wasn't my forever, I needed to get back on the horse. So I ignored his massive ego and I ignored the red flag of him wanting to go to a club for our date. What I couldn't ignore though was twenty minutes after we got inside the club, he was making out with some girl outside the bathrooms.

I should have left but something in me wanted to stay, to show him I didn't care. Then lo and behold Finn Jonas makes his way over and everything spiralled from there. If I had just gone home, who knows where I would be now.

It's no use to think about what I could have done. Instead I think about what I can do moving forward: I could terminate. It would be easier on my body, better for my routine. But the thought of it flits out of my mind as quickly as it entered. A woman has all rights over her own body, and despite the hardships ahead – I don't think I can make that decision.

Jack will be an amazing big brother. But if I really do this, I have to be ready to go back to the beginning. Midnight feeds, no matter how much pain I'm in. Every nappy change, no matter how big and smelly it might be. Constant crying; not just from the baby but from me too.

Having a baby is overwhelming, but from somewhere deep inside me, especially remembering holding Jack for the first time… I want to do this. Having a big family has been a dream since long before my diagnosis and I have already let it take so much from my life, I won't let it take this too.

I touch my stomach gently as I retrace the missed calls history in my phone log.

"Hi Liam, it's me," I whisper.

"El… Well, look at that, I never thought you would call me back." I can hear the smirk through the phone. It kills me to be the one to wipe it from his face, he might never offer it to me again.

"Yeah, it's… look, we need to talk."

Chapter Five

Ellis

My sweaty hands are shaking so violently I trap them between my knees for a moment of relief. Moments like this are supposed to be happy but instead I can still taste acid in the back of my throat after my latest trip to the bathroom. It could be morning sickness but I think it is anxiety. Seeing those two little lines after I've been in a committed relationship for less than two years shouldn't make me this scared, but every second that ticks by as I wait for Michael to come home seems endless.

When the front door of Michael's – or rather, our – flat opens, my heart pounds in my chest.

"No kiss? You're slacking Ellis." His voice fills the silence as I sit across the room from him. The only reason I'm not greeting him is because when I try to stand my knees buckle.

"Michael, we need to talk," I reply.

"I've just come home Ellis, can a man have one fucking minute?" His tone is full of warning, but today I need him to listen.

"Michael, please." I beckon him to the sofa. He lets out a sigh moving closer but I push through: "I'm pregnant."

Without missing a beat, he responds, "Who's the dad?" He sounds disinterested, but his unyielding glare sends chills over me.

"What?" I ask, sucking in a shaking breath.

"Tell me, who's the dad?"

"You are!" I exclaim with him towering over me.

He scoffs. "Don't lie, I always wear protection. I want a paternity test." His skin flushes red. One vein on the side of his forehead starts to protrude an ugly purple colour.

"I haven't slept with anyone else for nearly two years Michael, I wouldn't cheat." I want to soothe the situation. When he calms down from this he'll be happier. He'll hold me and kiss me, apologise for his outburst. It's the only way we can get through this.

"Oh please, don't try to tell me you've been faithful." He rolls his eyes.

"You want a life with me, right? Why don't you trust me?"

"I don't want to waste my life like this, I have plans. Fuck!" He lets out a bitter laugh. "You know you're not the only woman in my life, right?"

"Excuse me?" My whole body stills, breath catching in my chest. He must be lying. Trying to hurt me because I ambushed him, he loves me. He's always said he does.

"Oh, come on Ellis, we both knew what this was. Neither of us wanted the baggage. Now you're knocked up and want to lie to my face and tell me it's mine! You must think I'm stupid." His venom blasts against my skin, as much as I want to believe he's lying, I don't. Tears spring to my eyes, I feel so small on the sofa in front of him.

"It is yours! I'm not sleeping with other people. Tell me you're lying, please." I beg. "I thought what was between us meant more to you."

"Get rid of it."

—

I sit up in bed. The nightmare still fresh. The memory making me feel ill.

When I was pregnant with Jack, I had recurring nightmares of that day constantly. I didn't realise how bad the relationship was until I was alone. Completely alone. When Michael kicked me out I had no one to turn to. When we first started dating I had some friends, but Michael didn't like them. He hated how they would update me on Liam's career, said that they were disrespecting him and our relationship by bringing up my ex. I understood his grievances, so I tried to make him comfortable. When I chose to start distancing myself from them, I didn't realise I was going to lose them completely.

I don't blame my friends, though. They got a hundred no's when they invited me places. I would have stopped trying too.

The only thing that kept me from going back to Michael was Jack. On the day I was closest to calling him again, Jack kicked for the first time. Those little flutters pushed me to stay away. I wanted my son to have a good life, not one where he had to tiptoe around his father's emotions.

I lie in bed looking at the moon through a crack in my blinds. I have to do it all over again – tell someone I'm pregnant – and not know what I might get in return. Liam is expecting me tomorrow but I didn't tell him anything more, I couldn't do it over the phone.

For now, I push my nightmare to one side, preparing myself to face it once again.

Chapter Six

Liam

My house has never been this clean. I'm pretty sure it wasn't this clean when I bought the place three years ago. Every single large window along the right-hand wall is streak free, the hardwood floors are polished and smooth. My home is no bachelor pad, but it is still not where I wanted it in terms of decoration. There always seems to be something missing from each room, more art or another rug. Just *something* to make it feel like home. Still, every shelf has been emptied and dusted before being filled with trinkets again, pictures from childhood and my high school trophies lining the shelves. When my parents retired to Florida it was either I display them here or they go into storage. I didn't like the idea that just because it's old it doesn't have value.

In the past eighteen hours and twenty-three minutes since El called me I have scrubbed the whole place top to bottom. Twice. I have vacuumed every carpet and rug, even upstairs. I spent time on my hands and knees at six a.m. this morning cleaning between the bathroom tiles. Until yesterday I don't think I even realised how big this place is, it was just the one that felt most like home when the realtor showed it to me. Now five bedrooms and three bathrooms feels excessive, especially when two of those bedrooms aren't furnished because nobody's ever used them.

Usually, I don't get nervous. I don't get nervous on the ice. So far, women haven't made me nervous. Ellis Ainsley makes me nervous, though. She was the only one who did all those years ago in school and she still does now. Something about her biting sass just makes my bones itch. I guess in the same way some people feel butterflies, I get the bone itches. I sound insane even to myself, but that is the only way to describe the feeling: El makes my bones want to crawl out of my skin so badly that it made me want to clean. To make my space worthy.

When she was here last month it wasn't deep cleaned, but then I never expected to see her, let alone have the pleasure of having her in my space. Not to mention that it was the middle of the night, it's not like she was taking a good look around. But this time I want her to be impressed; I want her to notice the brown leather couch I had made especially for the main room – something I added because I wanted it to feel warmer than my team's bachelor pads, filled with blacks and greys. I have area rugs and pictures on the walls. This is my home, and I want Ellis to see me as a grown man now; not the little college boy who should have fought harder for her.

I know the boys would find this beyond funny, Ruin being given the run around by a woman. But she is not just any woman, Ellis was my dream woman. I still have to remind myself that our relationship was a long time ago. Now I wonder if too much has changed, and if I'm not the kind of man she'd want any more. Or maybe she has changed beyond what I knew her to be. But from that night we had, she felt the same.

Back in school, and even now given my career, women come to me without much effort. Something about the "bad boy" vibes with the dark longish hair and dark eyes, I guess. I knew the image I was giving off and I ran with it. But El didn't fall for that bullshit. My leather jacket was just a jacket to her and my smirk only made her arch her brows. From the minute I met her I knew I was smitten.

Getting my degree was not at the top of my priority list back then; all I had cared about was getting to the draft. But as soon as I spotted her tall frame from across lecture hall 320 for our first business seminar I knew I was going to start showing up to class more. It was my mom who made me promise to go to college and I could never break a promise to her. Meeting Ellis just made the promise a little bit easier to keep. Knowing I would see her if I turned up made waking up early worth it, even if I did it hungover.

I didn't approach her vying for sex or follow her around campus, I just knew I only had one year left with her in my life each week and I wanted as much of her as I could to tide me over for the rest of time. Dramatic college mind set aside, I was basically right. As soon as we graduated, she couldn't split us up quick enough and I knew it was going to happen. El was never quiet about her intentions to date me until I was drafted, but I had convinced myself I could change her mind. But there is no changing Ellis Ainsley's mind once she has it made up.

Ever mature and level-headed, she was right. Of course, she was right. If El told you something, she was giving you her word. If she told you something, it was her truth and there was nothing that would change it. I was drafted to the other side of the country to New York and I had the best four years there. If the distance hadn't broken us, the fame would have done it. I am mature enough to admit that I let it all go to my head, having millions of people screaming my name and women flashing me in the halls of the arena. From New York to Vancouver and now back in Seattle, it was a fucked-up dream that got old quickly. I still love the sport, but the pageantry was a novelty.

Admittedly when I heard I was being traded back home, Ellis was in the top five first thoughts I had. And she was not thought four or five. Stupid really, because I know we're in different points in our lives.

Watching her body change as she shared pictures online when she was having Jack was like a spiritual experience, I followed it so closely Edge thought that either she was a celebrity or that I was the dad. Both of which he found hysterical. When I explained she was my one that got away, he just felt sad for me, which was a million times worse. At least he was someone I could trust not to tell the rest of the guys. I didn't need any sympathy, I was happy for her.

Did I wonder why the dad wasn't in any of the pictures? Of course I did. Did I think about trying to get in touch with her to ask? Only once. But in my defence I was very drunk and we had just lost to LA, which sucked because do they even have ice in LA? It was just a sudden huge shift; her page went from couples pictures, dates and flowers to baby bumps with no man by her side. I'd always wondered how anyone could mess up so badly.

I know I need to focus on today and her impending visit that has been driving me up the wall all night long. I barely slept because I couldn't stop thinking about if I had time to mow the lawn in the morning, only to remember it's January so there is no fresh grass to cut. I've only eaten three meals instead of my usual five, and if my nutritionist hears about it he would be force-feeding me pasta before I could blink.

So, the house is in model home condition for the first time since it was actually a model home, and I am a pacing mess while waiting for her – now thinking that I should have gone to pick up groceries in case she is hungry. I offered to take her out for lunch but she insisted she had to speak to me here, in private. Which I think means we are not about to have sex? I'm not entirely sure. She might want to come here specifically because she liked the bedroom, but her voice was heavy with something that screamed we will not be having a sex repeat. There was also the fact she was clearly breaking her routine to do this and that only occurred on very special occasions.

Ellis has always been headstrong and her routine is a part of that, I always assumed it was because when she flared up her life felt so out of her own hands that she had to do what she could to regain that control. Her life would crumble when her fibromyalgia would rear its ugly head. One day she would be in a small amount of pain, enough relief to walk through the day with her head held high, and the next for seemingly no reason she would buckle. The pain was so bad it would cause her to vomit, to shake, to beg for it to stop.

There was nothing I could do. Hell, I was useless and no matter how much someone tries to google, it never offers all the answers. Especially with chronic illness, it is so personal and subjective that the things I read were often no help at all. I was a twenty-year-old guy just trying to graduate and become an adult, and Ellis had – still has – so much more to think about. If staying at home and reading is what helped her feel safe when the world was on her shoulders, then who was I to tell her to change? Yet she is doing it today.

From the moment ten years ago when I saw those long blonde curls bouncing around the room, I've been attracted to Ellis. Surely finding her again in December had to mean something? Yes, we were in the same city for the first time in a while, but I've been playing in Seattle for the past two seasons – still, seeing her was a surprise to me.

But I have no proper window into her current life; I've only seen her son through pictures online, but he somehow reminds me of her. And I can see she's done everything to raise him well, despite her own upbringing.

My childhood was different than hers. Both of my parents showered me with love. My mom was always open with affection and the perfect shoulder to cry on when things didn't go my way. On the other hand, my dad was subtler; it might have been because of his tougher Russian upbringing – hence the name Ruinsky. But as much as he loved me, he found it harder to show it. When I started playing hockey he found a way to connect with me. He played as a kid in Moscow, and seeing me on the ice reminded him of his childhood. Being the son of an immigrant made me want to fight harder; I wasn't just living life for me, I'm living it for everything that was given up for me.

I've never met my paternal grandparents. When they found out my dad was marrying an American they demanded he come back home. He chose my mom, of course. I want to make sure his sacrifice was worth it. He might not hug me like Mom does – but he laced up my skates, drove me hours to away games, and showed me he loved me in a million other ways. He wanted me to be strong when it was needed and my mom wanted me to have a softness in my heart. I owe it to them to be the best of both. Ellis, too, used to help me harness that strength when I felt weak.

I felt it again in that bar. Have those feelings really stood the test of time?

Knock. Knock. Knock.

The noise at my door interrupts my thoughts, which I open to a dishevelled looking Ellis. Her hair is thrown into a pony as she dons grey sweats.

"Hello there, beautiful." I smile, leaning my arm across the top bar of the door frame, I want to play it cool, but her eyes appear glassy and far off. My smile fades quickly.

"I'm not ready. Not yet. I need more time." She rambled the whispers more to herself than to me.

"Okay... take your time. I'm not going anywhere." I try to comfort her even though I'm completely lost, not moving from my place against the door jamb. Her eyebrows are furrowed and her lips are bitten red raw. I can't help but stare at them and the way they are opening and closing as she tries to find the right words. After a few seconds of her eyes bouncing anywhere but my face, they finally land there. Her gaze holds mine and the rest of the world stops spinning as we stare unabashedly. I feel myself soften from the inside out.

"Don't do that." She huffs before scrunching her nose – the way she always did when she was overthinking or uncomfortable. It's strange just how much I remember about this woman. I remember *her*. I remember how I've held this woman as she cried about her frustration and pain, and she has held me while I mourned a broken heart after a bad loss on the ice.

"Do what?" I ask with concern.

44

"Look at me with those stupid, beautiful bedroom eyes," she snaps up at me. But it's hard to not laugh at her obvious annoyance when she mentions *bedroom eyes*.

"Oh sorry, I'll just pop them out." I say deadpan down at her, stepping to the side to welcome her in.

"Don't do that either," she chastises.

"What did I do now?" I ask as my eyebrows fly to my hairline.

"You almost made me laugh and I don't have it in me to laugh today," she says, finally stepping through the door and stopping for a brief moment. For one small second I think she is going to hug me, but she doesn't. She walks into the living room and sits down on the couch – only to stand again and start pacing a hole in my white shag rug.

This isn't the woman I recognise. Ellis was always the one who was put together, even when things were bothering her. When finals season was coming up she had spreadsheets and flashcards, and I was the one last-minute cram studying in the library up until two a.m. every night. She didn't even seem this stressed when she thought she was going to have to drop out because her mother kept calling her non-stop for the first time in years and she feared Eleanor was actually going to show up in Seattle.

I don't have a lot of practice when it comes to being the rock in the room. On the ice that's Anders job – and he tends to carry that role off the ice too. He is the best captain I could have asked for, and for the past two and a half years he has made it a point to include me in the team antics. It helps that Edge and I transferred here together from Vancouver, and it probably helps that I know all the best bars to drink after a game where we won't be hounded by fans.

This though, I am not practised in. Being the steady person in a time of crisis is not my role in life. My role is the silent flirty type who makes things better by smirking and charming everyone in the room. But that never worked on El in college and judging by the look on her face, it sure as hell isn't going to work now.

Just from watching her I can feel myself spiralling again. Someone has to do something and it has to be me. I walk over to the pacing path Ellis is running in my living room floor and wait for her to start back towards me again. When she does, I'm ready to catch her and lightly hold her elbows. Her eyes are rimmed red.

If she's truly in crisis, why has she turned to me? She never answered my previous calls, and she was so adamant about only spending a single night together. I'm certain there are people she is closer to whom she would rather lean on, so why come to her ex? Why now?

"Ellis, what's wrong?" I ask while she moves to start pacing again.

"I can't just blurt it out." She gasps as if I'm asking her to do something absurd.

"Rip the Band-Aid off El."

"They're called plasters, silly American." She chokes out between her heavy breaths, I can't help but laugh because *there* she is. Full of sarcasm and wit.

"Liam I'm pregnant. You're going to be a dad." Her hands fly to her mouth as soon as the words slip past.

Then silence.

Nothing but silence.

Strangling, deafening, charged silence.

Chapter Seven

Ellis

"*You're going to be a dad.*"

Why the hell did I say it like that? I had a whole speech prepared in my car. Not only was I prepared, but I had rehearsed it when I sat in the driveway for twenty minutes before knocking. But no! I ignored all the prep work I did and instead just blurted out the words like some inexperienced teenager, never mind an adult with a business.

Liam is going to hate me and kick me out of his home, I'm sure of it. That's the main reason I got myself so tongue-tied in the first place. Why does his place have to be this fancy? It looks like a ready-made home straight out of a magazine and I am supposed to behave like a *mature controlled woman*. Not a chance, the man has what look like *very* expensive sconces for crying out loud. This is not some bachelor pad, it's a house where I can picture a family. Therein lies the problem: I saw it and pictured our family here.

Our family? It's ludicrous. But I'd love to have a home like this. I can see Jack's bike on the path. A little row of shoes by the door arranged in size order. I can feel myself melting. I blame the hormones. I give it two more seconds before he comes to his senses and throws me out and wishes he never let me in the door today – or last month for that matter.

I'm waiting for the scenes to begin when Liam's body falls to the couch behind him. The sound of him hitting the surface seems to echo through the space around us. After that, all I can hear is my heartbeat thumping. He touches a hand to his temple.

"You mean it? You're pregnant? Have you spoken to a doctor?" His eyes are filled with bewilderment as he stares at my body stuck in place. From his position, his eyes are level with my belly button.

"Liam," I begin, but I don't know how to follow it up. There should be yelling and panic, but instead there is steady silence filled only with heavy breathing. When I don't answer his questions, he looks up to my eyes again.

"I have an appointment in a few days, but I'm sure. I haven't slept with anyone else, I swear to you," I explain. Liam nods, allowing his gaze to drop back to my stomach.

"We're going to have a baby, El?" His tone is serious as his eyes flick up to mine before he rises from the sofa, striding back to where I stand. "Thank you… for trusting me with this," he says softly, pulling me into his arms. He buries his head in the crook of my neck.

I'm almost paralysed with shock. There should be some kind of fight. I expected at least some more questions, definitely not *thanks*. Why is he thanking me? You don't thank a decade-old flame for a one-night stand.

"Why do you seem… *happy*?" The words feel heavy on my tongue, and even heavier once they are in the air.

"Are you not? If you don't want his baby I–I'll under-stand. It's your choice. I should have asked first." He pulls back, shaking his head. "Fuck. I'm doing this all wrong."

"I don't know exactly how to feel, I guess I just expected something different," I reply. Liam's eyes have a glow that I hadn't noticed until now. Have I been wrong about him? Maybe he isn't the aloof womaniser I worried he would be now that he's famous. Even when he had a bad boy attitude back in the day he was still a great guy. Sometimes he was too scared to show it.

I wanted Liam to stay the same when we broke up. But maybe this version, matured and experienced, is something better than I imagined.

"Ellis, you know I'll support you. I care about you, even if we are technically exes…" His voice trails off slightly. "But if that isn't what you want, I will support that too. Having two kids is a lot of work and if you don't think your body can handle being pregnant… Or shit, if you just don't want this baby right now, I will be right there with you. Just tell me what you need." His words become a ramble as I drop my head to his chest and the tears begin to flow.

"I want to keep the baby." I muster the courage to say. "I thought about it all, I thought about Jack… But how can you want this? You have a life and a career and you are so busy, it's the middle of the hockey season and I just dropped this bomb on you." I speak into his jumper.

"You want to do this, so we're doing this. Don't worry about hockey, we can figure that out as we go." He strokes my hair as he continues. "We need to put you first, not hockey. I know the team will offer whatever support we need…" He stops for a moment, and I wonder what he's thinking. I processed my emotions alone in my bathroom. But in real time, I'm watching Liam do the same, wondering who he's going to tell, and how. How his life will change. What this means for both of us.

"I suppose we need diapers," he says quietly.

"They're called nappies," I squeak.

"Shut it, little Brit." He chuckles. "I think you should sit down," he suggests, directing us both back to the couch. He takes me in his arms again when we flop down. "There's a lot we need to talk about El." I look up at him, waiting for him to begin.

"We might have to figure out if we are going to raise the little one to be British or American." He raises an eyebrow jokingly.

"British, we came first," I say decisively.

"Well, *you* sure did," Liam quips.

Clocking onto his reference, I scrunch my nose. "Liam, oh my god." His eyes are still shining, now with a tint of lust. "You're a pain in my arse." I pause, biting the inside of my lip. "Are we going to be okay?" I ask. "Co-parenting is hard for a couple who are actually dating, all we did was sleep together."

I want us to be okay, but our lives are going to be tied together forever once we get up from this couch. My biggest fear is that he will one day hate me for dropping my life onto him and bulldozing the future he had pictured for himself. Having a baby is a lot of work, but I come with my own little family already and I don't think Liam is ready for everything that is going to bring his way.

We can't be more than co-parents; it just wouldn't work. Between his travelling, my florist business, Jack's needs, my own health… it would be a headache to even think about aligning our schedules to form a relationship again. I need to keep that wall between us, for both of our sakes. Even if we did date again, I can't take another possible heartbreak. How could I care for two children while mending my disappointment? I can't let my selfish desire to kiss him again cloud what is best for the baby.

"You don't know Jack, and it's been a long time since we spent time together. *Real* time. There is going to be crying. Not just the baby, me too. I cry a lot these days," I admit on a watery hiccup.

"I'll have to step up to it then, won't I?" he confirms. "For the baby and even for Jack. But for now, I think we should stop catastrophising and talk about the next steps." He shifts on the couch, sitting up slightly. "If you want us to figure out how parenting is going to work for us, you need to let me help where I can. You know more than me when it comes to babies, so I want to follow your lead. It's your body, I want to support you."

For once, I'm the one with the expert knowledge. Liam must remember how much I enjoy being in control. It's why I run my life on a schedule, it makes the pain easier if I don't have to think about the rest of my life as well. Meaning when I got pregnant the first time around I made sure to read every book under the sun that even mentioned pregnancy or birth. I joined a bunch of forums so I knew I was getting the real information and not just psychobabble about how I was going to glow and that the whole thing was going to be sunshine and rainbows.

Over the next two hours I relay all of the information he is going to need. At least for the first few months. I save the gorier details for another day, maybe when he starts to annoy me I will show him that diagram that shows how big ten centimetres really is just to see him squirm.

As I talk, I can't help but smile watching him learn. Big bad Liam Ruinsky sat like a schoolboy on his couch with wide brown eyes, taking notes in his phone, while I ramble on and on about getting an appointment with my ob-gyn, and about how far along it will be before we hear a heartbeat, or find out the gender, about swollen feet and cravings.

I also tell him about how fucking scared I am. Having Jack wasn't all fun and games. Pregnancy and fibromyalgia don't exactly mix. In fact, they are oil and water. I tried so hard to hide how much I was suffering last time so other mothers around me wouldn't think I was going to be a terrible mum. But Liam is going to see it all. To see me not be able to stand unsupported for more than a few minutes, to see me shake because it's taking that much out of me to do simple tasks like brushing my teeth. He will see me wearing sandals in rainy Seattle because I can't bend over to tie my shoes, even before my belly starts to get in the way.

"And what about Jack?" he interjects. "If you're in too much pain, should I be put on his pick-up list for emergencies?" He's hesitant as he finishes his sentence.

I struggle to hold back the tears again.

This time I cry for twenty-five-year-old me who was pregnant for the first time with no family around her, who just wanted a hug and was instead kicked out of her cheating boyfriend's apartment. I cry for Jack who has never had anyone other than me put him first or think about his well-being. I cry for our little baby, the one that is going to have their dad to help them no matter what happens between me and Liam.

I fall into his arms to cry as the realisation hits that until today I didn't have anyone to hold me. But that isn't the case any more.

Liam will catch me.

Chapter Eight

February

Ellis

Despite their purpose, hospitals have never made me feel safe and secure. From the bright white walls that shine a light on all the harsh realities of illness to the painfully uncomfortable chairs that punish you for needing them… it all creates an atmosphere that fills me with trepidation.

My body has been aching all day. The combination of chronic pain with the pains of early pregnancy is already prevalent without the added uncomfortable chairs. This wait is like a small torture on my body. It is a reminder of the things my body had to endure the last time I was pregnant, the things I'm going to have to face again.

Posters line the walls around me; I suppose to give the room some much needed colour. But instead they just add to the doomsday feeling that ruminates around waiting rooms. Back as a kid in England I would have taken the time to read all of the signs, but I'm not the naive young girl I once was. No more do I bother with filling my mind with the anxiety-inducing statements about cancer scares or take the time to remind myself that the hospital staff will not take abuse from patients. The posters in my current waiting room are slightly different, highlighting the joys of growing a child, not that I have to read them to know. I remember them from when I was carrying Jack. All those years ago I needed the medical jargon to lose myself in, to hide from the fact I was alone and scared and so lonely.

Realistically, I have been alone most of my life. My mother, or as she demands to be called by her daughter, *Eleanor*, was never a nurturing woman. She wanted to have a sophisticated, high-brow, young English lady. She seemingly forgot she lived in Reading in the early Nineties and not Victorian London. After my dad died of a heart attack she was even more highly strung, but she was the only parent I had. Dad died when I was so young that my memories of him are very lacking; when I think back on my childhood it is her I remember.

I wore what she told me and attended the best private schools, but all I learned was how to climb out of my bedroom window without detection. I also learned that men are pigs, even little teenage private school boys. Frankly, they were probably worse; because along with raging hormones and huge egos that must have been compensating for *something*, there was the added entitlement of being daddy's little boy who is going to inherit millions of pounds without working a day in their life. Basically, they were insufferable future prime ministers who wanted women to kiss their feet without doing any of the groundwork. You would think with a (supposedly) high-value education I would have picked better boyfriends over the years, but I still managed to pick the worst of the crop multiple times.

If I were a different – maybe better – person, I could attribute all the good I have achieved for myself to Eleanor's child-rearing, but I am not a liar. Me getting an education was not her priority, she wanted me to *appear* educated so that I would appeal to her peers as a possible future daughter-in-law. Everything was a storm, from running from my old life, to starting anew in Seattle. But then I met Liam in university, and I was found again.

Until that, too, had to inevitably come to a heart-breaking end. Life, as it always does, continued on. Since then, I ran a catalogue of heartbreaks – including Jack's father. That loneliness was different. It was deeper, all-consuming. I was growing a baby, but I had not a soul to tell; no friends or acquaintances left.

Coming home to an empty flat day after day was the second worst time of my life. Living in dark rooms that were cold both figuratively and literally because I refused to use my gas to cut down my bills.

Then came the hospital appointments. Sitting in the prenatal waiting rooms with all the happy, expectant couples huddled over big bumps with smiles as blinding white as the walls. I know that in my soul they must have been having their own issues, but from where I was sat, I felt like a leper, cast off to the side of the room for being a single mum with nobody to hold my hand when I was listening for a heartbeat. There was no one to talk to about whether or not we were going to find out the biological sex of the baby: it was just me.

This time should be different. I told myself if I ever got pregnant again I wouldn't be as alone, I would have a support system and be in a healthy relationship. But today it's just me and Jack. Again.

I *do* have Liam, but he had to travel to an away game in Las Vegas. Though he has demanded that from the moment the nurses call my name I must FaceTime him so he can be in the room. I could see on his face when the first scan date was booked that it hurt him.

It's a scary thought, to think how much he might miss because of his games. I don't want to look at it is a bad omen – that the first scan lined up with him being away. But a small part of me worries this is a sign of things to come.

It's an unfair thing to think, it's just one scan. A scan that's taking place earlier than usual, due to the medication I take. My ob-gyn wanted to make sure the baby is okay, given that I was still taking non-pregnancy-safe pain relief for weeks into this pregnancy. If the first scan was at the usual point, around twelve weeks, then Liam would have been here. He apologised and apologised relentlessly; so desperate to let me know he would love nothing more than to be holding my hand.

A month ago, babies would have been the last thing on his mind. And now his world is revolving around one. A part of me feels bad for forbidding him from telling his team about the baby yet, but I know it's too soon. I just worry that by making him keep it a secret I am subjecting him to the same loneliness I felt. The Seattle Spears are his support system and he will want to lean on his team for support, especially being on the other side of the country.

We did call his parents though, Tracy and Alek. To be specific, he called them while I listened in from beside him. I didn't even want to be in the room. I begged for him to call them when I wasn't around but he assured me they would be ecstatic about becoming grandparents. I was reasonably worried about what they would think about him, about me. Would they look down on me because I hurt him in the past? Would they admonish him for being foolish enough to sleep with an ex? I didn't want to be by his side when they scolded him, pretending to be happy about the news.

They retired a few years ago to Florida in a home Liam bought for them with his first transfer bonus when he traded to Vancouver. They are proud of their son, but to them it could have looked like he was moving backwards instead of looking to the bright future parents want for their kid.

They were surprisingly supportive of the news. Understandably confused and shocked at first. But once it settled in, they began gushing about finally becoming grandparents and asking him if they could fly up to meet me and Jack before the baby is born. But Liam gave them a non-committal answer. I was grateful to not be put on the spot. It was strange to hear a mother so excited about her son's one-night stand getting pregnant, but I guess it helped that I'm not a complete stranger to them.

We met a few times when Liam and I dated, so there was probably some relief that I'm not just around Liam for his athlete status. Still, I wonder if they called him after the fact to ask more questions. To interrogate him about me and my intentions. But I've had to remember that not all parents are like mine. Some are genuinely happy for and supportive of their children, no matter what. It's refreshing to see, and now I know exactly where Liam gets it from. I saw it especially when Liam met Jack, and it somehow didn't go horribly wrong. As I sat twiddling my thumbs in the waiting room, I run the event over in my mind.

–

"Mum, come look at my train!" I can hear Jack yelling but my brain just can't focus. So many thoughts are running through my head, I can't keep still. I pace in front of the front door, my mind whirling a mile a minute.

"Mum!" Jack yells, clearly unimpressed by the lack of attention I'm giving him.

"Sorry, what's up, bud?" I wander over to where he's set up his newest train set on the living room rug. I sit on the couch but as soon as I do I bounce back up, unable to relax.

"Why do you keep walking around?" Jack quizzes me. I wish I had an answer, but how do you explain to a five-year-old that you are so anxious that your hands have started to sweat and your mouth feels so dry it is hard to talk?

"Just got a lot of energy to shake off, my friend is coming over remember?" I tell him. I explained before that Liam is an old friend from school who I haven't seen in a long time. I don't like lying to Jack – actually, I hate it. But I'm also not going to dump all of my history with Liam on his little shoulders. He is going to be in Jack's life for a long time, and I need Jack to like him.

"I didn't know that grown-ups had play dates. Is he fun?" There's that childhood innocence again. He's half right. It was a damn play date that got us all into this mess.

Knock. Knock. Knock.

"Here we go," I mumble to myself, knowing it's Liam behind the door. I take one last large breath as I swing it open. And there he is. Liam is wearing a pair of loose-fitting black jeans and a tight grey T-shirt, the perfect picture of muscle and smiles.

"Hey Sunshine, how you feeling?" he asks, eyes scanning me from head to toe, cataloguing all the small changes that have happened since the last time he saw me. I'm not showing really, but my boobs have definitely swollen. I wonder if he notices as his eyes pause there for a second longer than usual.

"I feel sick," I tell him truthfully.

"Oh no, has morning sickness kicked in?" He comes forward placing a hand on my shoulder, digging his fingers into the tight muscles there.

"Yes, but also I'm just anxious about this." I melt under his fingertips. He gives me a small smile continuing to massage me slightly. When I finally give him a smile in return, he drops his hand to pick up a bag from between his feet that I didn't notice yet.

"I bought Jack something," he tells me, straightening back up.

"Liam, you can't bribe him," I tell him, tired. I don't know what I expected. Liam is using his money to get his way. I should have known he would try this but this can't be how this goes. I need him to try and get to know my son, not buy him with building blocks.

"I know!" he interrupts me, jumping to his explanation. "That's why I'm giving them to you and not him, if you want you can hide it and give it to him some other time, but I saw it and bought it without thinking."

"Oh." I'm not often lost for words, but that is really thoughtful.

"Don't sound so surprised." He laughs, his eyes darting into my flat. Only then do I remember we are still stood in my doorway.

"Sorry, come on in." I finally step out of his way shutting the door behind him, it's time to get this over with. "Jack! Come here, bud."

Jack comes running from his train set, sliding to a stop at Liam's feet.

"Do you like trains?" Jack asks bluntly, staring down at his feet.

"Jack!" I chastise. "We introduce ourselves first."

"Right. Sorry." My son holds out his hand for Liam to shake, and I see Liam's shoulders shake up and down with suppressed laughter. "Nice to meet you, I'm Jack. Do you like trains?" he repeats.

"Hi Jack, I'm Liam and yes, I love trains!" Liam gives Jack a magazine-worthy smile.

"Cool!" Jack nods taking Liam's hand and dragging him into the front room before tugging him down to sit next to his train set.

The pair of them sit together for over an hour, and Liam listens to Jack tell him everything he knows about trains. Which is a lot. Liam tells Jack about the model train set his dad helped build as a kid. Jack's eyes are full of awe looking up at Liam and my heart splutters. Seeing them getting along is everything I needed, but never expected. I thought it would be stilted, that they would feel awkward around each other, but I should have expected Liam to win him over. It's clearly not just women he has a way with, we can add kids to that list too.

My mind still can't be quiet. What does this all mean for us? Will Jack be jealous when the new baby arrives, and Liam isn't just his play-date buddy – but his own sibling's father? Is it going to confuse him? Or confuse me, even?

–

As I think over the first meeting between Liam and Jack, I'm reminded of how much I appreciated having Liam there when I first told Jack he was going to have a sibling. I think in some messed-up way, I wanted to prove to my son that I could pick a man who wanted to be around. That I wasn't going to make the same mistake twice.

Realistically, I know Jack won't really have noticed yet how much not having his dad around will affect him. He is still so young, but I think having Liam by my side for that chat was a way for me – for *us* – to show a united front. As Jack meets other kids, watches them get on their dad's shoulders and play sports together, I know one day he'll want the same. And again, I won't be enough for him.

"Mummy what is a feet-us?" Jack's little voice breaks me out of my head as he points at a poster on the wall next to him.

"It's what the baby is called when it's still in my belly, when they are still growing." I made a foolish promise to my son while we were alone in that delivery room that I would always answer his questions with as much honesty as I could, and it has been one promise I have tried my hardest not to break. The problem with that is Jack sure knows how to ask questions that I don't know how to answer. *Where do stars live? What does yellow taste like? Why does Tom have two dads and I don't have any?* They should warn you about all the questions your kid is going to ask in those *Parenting for Dummies* books but they don't – I checked.

"Oh, so where—" *please don't ask were babies come from please please please,* "is Liam going to be when we call him?"

I gasp a sigh of relief. "I'm not sure, maybe in his hotel or at the rink getting ready. His game isn't until tonight though, so he promised he would be waiting for us." Jack hasn't asked too many questions about Liam yet, but I know he's mulling them over. I'd love to be inside his infant mind and see how he perceives this whole situation. I wonder if it's any clearer than my own.

"Miss Ainsley?" A nurse in pink scrubs calls for me from down a corridor. I actively try to avoid looking at the other expecting mothers as I pass because I know I will find nothing but pity in their eyes: a woman having to bring her son to a baby scan because she has nobody to look after him for a few hours. Usually my neighbour

Mrs Lewis would look after him, but she has gone to Montana to visit her sister. She has been someone I have connected with over the years, when I have to work of a weekend or if he has to stay off school because he doesn't feel well. She is always happy to have the company. I feel the eyes around the room watching, so to distract my mind from the feeling of being watched so closely I pull out my phone and call Liam. He answers on the first ring.

"Hey, we going in already?" His voice is low and calming, through the phone I feel his support. It fills my bones all the way from Vegas but beneath the question I hear the tremor in his voice. I nod in response. He must be freaked out. He has been far too calm over the last two and a half weeks, an anchor to my spiral – pulling me back into the real world. But it's new to him; becoming a dad isn't easy, and it's not like he planned for this, especially not with me.

I let Jack hold my phone, keeping Liam on the line, while a nurse takes my blood sample. I settle onto the bed where Jack hands me my phone back, and I get my first real look at Liam. His hair looks wet from a shower or a sweaty practice session, and I can see he is lying amongst the plethora of pillows in his hotel room bed, a complete opposite to the one I'm lying on.

"You okay, El?" he asks.

"Yeah. I just wish you were here," I admit. Something about being in this hospital again with my still flat belly out must be making me more vulnerable than I anticipated, because I never planned on telling him that. Maybe it was reminiscing in the waiting room about being alone that tipped me over.

"El—" Liam starts, but is interrupted by my ob-gyn coming into the room. Dr Horne was my doctor when I had Jack and it was a no-brainer for me to come back to her this time around. She was a rock in the room when I needed that support and there is no other doctor I would want to help deliver this baby.

"It is Ellis, yes?" Dr Horne asks.

"Yes, hi," I reply quietly.

"It's good to see you again, so: are you ready to see how it's going?" she asks with a smile. It takes her a second to notice Jack sat so patiently in the chair next to me, but when she does her smile doubles. "And this young man must be Jack," she says as she glances at my notes. "You ready to be a big brother?" she asks in a faux serious tone that my son falls for straight away.

"Yes ma'am, I'm ready, I have to be gentle and kind when the baby comes but Mummy said if I am just myself then the baby will love me because I am easy to love," Jack speaks with so much conviction you would think he was under oath. My eyes mist at the sight of my little baby boy looking so grown up and excited.

"You, young man, are going to do just fine. So, who do we have on FaceTime?" she quizzes, eyeing my phone a little sceptically as though she were worried about asking. But Jack must still think he is under the spotlight because he tells her.

"That's Liam, he is the baby's dad but he isn't my dad… but that's okay, because I have Mummy to be my dad." I grit my teeth to swallow the lump in my throat as I turn the phone for Liam to introduce himself to Dr Horne. I hesitate for a second – she could recognise him as a star ice hockey player and let it overshadow the appointment, but it would be rude to not allow him so much as a hello.

Even if I want to keep him to myself for a little while, there is an ever-present fear that word will get out. People

63

will find out that Liam Ruinsky has gotten me pregnant. As much as I wish we could keep it a secret forever, that wouldn't be fair to either of us, nor realistic. I do see a spark of recognition in her eyes when she fully takes in my phone screen, but ever the professional she doesn't ask. Instead she moves her eyes back up to me with a small nod before moving the ultrasound wand and the jelly to my awaiting stomach.

"You know the drill mom – I'm just going to talk it through for the boys. So, there won't be a lot to see here so far because you are still so early on, we are estimating around seven weeks since conception. But with your medical history and fibromyalgia, we just want to be sure we have a viable pregnancy and detectable heartbeat, especially with the medication you are taking – it's better to be safe and check now rather than later," she explains delicately.

Viable pregnancy. The words ring in my ears, I barely hear the rest of her sentence as those words echo around my mind. It's a clinical, terrifying question to pose. Is this cluster of cells going to become life, or will my body potentially fail me? Am I enough to host a baby? If anything is wrong, is it my fault? Will Liam grow to resent me and my body even more if I fail? These are the questions I've asked myself since seeing those two lines on the pregnancy test. The computer screen whooshes and warps around the room and the three of us all sit in silence waiting for her to talk again. I don't know if Jack is waiting on tenterhooks like Liam and me but he is quiet as a mouse.

It takes the doctor a few minutes to find the right spot as she firmly pushes the ultrasound probe against my stomach. It's uncomfortable against my bladder after I was told to drink as much as I could before the appointment.

"Okay, here we are." Dr Horne spins the screen around to face me. I hold my phone up so that Liam will also see the little black blob that will be our child. "The baby looks to be the right size for seven weeks, around six millimetres, so still itsy-bitsy, but they are going to start growing faster and faster," she explains. "Stay very still for me now, you're still very early so it might not be as easy to find…" She seems to trail off as I follow her instructions.

She squeezes the probe tighter against my belly while she frowns at the screen. Liam is silent on the other end of the call, but I wonder if he's thinking the same as me. *Why is she frowning? Is everything okay? Why do I need to be still?*

As I begin to spiral, Dr Horne looks at me with a reassuring smile. Behind her on the screen are waves flowing underneath the image of my uterus, dramatically large and rhythmic. She twists a dial near her lap, and suddenly the waves are connected to a thumping sound. *Dun-dun, du-dun.* "That's the heartbeat there," she tells us.

"That—that's our baby?" Liam's voice is quiet coming through the phone, but I hear him over everything else. I turn the phone around so we can see each other, but the sight that I find would knock me off my feet if I were standing. Liam has tears streaming down his reddened cheeks, his lip is quivering. There is so much hope and excitement on his face that he looks as though he was just handed a star plucked right from the sky. "Fuck, Sunshine, that's our baby." He says, wiping his hand down his face to clear the tears but just as quickly more fill his eyes.

"That's our baby." I am nodding like a bobble head. It's the only part of my body I can seem to move. I wanted this time to be different, and despite being in that waiting room without him, it is.

On a fundamental level, something is very different; this baby is *ours*, not just mine. Liam wants this baby. He wants to be here.

Liam is more than making it different.

He's making it better.

Chapter Nine

Liam

Other than getting drafted into the NHL, I've never had some grand life plan. From the first time I had skates on my feet I knew I had found my calling. But beyond making that a reality there was not much else I dreamed of.

As a kid my heart beat for getting on the ice. The rush of scoring, the adrenalin of having people wearing my number eight on their jersey and knowing they were putting their faith in me. Nothing has felt better than my first official game as a rookie in New York all those years ago. Until I saw that little black blob on the computer screen this morning.

Coming back to Seattle felt like a step back. I thought by playing for the Spears I was giving up on my dreams of travelling the US and seeing the world. A stupid thought when really I *am* travelling now just as much as I did in New York and Vancouver, but I guess something about being at home again felt wrong. It felt like perhaps I was reverting back. But I suppose something bigger was at play than just my career. Fate was bringing me back home so I could find a way forward, so I could find something worth moving forward for.

There's no denying that I'm scared. Scared for Ellis especially. Being pregnant is scary for most people, but for her it's going to be even harder, and I have to step up. Jack is going to need support when Ellis is in pain, so I'll need to be there for him too. All this while trying to keep the Spears winning, I'm going to be pulled in one hundred different directions.

With my thoughts running wild, it's no surprise to me that my body is still buzzing with electricity when I make it to the arena in Vegas. Suited up, I feel constricted in the tailored fabric, but rules are rules. It was not unlike me as a rookie to walk into the locker room with enough ego to fill the seats, but today, something feels different. There is a distraction pulling me away. I'm having a goddamn baby. I'm going to be a dad.

"Afternoon boys, we ready to play some hockey?" I yell as I walk in, hiding my fear and anxiety behind a confident bravado.

Rook sniggers. "Who are you and where is Ruin?" he says as he stands on a bench blasting terrible dance music.

"Hello to you too, Rook," I reply. With my current mood, and the attitude from Rook, I'm determined to push any negative thoughts to the back of mind. I think about my future baby – what would that kid want me to do?

Suddenly, Rook's shitty music taste is actually not so horrible. Still sucks, but I could dance. So I do.

Edge takes notice and looks at me as though I lost my mind. He knows me well enough to know there has to be something behind my change in behaviour. But Rook shrugs and joins in.

"Ruin I swear to god, you best not be enjoying this shit with Rook right now, because I don't think I could handle two of you." Edge glares at the two of us, but it just makes me dance harder to push the focus onto him. Before I know it, I'm up on the bench next to my favourite rookie in the NHL trying to twerk. If Ellis could see me now she might rethink our co-parenting arrangement.

"What the *fuck* is happening?" Anders's voice comes from the doorway. Rook jumps from the bench, leaving me lonely and twerking. A very sad sight. I have gone so far in trying to seem normal that now it feels impossible to rein it back in.

"Don't know, Cap," Rook begins. "I think Ruin might have gotten laid, eh? He might finally be over Ellis, no more quiet brooding like Edge." Rook laughs as I throw my shoe at him. My heart beats fast when they mention Ellis. They are too close to the truth for comfort.

"Well, I haven't ever seen you like this." Anders raises a suspicious brow at me, but now I want to guide the conversation away from Ellis.

"*Nothing has happened*, I just needed some time to get over her. She meant a lot to me. Let's change the subject." I jump down to the floor and walk to Anders and Rook.

Edge joins us over from the bench. "Can you try to make it look like you are getting ready for a game?" he urges.

Before I can find an inconspicuous reply, Anders grabs me by the elbow and pulls me into an unused corner of the room.

"Liam what the hell is going on with you?" he asks, an accusatory tone in his voice.

"Is it so crazy that I might just be happy?" I ask, frustrated I might have pushed myself to seem so calm that I tipped the scales in the wrong direction. I may not be made of rainbows, but I didn't realise the team saw me as some downer the last few weeks.

Anders narrows his brows. "Dude there is happy then there's *this*. You're completely out of character right before a game. Have you been drinking?" His words shock me. Does he really think I would do that?

"What? Fuck, no, I wouldn't drink on game day. You know that. You know me. Where is this coming from?" Anger rises in my voice as the rest of the team continues to get ready amongst themselves, oblivious to our conversation.

Anders leans closer, speaking in a hushed pitch. "I love you, you know that. But you have been kind of a mess since everything with Ellis, and then the last few weeks you have been super quiet… now suddenly you're on top of the world. It doesn't make sense."

I can't deny his logic. Ellis left me with a shitty note and wouldn't answer my calls; I wasn't going to ambush her at work, so I lost her again. If he thinks I've been bad now, he should have seen me when I first traded to New York, I was a mess. The only time I didn't drink was before a game.

"Shit, I know I've been different but I didn't think it was that noticeable. I mean we have still been winning. I didn't think you would care." My words are bullshit, even to me. Of course he cares. Anders cares too much for his own good, though it is what makes him a good leader for our team.

"Ruin, of course I care. I'm not just the captain, I'm your friend, right? Talk to me." His eyes have softened and are full of genuine care. He's right to be suspicious. I wish I could tell him everything. In the two years I have been back here I have spent more time with these men than I have with anyone else; and not just training. Anders and Edge, even Rook, are a big part of my life. I want to lean on them now. But I agreed with Ellis that we would wait.

"She'll kill me," I say. My heart is screaming for me to tell him. Just him, no one else has to know.

"Who?" He asks.

"Ellis." I grimace. *I'm going to tell him*. My mind is already made up. I just hope she will forgive me.

"You have been speaking to Ellis?" he asks. *Say yes. Say yes. Just say yes.*

"More than that." The words leave my mouth before I have time for regret.

"What do you mean, more than that?" Anders's pitiful expression has turned to one of pure confusion.

I take in a deep breath before revealing the biggest weight on my shoulders: "She's pregnant."

I've never actually said the words out loud. I told my parents "We're having a baby." But Ellis Ainsley is pregnant right now. I saw the blob baby myself.

Anders couldn't suppress his small gasp. "I'll be damned. You're serious?" His jaw is nearly mopping the locker-room floor. His voice is tight and concerned. I can't blame him for the reaction. Sometimes I think I should be more worried or shocked.

"Nope. She's having a baby. *We* are having a baby. My baby."

"Wait, you're gonna be a dad?!" I shudder at the sound of Rook's voice reverberating across the room. It's already too late – news is out. I should have noticed his music had stopped, but I was so engrossed in telling Anders that I wouldn't have noticed an earthquake.

"I'm going to kill him," I seethe.

"Rook, shut your mouth!" Anders warns. Better him than me. If he says anything stupid, I might live up to my threat.

"What? I didn't know it was a secret, eh!" His voice goes up an octave in defence, and if I didn't want to kill him I might laugh.

"That's because you're an idiot." Edge joins in the chaos. I don't know how much he heard, but this is definitely enough for Ellis to kill me. She's a charming Brit with a butter-wouldn't-melt smile – I think she would get away with it.

"If this gets back to Ellis – that you all know – she will put my balls in a blender," I admit after a blanket of silence falls over the room. I silently thank every deity out there that it's only the four of us in here right now, because if the whole team finds out then it will almost immediately be told to their wives and girlfriends, and the whole of Seattle will know before the plane even leaves Vegas.

Edge's face spreads with shock-horror at the sound of Ellis's name, but he quickly shakes it off before continuing, "Forget Ellis for one second, Cassie is going to kill you when she finds out."

He has a point. Cassie Fitzgerald is the head of Spears PR and she scares the shit out of me. Five foot of pure rage, she gives the coaches a run for their money when it comes to who can keep us in line.

"Well, Cassie doesn't need to know anything yet, got it? I want to talk to Ellis about everything first, tell her what to expect from the public." I give them each a pointed look as they all nod their agreement.

"Just between us here. Is this happy news or not so happy news?" Edge asks.

"Good news, right? Isn't that obvious?" I snap back, going right on the defensive. I understand his question, but I never want to think of this as anything but good.

"Okay, you know I had to ask," he tells me, placing a hand on my shoulder to calm me. But I know they'll be wondering more to themselves.

"And before any of you ask, yes, the baby is mine. Ellis wouldn't lie about that. Everything... lines up," I assert. They can ask questions about my own morals and choices, but I won't have them accusing Ellis of anything. They might not know her, but if she is half the woman I remember she would never dream of lying about something like this.

"Then we're happy for you Ruin. Seriously dude, y'all need anything just ask. We might not have kids, but I'm sure we can read a book. Maybe I can come tell Coach with you, be a buffer?" Anders offers as he pulls me into a bear hug. There are not many men who make me feel small, and even though I'm around the same height as him, Aiden Anders feels like my hockey dad. With my real one off retiring in Florida, I might need to seek some wisdom soon.

"She has a kid, right?" Rook asks. I'm waiting for him to make a remark about Ellis being a single mother, before he shocks me. "You should bring him to the rink back home and we can teach him to skate, you know, so Ellis can have a break."

My eyes widen at Rook's startlingly mature suggestion. "Look at you being helpful for a change, I might just take you up on that. Jack is great; he's five and I can already tell he's just like his mom." I tell them, strangely full of pride. Jack was nice to me when he could have thrown a tantrum or demanded I leave. Instead, this little guy took my hand and showed me his trains.

"You're fully in for a ready-built family? Especially with your ex? That's a lot." Anders asks but there isn't really a question in the way he says it. He knows my answer. I think they all do. As if my little outburst in defence of her wasn't a clear indication of my feeling on this whole thing.

"They are my family. Well, if I get my way they will be." Ellis is my sunshine, always has been and always will be, but I know it will take time for her to get used to the idea of me being around. There is no way I am going to push the idea of us in a relationship for a while yet. I need her to know once she says yes to that she is saying yes to forever.

"Damn Liam, you're going to be a *dad*," Anders repeats again. "A good one, I'm sure. You're one of the most even-tempered people I know. You need that in spades with kids." The rest of the guys nod along with him, showing their support for me too.

"She had her first scan today, you wanna see?" I ask, but I don't care about their answers; I'm already pulling up the pictures.

The three of them stand around like good dutiful friends and look at every picture I show them. But I don't stop at the scans. I show them pictures of Ellis and of Jack and a few I found of Ellis and me in college. Those ones they love the most – mocking my old haircuts and laughing at how young we both look.

My favourite picture is stashed privately in my wallet. It's a polaroid Ellis took for me of her newly pregnant stomach. Her plan is to take one every month so she can see how much her body changes and I plan on stealing them so I can bring her with me when I travel.

After a while the rest of the team start to arrive, so I put my phone away. But at least it isn't just me holding onto the secret any more. I do wonder why they have so much faith in my fathering abilities, though.

Regardless, their faith in me makes me think I must be doing something right.

Chapter Ten

Ellis

Every morning, weekend or weekday, summer or winter, having my routine is one of the only things that makes me feel as though I am in charge of the day. There are days when my routine is thrown out of the window, I have no input on when my body decides it will flare up, but when I can, I cling to my routine like a lifeline. This morning is no different from the rest.

When my alarm goes off each morning, I take a few minutes to stare at the ceiling and just breathe, centre myself and assess my body from bottom to top; cataloguing where hurts and what I have to do during the day. When you are chronically ill, doctors give you advice that at the time seems like a bunch of bullshit. *Try getting exercise, eat well, fresh air will do you good*. When they are saying it, all you want to do is throw something at them. But the worst thing about it is that they're right. It doesn't fix everything; nothing will ever fix it completely. But a curated medication plan and taking steps to try and feel whole really do help.

Then you get pregnant, and suddenly a lot of the work you have done to better yourself gets thrown out of the window. That carefully selected medication plan is tossed because of how much medication can harm the baby, and you're forced to decide what to sacrifice to help your baby develop while also needing something to help you survive your day. The other stuff is easier to continue; eating well is the easiest to maintain. Jack is not a picky eater (thank god) so he's good with pretty much anything I make.

Each morning, I make breakfast before I wake up Jack so that I can take my medications and give them enough time to start to work. One of the first things I did when those two little lines popped up – both before and now – was book an appointment with my doctor to figure out what I can still take and what I have to give up.

Despite my feelings towards it, objectively from a medical stance, it would have been a lot easier on my body to not go through with this pregnancy. One reason I did was because of Eleanor. When I was young and being ignored by her, I wanted a big family that I could love and surround myself with, the life I want to believe my dad would have wanted for me. Long before I was diagnosed with fibromyalgia, I wanted a family. I still want to be able to live the life I always dreamed about, despite my limitations.

By the time I finish eating my breakfast it's time for Jack to wake up and get ready for school. After some groans and arguments about what shoes he's going to wear, we're finally out the door.

Once I wave Jack goodbye, watching him disappear through the school doors, I immediately switch into business mode. Having my own business was another one of my childhood wishes, right alongside having a family. But I never expected to truly have both – or to make another family *at* my business.

Lyndsey has worked with me for nearly six years, and she is the sister I never had. After all this time we have developed a routine of our own. I open the shop after dropping Jack off and start getting everything ready for the day. I begin by checking deliveries that need to be made each day and taking any dead flowers off the shop floor. I spend some time answering query emails about pricing – for funerals, for weddings, for boyfriends begging forgiveness.

Lyndsey starts her shift at two p.m. when I leave to pick up Jack and works through the afternoon until we close. Liam came into the shop when he got back from Vegas and the poor girl nearly passed out from excitement. Not only is Lyndsey a huge Spears fan, she's also a straight woman – and a man like Liam sure makes an impression.

I was in the back room at the time, and she walked to me with cheeks redder than ever. Of course I panicked at her state, until she muttered, "Your baby daddy is fine as all hell, and if you don't go out there I might climb him like a tree." I told Lyndsey about the baby in a moment of anxiety. The words burst out of me and I couldn't take them back. It is probably hypocritical to ask Liam to keep it a secret when I told her but if word got out on his end it could end up in the press. Lyndsey wouldn't tell a soul and she is pretty contained. She is single so there isn't a partner that could slip up. She doesn't really talk to her family much any more. If Liam told his team I don't know how tight-lipped they would be. Would they tell their families? Their partners? It would get too big too quickly. There is so much we have left to figure out before word gets out.

Safe to say I have that memory vivid in my mind. Even though it makes me laugh, her reaction is a stark reminder of something I can't ignore. Any woman would be lucky to have Liam, and it would be so simple for him to find the next best thing. He travels so much and there are so many women that would offer themselves to him on a silver platter. It can be hard to imagine him always coming back to little old me and our baby.

One day I might have to accept another woman helping to raise our baby. A step-parent. It wouldn't be fair of me to stop him from dating. He will find his true love eventually, and who am I to stand in the way? Selfishly, I hope it's far in the future. I want him by my side for now, even if it is just for the moment.

Aside from Lyndsey, there are certain regulars at the shop that make my week brighter. I like to think I have become a staple of the community, not only because of the beautiful bouquets we sell but also because of how I designed the shop. It was a must for me to make this place as accessible as possible.

The shop is set up in two aisles that are wide enough for wheelchairs to comfortably pass between and the front counter is low enough that if someone is sat down they can still see over the top. At the end of the two aisles there are small bench seats for people who might need a break, and there is always a pot of coffee brewing in the winter for anyone who needs it. Making Bloom and Blossom as comfortable as possible not only for me but for people who are often overlooked was a large passion of mine.

Flowers were one of the few things my mother and I both appreciated together. Without even trying she taught me how there is a flower for every occasion, each one with a meaning and a story to tell. Eleanor always wanted the fanciest in-season flowers she could get. But the way she spoke about flowers always stuck with me. I wanted to help people show their feelings through flowers. I get to be a tiny part of people's everyday lives, when words aren't enough – the flowers speak for themselves.

As February comes to a close and we get closer to spring, the flowers around me are shifting colours from the passionate reds of roses and chrysanthemums to bright tulips and hyacinths. February is both a dream and a nightmare, roses of all colours line the walls and I make bouquet after bouquet for Valentine's. March is always a nice reprieve, a slower time filled with Easter excitement.

By the time afternoon starts to draw closer, I have made a beautiful arrangement for a birthday gift as well as met with a soon-to-be bride to discuss what flowers will be in season for her autumn nuptials. When Lyndsey walks through the door I barely feel like any time has passed.

I'm eating lunch at my desk when she saunters through the doors. "Hello," she says cheerily.

"Afternoon," I reply. She parks herself in the chair next to me, pulling out a tub of leftover pasta. She waves her hand at me like she is waiting for me to speak, but I have no idea what she wants from me. I've already told her everything: Liam and I are going to co-parent and we have spent time together getting to know each other again. That is really all there is to tell.

"Well…" Lyndsey prods.

I roll my eyes at her as a smirk spreads across my face, "I promise, if anything changes you'll be the first to know, but it's still business as usual."

She scoffs in response, clearly disappointed. As her anticipation for news dulls, I fill her in on what I need her to do this afternoon. Lyndsey was built to work with the public: she has a smile that lights up a room. Her only downfall is how much she hates paperwork. I do as much of it as I can so she can shine in front of our customers. But since my bridal appointment ran over this morning there is more for her to do than usual.

"Yay, my favourite," she says sarcastically, looking at the computer screen on my desk.

"It isn't all bad." I try to sweeten her up. "When Liam is ready to introduce me – and I suppose our baby – to his teammates, I'll make sure you're there too." I pop some of my painkillers in my mouth as I stand up from the desk, closing the lid on my lunch. I see her try to restrain a grin. Suddenly the paperwork must seem less daunting when she can daydream about the Spears players to get her through.

Late afternoon starts to creep in by the time I've collected Jack and driven home. I'm still clinging to the relief of my last dose of pain meds, so I use the last moments of that relief to tidy up our home.

As I sort through the washing, Jack's favourite time of the day approaches: screen time. I was never the person who was going to be able to parent without some kind of distraction. Now that school takes up a lot of his day, I have cut his time down to an hour before we eat dinner. Before I was pregnant I would use this time to clean up more or to read, but now I use it to try some non-medicated ways to reduce my pain. First, I attach a TENS machine to my back to reduce the pain signals in my spine in an attempt to help relax my muscles. It does what it should, but only while the machine is running. Once it powers off it doesn't take long for the pain to come back. But even small relief is a win in my book.

Other doctors have recommended yoga to help my pain, but I've never been particularly bendy. I had pretty much forgotten about that suggestion until I read it can be a good way to prepare the body for the difficulties of pregnancy. I've tried meditation in the past, but my brain is too loud to turn off. The moment I try to centre myself it decides to run through every embarrassing thing I have ever done or conjure up new embarrassing things that could happen in the future. Not exactly the relaxing time I was promised.

I know I could try these things once Jack is tucked in bed, but since I'm cutting down my medications I won't be taking any more until I go to bed myself. Besides, when Jack is in bed it's my time to focus on what I need to do for the baby. I am going to have to start looking for a bigger place eventually. The baby can sleep in my room for a while, but both Jack and the new baby will want their own space soon enough. My evenings are now spent scrolling through housing listings and baby furniture sites to find everything we are going to need.

After cooking whatever is on the menu for the night, Jack and I sit and talk about our days. He tells me everything he learned and the dramas of being a five-year-old, and I tell him stories about eccentric customers who visited the shop – embellishing the stories with some magic to keep him interested.

After our debriefs, it's his bath time. I struggled with bath time for a long while. When he was very small I used to just wash him in the sink so I didn't have to bend over the side of the tub, but he quickly grew too big for that. I tried sitting on a stool next to the tub, but it was hard to reach him. Now that he's five he likes to bathe himself, so I thankfully only have to supervise. I know in the back of my mind I'm going to have to find a better way to deal with it for the next baby. My daily routines are making me realise how much I have forgotten about early motherhood – it all becomes a blur after so many years, but I can feel the problems creeping back over my shoulder.

Once Jack is all clean we snuggle up together in his bed for story time, which has long been my favourite time of the day. Books are where my escape is. When I was a kid I would read constantly. Eleanor was never interested in that side of parenting or parenting at all really. Jack's favourite book at the moment is *The Little Prince*. Spending this time with him is another reason I wanted to have this baby. Watching him become a gentle and strong little boy has been the highest of honours, and I want to see him love his sibling fiercely.

In bed alone, as I hear Jack softly snoring, I scroll and scroll through listing after listing, getting increasingly frustrated. I think if I have to look at one more house that I can't afford, I might have a breakdown. I throw my laptop aside and click on the TV to the sports channel showcasing the NHL highlights.

Back in university, hockey wasn't my thing. I wasn't dating Liam because he was the popular, athletic guy on campus; I was dating him because he was funny, kind, charming. He was *good* for me. He made me feel beautiful. Sure, there were other people who had decided that I was only with him for when he made it big, but I knew the truth. Still, I have all but avoided hockey over the past decade. At first it was because it hurt to see Liam living the high life, but also because if I pretended it didn't exist then I could try to ignore my lingering feelings.

Yet every game he has played since December is available for me to watch, and I can't help but indulge myself. I watch him celebrate his goals and I see him hold it together after a loss. Aside from Liam, the viewing seemed like an easy way to get to know his teammates. After watching press conferences and seeing how they blend together as a team, it makes sense to me how he sees them like his family. Between Anders, Rook, and Edge – as Liam calls them all – they each share a look and the other instinctively knows where to go and what to do. Edge is an enforcer, and admittedly I had no clue what that meant until a couple weeks ago. But seeing him engage in brawls on the ice to protect the team is frightening.

I can also see how much they respect their captain, Aiden Anders. And I also understand why Lyndsey drools over him. He commands the ice as one of the biggest men on the team. His strength is a given, but there is also a mental toughness that can be felt even through the TV screen. If he asked me to lace up some skates and take to the ice, I would have trouble telling him no.

I might not know the team yet, but I know their bond. It gives me some reassurance to know Liam has them in his corner as he also navigates this strange time in his life.

As the NHL portion of the sports schedule comes to an end, I can't help but think about doing it all again tomorrow. There are parts of my day that I love, but I know the further along I get in this pregnancy and the bigger my bump gets, the harder it's going to be to live my life. I know I'm going to have Liam's help, but there's still so much distance and there are so many obstructions between us that I'm not sure how much good it will really do.

In the later stages of my pregnancy last time around I had to put the business on the back-burner because Lyndsey wasn't ready to take over fully. This time Lyndsey will take over if – and when – the time comes that I have to step away for a few months. I count my blessings that I can afford to take time off for myself and for the baby, I know so many others aren't given that luxury.

As I lay back in bed staring at the ceiling again, I think of the ways I could benefit from taking time away from work. I could use it to find more holistic therapies to ease my pain. I could find time for massages or acupuncture. Stepping back could also benefit mine and Liam's relationship. We could have more time together before the baby is born – to get to grips with what co-parenting will look like. The thought raises goose bumps over my skin.

When Liam and I are alone I feel like the tension could be sliced with a knife. I see us that night, after the bar – all over each other, hot and heavy. The images make my breath quicken. I try to ground myself, placing a hand over my slowly swelling belly. There's no relationship for Liam and I. No matter how much my hormones try to sway me.

It's times like this, when I'm lost in my own thoughts and worries, that I wish I had a mum. A *normal* mum, one who wants to be there to meet her grandkids and hold my hand through this. Liam's mum, Tracy, has called me a few times to check in. I was nervous at first – talking to my ex's mother on the phone, while pregnant with her grandchild. But the conversations only cemented what I already thought about her; she is a lovely, supportive woman. It's no wonder Liam has turned out to be so similar.

I only wish Eleanor could show some love the same way. I wish she could have prioritised me and our relationship over finances and luxuries. I often think about giving her a call, but last time I did it went straight to voicemail, one than was never returned. Foolishly, I have this image of her coming back into my life. Being there for me the way a mum should.

With my final dose of painkillers starting to kick in, I burrow down into my blankets. March will be a new month – hopefully one filled with new opportunities, I tell myself. Another month into my pregnancy.

Another step closer to an unpredictable future.

Chapter Eleven

March

Liam

Hospitals are a place where I feel secure. I hate them when it means I have to be off the ice, but I know this is the best place to be. It's a symbol of recovery and safety. There is something comforting about the bright open space. As uncomfortable as the chairs are, it is a comfort to know I won't have to sit in them for long. This is very different to any other hospital waiting room I've been in before. The medical rooms in stadiums always have the best equipment and the top minds in sport medicine are at our beck and call. I have been incredibly lucky in my career not to have received too many hits. I've dislocated a few shoulders and bruised every rib, but there has not been a time when I have needed to worry about my career ending.

A prenatal ward is unlike anything I've seen. The walls are plastered with informative posters about the dangers of smoking while pregnant and charts displaying foetus sizes compared to fruit. Apparently our baby is the size of a lime. These types of posters never really made sense to me. I've looked at them online, but it's confusing because no two limes are the same size, so what size lime is our baby exactly? A big juicy lime ready to eat, or a little lime left on the shelf? I guess Ellis will know by how much her back aches.

Unbeknownst to her, I've got a little pile of pregnancy books on my bedside table. Just because this is the first scan I could come to that doesn't mean I haven't been trying to find out as much information as possible. That is how I know our little lime is fully formed in there. All its bones and organs are inside Ellis.

Even the thought amazes me. She's growing someone else's organs and acts like it's not a big deal. It is a *huge* deal.

As we wait I can't help but notice the other couples around us. To our right there is a pair who I think might hate each other. I know some people just co-parent, hell it's what Ellis and I are doing, but these two have barely spoken a word. I have scripted a whole morning for them where they were trying to paint the nursery; he wants blue and she wants something more neutral like a beige. He threw a fit about how nothing he suggests is good enough and she told him to stop yelling at a pregnant woman (as she should) then he stormed out of the nursery to calm down, but she is still holding the grudge.

Of course, these are strangers who might be madly in love. But they are sat more or less with their backs to each other and he has sighed every five minutes. Could I be staring at the view of mine and Ellis's future? She has no reason to have any loyalty to me, and she even has some reasons to hate me, my travelling is one. I will miss a lot of midnight cries that she is going to have to deal with alone. I can imagine that causing some resentment. The thought of it makes me shudder.

Ellis thought it would be a good idea to set some clear boundaries in our relationship. A strictly co-parenting relationship. We decided that we have to keep the lines clear. We can't indulge in a relationship because if things didn't work between us it wouldn't only affect the baby, but Jack as well. She doesn't want him getting attached to me if I'm not always going to be around. When I tried to argue that I always would be, she pointed out how I travel so much already that I can't make that promise. That stung. I know my job is going to create difficulties for us, but I don't want to seem like less of an involved dad because of it.

I kept to myself that I'd be willing to try more than just co-parenting. Some selfish part of my brain wanted to push her into admitting that we could be great together, just like how we were before. But I don't know if that's true. As much as I like spending time with her and Jack, I don't really know the woman she has become. I know she is strong and protective and her heart is hidden behind a hundred walls, but how can I tell her we would be perfect together if we haven't been together in a decade? I don't know if my nostalgia is making me want something that doesn't exist any more. Maybe I'm delusional, but I can feel the chemistry between us. It isn't all just sexual. And despite all of that, I want her to at least know that she can depend on me. That I'm not going to leave when things get rough.

In the corner opposite us sits the epitome of a happy couple. His hand has been rubbing circles on her large bump while she has been going through every baby name she can think of. I think they must be early twenties, with a youthful glow about them. I personally have hated every name she has suggested; you would think she was giving birth to a pensioner. I mean, is Gerald a real suggestion?

The man seemed to very kindly shoot that down in a way that made it seem like it was her idea.

I wonder if they already have a child because he seems practised at keeping her balanced. As I listen in, the man darts his eyes to me every once in a while. I look away, thinking he is probably annoyed that a stranger seems to be listening to their conversation. But from the corner of my vision, I see him nudge his partner and nod in my direction. That's when I realise I've probably been clocked for more than just being nosey.

I knew a cap wouldn't be a good enough disguise, but I wasn't exactly going to turn up in a mask either. The chance of being recognised is never zero, no matter how much preparation I do. The man leans forward and opens his mouth as though he is going to ask me something, but I give him a subtle shake of my head, hoping it deters him.

"Jesus, it's really you!" he exclaims. Ellis jolts at the sudden noise.

I shush him lightly as some others around the room draw their attention towards us. "Hey," I speak quietly, edging forward on my chair. "I'm more than happy to sign something, but I'd like to keep it low profile."

"Oh! Yes, sorry! I'm just a huge Spears fan," he whispers back at me, pulling a baby book from his satchel. I glance at Ellis who smiles shyly, rummaging through her handbag for a pen. The irony of me signing a baby book isn't lost on me. The idea alone makes me chuckle.

"It's great to meet you… what's your name?" I flip to the front of the book. I eye Ellis over my shoulder to gauge her true reaction, I can't read the look on her face. I don't know if she's mad or just observing me.

"Oh, yeah right, sorry – it's Tom."

As soon as I catch his name I scribble a message in the book, sign it, and hand it back to him. His hand darts out to take it from me but I keep my hand locked around it, not handing it over just yet.

"Tom, can you keep this between us?" I tell him in a low voice. I raise my eyebrows wanting him to understand. Ellis isn't ready to announce to the world that she is having a hockey player's baby, and until she is I will do what I can to keep this under wraps.

Though I would have paid for the most private treatment available, Ellis is insistent on seeing her usual doctor – and who can blame her. Her doctor knows her well, her condition, and her previous pregnancy. It would be selfish to take her away from what she knows for the sake of my identity being hidden.

"My lips are sealed. Thanks dude." He winks. When I finally release my grasp on the book he seems overjoyed. I really hope he is a man of his word.

I look back at Ellis, not saying a word. Silence is so much easier when there aren't so many things I want to say. On one hand I want to apologise for the disturbance, but I also know it's probably going to happen again. It's part of the deal of being around me. But right now, I'm not ready to hear Ellis tell me I am too much to take on. Instead I go right back to observing the final woman in the room.

Across from us is a woman sitting on her own. It's a visual for me of how Ellis has looked every time she has been in this waiting room. The brunette is reading a book yet her phone pings every couple of minutes, and every single time she puts her bookmark in place and texts back whoever is looking out for her. When I was sat in my hotel room waiting for Ellis's FaceTime I thought about nothing else apart from the fact Ellis would have done this all alone for Jack. I know she brought Jack to her scan at eight weeks, but she could have found out some bad news and I would've been in another state unable to hold her. Being here and seeing the posters reminds me just how excited I am to not only be a parent but to be one alongside Ellis Ainsley.

"I need to pee so bad," Ellis announces, shifting uncomfortably in her chair. "I can't believe how much we have to drink for the scan to get a clear picture, I mean with today's technology? Surely we don't need to make already bloated and heavy women *more* bloated."

"Hmm." I try to focus on Ellis's words and muster up a reassuring response, but nothing comes. I am too distracted by my inner monologue to engage.

"Why are you so quiet?" Ellis's voice shocks me out of imagining a backstory for the solo woman in front of me.

"A few reasons."

"Come on Liam, I thought your mouth would be going a mile a minute." She laughs.

"Honestly? The first reason is because I'm so fucking scared, about seeing the baby, about becoming a dad, but also because—" I can hear my own voice crack as I try to speak honestly, "I think I might cry if I talk too much."

It's the real reason I have been losing myself to these strangers' stories, it's so much easier to dissociate than face the fact I am a *dad*. Ellis has already warned me about her health, about the worries she has with carrying a child in her condition, and the higher possibilities of tragic occurrences. But even if something were to happen with this pregnancy, if the very worst happened and we somehow lost the baby, I would still be their dad. The emotions haven't escaped me from the very first scan. I didn't think love could come for something you haven't seen or even felt, but I love this baby.

"Liam," Ellis's eyes are filled with sympathy.

"I'm sorry." I pull her to me in a second. I smell the mix of her shampoo and perfume. She has always smelt the way I imagine a tropical island smells when you wake up in the morning. Fresh and floral with something fruity like mango or peach. When I woke up alone in December I could still smell her all around my home; she was buried in every atom of my being.

"I'll cry if you keep being so cute." Her words are muffled against my chest as I laugh.

"You think I'm cute?" I quip. Before Ellis can reply, a voice captures her attention.

"Miss Ainsley?" the nurse calls from the door.

-

Pacing around the room as Ellis has her blood drawn and weight taken, I go over all the questions I have for the doctor in my head. I could ask Ellis but I don't want to bombard her and risk making her more anxious than she probably already is. She is a pro at this by now and I feel like a fish out of water begging for some guidance.

"You're making me sea sick." Ellis breaks my concentration.

"I didn't think you had any nausea any more?" I rush to her side in a second.

"I don't, but your pacing is making the room feel like it's spinning, so can you sit down?" Her hand captures my elbow on my next walk past.

"I have too much energy El, there's a baby in you and I'm about to see it for the first time in person. I feel like

I'm about to go out on the ice." I shake my hands out as though that's going to do anything to help.

"What do you do to calm down there?" she asks.

"Push a dude against the boards, but I don't see that as an option here."

"Please don't body-slam my doctor," Ellis jokingly pleads as the door clicks open again.

"I second that," Dr Horne announces with raised eyebrows. "Hi Ellis, and it's good to see you in person, Liam. But if we can refrain from fouling me during the scan it would be appreciated." Dr Horne looks different in person compared to a phone screen, she is human-sized for one, but her smile seems so much wider and more genuine in person. With her round face and round eyes she reminds me of the garden gnomes my mom has on her lawn in Florida.

"Sorry Doc, just filled with nerves," I reply, only marginally embarrassed.

"You're a first-time dad, you get a pass. So, Ellis, before we get the ultrasound out is there anything going on that you're worried about?" Giving Ellis her full attention Dr Horne takes a seat on a rolling stool and I move to stand next to Ellis's head so I can hold her hand.

"Heartburn is kicking my arse but I'm doing good, no more sickness really, it's just around certain foods." I fail to stifle a laugh as I remember an incident earlier in the day.

"I wanted to have a tuna sub for lunch and she tried to murder me," I explain quickly, my smile falling fast. Ellis looks up at me with slight irritation. It's my cue to keep some thoughts to myself.

"No more tuna for you then, Dad." Dr Horne continues to talk but I think I black out at her words. It's the first time someone has called me Dad. Dad is going to be my new name. I am no longer just Liam or Ruin. I'm *Dad*.

The thing that pulls me back into the room is the whooshing noise from the computer's speakers. Dr Horne is moving the probe around to find the baby as I wait on bated breath for a glimpse.

Then there it is.

Our baby takes up the screen. Everything else ceases to exist. Nothing but the image of my baby and the feeling of Ellis's hands tightly wrapped in mine. So much has changed since last time, it's almost hard to believe it's the same baby. What was once a small blob now appears to have limbs and a rounded head.

After typing for a few seconds, the screen changes slightly and a different sound falls into the room. Quick heartbeat sounds thump through me. My heart stopped so my baby's could beat. It feels as though my heart will always beat in tandem with the little person on the screen. The sound is faster than I imagined.

Dread slips over me when Ellis slips her hand from mine. My eyes snap to hers to see her thumb reaching up to wipe tears from my cheek. I couldn't feel the tears coming, but they don't surprise me. I have never felt this many emotions at once.

Excited.

Scared.

Thrilled.

Awed.

But mostly so damn scared.

There's also the intense need to show Ellis how much she means to me. It's really because of her that I feel any of this to begin with. She looks radiant laying on the bed.

Despite how she's been feeling, I can't help but think pregnancy suits her. I can see a glow about her. There is a second where I contemplate kissing her, but I know that isn't what she wants from me. That would muddy the clear boundaries she wants. Co-parents and nothing more, Liam, remember that. Instead, I take her into my arms.

"Thank you. Fuck, Sunshine, thank you," I mutter. As soon as Dr Horne leaves the room and Ellis has wiped the goo from her stomach, I lift her off the bed and spin her around, the dress that was pulled up over her stomach falling down and around as we spin.

"Liam! Put me down!" Her shrieks are peppered with laughter.

"You have precious cargo, I think I should carry you everywhere."

"Ask me again when my ankles swell, I might take you up on it." She pulls my earlobe until I put her down. Nobody has done that to me since college. It was her favourite way of pulling me off the sofa when she wanted to study but I was too busy staring at her. Her other technique was to kiss me until I was putty in her arms and then sneak attack by putting my textbooks on my lap when I tried to pull her closer.

"I'm glad it's you who I get to co-parent with, Liam," she says with sincerity. I nod in response. No words will describe how much I love and hate what she just said. Instead I watch as she zips up her jacket and goes to leave the room.

I wish I could tell her that isn't what I really want. Co-parenting isn't enough for me, especially not after how I felt when we reunited at that bar. But something in her doesn't want me – doesn't want *us* like that. I debate with myself whether or not to be honest about how she makes me feel. But risking what we currently have, the steady, easy-going bond… it seems selfish.

So I stay quiet, and follow her out the door.

Chapter Twelve

Ellis

I can feel it the moment it happens. When my brain drains of the adrenalin from hearing the heartbeat and we are back in the car. I feel the second it all saps away. The high of seeing the baby and having Liam by my side crashes as I stare at the sonogram picture the whole way home. So wrapped up in the feelings of anxiety digging its way into my heart that I don't know if Liam is driving to my place or his, but I know I have hours until it's time to pick up Jack so I don't care. I care about the fact my life is about to be splintered apart and there is nothing I can do to stop it.

Jack for the most part was a happy baby, his birth was scary, I was going in blind and alone but it was a straightforward labour. There is no way to guarantee it will happen like that this time. There are so many things that can go wrong.

One of the things Jack struggled with when he was first born was sleeping. He just didn't want to do it. I would feed him, change him, hold him. But he would cry relentlessly. All through the night. All through the day. It felt as though I went months without more than two hours' sleep. Every feed was my responsibility, every nappy was mine to clean up, and nobody told me how many loads of clothes I would have to wash.

Now I'm going to be doing that again, alongside raising a small child. My routine will be out of the window, there will be no full night's sleep to replenish myself for the next day. The days will roll into each other and I am going to have to find a way to still be a parent to Jack.

I can hear Liam talking to me from the driver's seat, but the words don't penetrate my spiral. I don't hear the car stop or him getting out. It isn't until he opens my door for me that I am pulled back to the present. I can see the concern in Liam's eyes but I don't have the strength to pretend everything is fine. Because it isn't. I am in so much pain already and I am only one third through. There is so much left to go and so much I will have to do and change even once the baby comes. Everything is spinning out on me and there is nothing solid for me to hold on to.

Frankly, I don't care if he is concerned. Neither of us are to blame for my contraceptive failing because I was ill, that couldn't be helped. But that is too logical for my brain. Liam is the reason my head feels like it may fall from my shoulders and he gets to smile and watch as my body goes through anguish to give him a child.

It's true that I wanted another baby one day, and I know that if I didn't want to do this I could have waited and given myself more time, but those are not the thoughts I care about right now. I care about the fact Liam Ruinsky has ruined my normalcy. Maybe it wouldn't be too bad if he was actually going to be around whenever I need him. But in typical Ellis fashion, I had to get pregnant by a man who is going to be gone half of the time to play stupid hockey with his stupid team.

I am scared and mad, and I don't know which one I feel most. Somehow they are both his fault. I could blame the resentment on my hormones, but instead I blame him. My hormones are crazy because I'm pregnant, and I'm only pregnant because of him and his stupid perfect face.

"So, are we going to talk about what's bothering you?" He asks through a tight jaw. We've pulled up outside of his house and I jump out of the car slamming the door on my way out, it doesn't help my simmering emotions the way I wish it would.

"You are," I answer bluntly. I'm aware I sound like a stroppy teenager, but I'm too far gone to turn back now. I look away from him and throw my jacket onto his couch. I can feel my fear brewing into anger.

"What did I do?" he asks with his arms outstretched in confusion. *Isn't that the million-dollar question, Liam?* He asks it like he really thinks he has said or done something today to upset me. The reality is, I'm upset about how he is managing to stay so damn strong and steady when I can't even see straight.

"You got me pregnant, you arsehole!" I yell and throw my bag onto the floor.

"What? That's what's bothering you?" He frowns, shaking his head. I would feel sorry about how confused he looks, but he should be keeping up.

"Everything is going to change because of this baby and my whole world is going to crumble." I point my finger at him to show him how much this is all his fault.

"It's not going to crumble, Sunshine." He has no right to try and be sweet right now. My lips lift in a snarl and I move away from him.

"You have no idea, do you? Jack is going to be a brother and there is going to be a baby, a *baby* that isn't going to give a shit about my schedules." I am rambling and I see him try to interrupt but I'm not letting that happen, he just has to listen. "You're going to get to waltz in whenever it suits you and tell me everything I'm doing wrong. There are so many things that I could do wrong. I mean, what if I get taken into hospital with a flare-up? What if I have to stop working? What happens if it's a premature birth and you're miles away? Or what happens if Jack hates the baby? Or if the baby hates me?"

"Ellis, stop for a second. You're catastrophising and you need to come back to earth." His voice is tired, I can hear all of his earlier joy has fallen away. When I turn to look at him, I can see worry for me in his eyes, but I don't stop pacing. It's like he didn't hear a word I said, nothing about that is catastrophising. All of it is a real possibility and now he wants me to *calm down*. Fuck him.

"Oh, that sounds so easy, don't know why I didn't think about that. You are so fucking helpful." My teeth are gritted and the sarcasm tastes like poison against my tongue, but there is no stopping it.

"What can I do to help?" Liam asks, reaching a hand out for me that I bat away.

"Nothing! It's too much. Everything hurts. I don't want to be alone again." My voice falters over the words and I can feel myself shaking. Tears fill my eyes as the emotions continue to pour out of me. Every thought I have had over the past twelve weeks is pouring out of me in the middle of his living room floor. Liam looks tortured through my tears, but I can't find it in me to look after him as well as me when I am crumbling onto the cold floor.

"Sunshine, please get up." Behind the fog of my tears, I see him close in on me, so I scramble back even further. His voice is soft and kind, trying to put me at ease, but it doesn't work. It still sounds like static to me, a background humming in a deep corner of my mind. Unable to focus on it.

"Don't touch me!" I hear my voice but I don't recognise it. I need Liam to put me back together again. I wish he could, but I know if he touches me the fragile remains of me will turn to ash.

"Ellis, please." He is on his knees in front of me now and it makes a small part of my heart long to reach out for him, but my brain is not ready for his comfort.

Instead I yell out, "Liam, I'm scared!" I am pulling at my clothes and my hair. Everything feels too much. My hair is sweaty on the back of my neck, my clothes feel constricting around my barely showing bloated belly.

"Ellis, stop." He tries to pull my hands from my hair but as soon as his hands settle around my wrist I tug them out of his grasp. The words are desperate when he speaks.

"No, you don't understand! You can't understand, I don't know why I thought you would. Fuck, I'm such an idiot." My words surprisingly come out with a manic laugh that goes against everything I am feeling. The last time I felt this stupid was the day I told Jack's father I was pregnant. Just the look in his eyes was enough for me to know that I was an idiot to think he cared.

"El, just take a breath." He now stands a few feet in front of me. I know he wants to come closer. His hands fist at his side, but he holds himself back from stepping closer. I probably should breathe and think about what I'm saying, but every possible future is running through my head and none of them look good.

"Oh, get fucked Liam. I'm going to have to do this by myself while you're off fucking other women across the states." My chest is heaving as the venom spews out of me, sounding more like my home accent than usual through the emotion. "Every midnight cry will be *me*, every nappy and every bottle. It's all going to be *me* while you spend your days living your rich and famous life away from us."

"Is that what you think? That I'm going to be doing anything except wish I was home?" His body becomes stiff, a tension flowing through him, from his feet right up to his clenched jaw. I can see the effect my words have had. I've hurt him and it shamefully feels good. There is shock and an ebbing anger in his tone and I feel vindicated in hurting him the way I'm hurting. So he might understand for even a second how it feels when my world is fuelled by pain.

"I don't know Liam, I don't know what the fuck is going to happen… but I'm going to have a son and a baby and I'll have nobody."

"You have me!" Liam yells. Finally, something is getting to him, he is losing his cool, his hand slices through the air. I want him to feel as untethered as me because of how lost I am in all this. Lost and alone – completely trapped inside my own head.

"No, I don't. You won't be here!" *I will still be alone*, I think.

"Because you won't let me." He points down at me alone on the ground, as if it proves his point. His voice is still rife with tension when he spits out more anger. "How can I help you if you just yell at me instead of just telling me what you need like an adult."

Fuck him for trying to rationalise what I'm feeling. If I could tell him what I need I would, but that isn't an option because all I know is I need a steady shoulder to lean on.

"I'm scared." It hurts to say the words. It hurts to admit my world is spinning with no end in sight.

"Scared of what exactly, Sunshine?" he says softly. I don't know when it happened, but his arms are around me. Liam is sat by my side with one hand steady on the back of my neck pulling me to him.

"Losing you. Being alone!" Finding the words is difficult. Coming from a family like mine meant that emotions were mine to hold, not to share. But suddenly in waltzes Liam, demanding my heart beat for him. "Doing this again wasn't something I planned on and I will still have to look after Jack and that takes everything in me already without a baby and sleepless nights."

"I'm not going anywhere, if you aren't sleeping then neither am I. When the baby wakes you up I will sit with you until they fall back asleep, you need someone to pick up Jack you ask me, ask and I will do anything to make it happen." He makes it sound so easy but he has not done this before. If I try to wake him every time he will hate me before the baby is even a month old. The season will be starting and he thinks he can win at hockey on zero sleep, he is not invincible.

"What about when you're away for games, Liam? You can't promise to be here when your job demands you leave." I need him to see, to understand how difficult this is going to be.

"Then we hire a part-time nanny for while I'm away if that's what it takes. I'll buy a damn jet so you, Jack and the baby can travel with me if you want. You know Lyndsey would love the extra hours."

They say money can't buy happiness, but it sure helps give me peace of mind. Without Liam there is no way I could afford a nanny, the thought never crossed my mind.

Before Liam, I couldn't even think about money as a solution to my fears because every cent I earn goes towards keeping me and Jack fed and housed, frivolous expenses like a jet are not even in my imagination.

As I sit wrapped in his arms, somehow my tears stop falling and it hits me how much better he makes me feel. Even against my own wishes my body feels centred when he holds me.

"Why are you so calm about all of this?" I ask. Through everything over the past three months there has not been a moment where he has wavered. I have been teetering on the edge and Liam has been a pillar of calm and strength that I am fighting to rely on because nobody has ever supported me. Liam doesn't gain anything from me, he should think I am ruining his life.

"Because you are my family." There is conviction in his voice and his eyes as he looks deep into my eyes making sure I am hearing what he says: "I have to be strong for you."

"Do you regret taking me home that night?" I feel him freeze beside me. I didn't realise it until I said it out loud, but it is one of my biggest fears. I know Liam is here because of his duty as a good man who is about to be a father and not out of love, but I wonder deep down if he would take it all back.

"Never. It's the best thing I've ever done." His voice has so much conviction that I almost melt into his embrace fully, but my doubts surface anyway.

"But now you're tied to me forever, you're going to be out there trying to date as a dad with a baby momma as baggage." His body shakes against mine slightly, so I pull my head from its resting point against his neck to see him trying to bite back a laugh. I raise my brows at him in question.

"I don't think about that... besides, being tied to you forever doesn't sound so bad. Come on Ellis, we aren't sworn enemies. We have it better than most," he admits with a kiss to my forehead. That one little kiss, a small sign of affection, pulls together some parts of my shattered soul that lay in shards around us.

"How do you do that?" I ask.

"Do what?" he asks, mimicking our interaction from way back in December.

"Make me want to kiss you," I say tentatively.

I want him to pull me in, to claim me as his with his lips but he doesn't. Instead he pulls my cheek against his chest and I hear the quick thumping of his heart against me. The clear rejection stings, but what did I expect? I yell and scream at him and then ask him to kiss me when I have told him I only want a co-parenting relationship. It's just my hormones talking, it has to be.

"I'm sorry, El," he begins explaining. "You know I—"

"I get it," I interrupt him. "I'm overstepping, just ignore me." I force a smile.

I'm painfully embarrassed. But I can't let it linger over me like a bad smell. Over the next few days I'll be entering my second trimester. I worry that if it is anything like last time my libido is about to go through the roof.

Liam can help me with so much, but I wish there was a way that he could help sate that one need for me. I respect his restrain. He's too gentlemanly to play with a pregnant woman's emotions.

It's probably for the best. Getting tangled in the sheets might sound fun, but getting my heart broken by Liam and having to continue to raise a child with him would probably kill me.

Chapter Thirteen

April

Ellis

I am adult enough to admit I'm acting crazy. My hormones are changing so fast that even Liam is having trouble keeping up. One moment I feel like I did after the scan: like an earthquake is rumbling from somewhere in my soul. Then moments later I'm on cloud nine, excited to be on this journey. One big moment of anger was when he admitted the guys know about the baby. I hit the roof. I asked for one thing, for some time to come to terms with anything and he couldn't give me that. If he can't follow that simple boundary I can't imagine how co-parenting is going to work. Obviously he apologised, and his teammates promised to keep it a secret, but it still hurt regardless.

I'm also craving crumpets. I haven't eaten a crumpet since I left Reading at eighteen, but right now, the warm, buttery taste is all I can think about. I'm lucky that Liam will do anything in his power to make me comfortable, because shipping costs to get British crumpets over here is super expensive. He covered every penny.

I eat them by the packet-full. It feels like each time I blink my emotions switch. There's an aching need to find some balance. Some stability in the hurricane of my mind. And that is why I have spent the better part of a week trying to convince Liam we should find out the baby's sex.

To give him credit, Liam does have some good reasons why we shouldn't, but I just *really* want to know. Every new polaroid I take to compare my bump growth makes me want to find out even more. There is a baby in there and I don't know anything about them except their size. I have had Liam all but running between my flat, where he spends as much time as he can, his place where he sleeps, and the rink for training and games.

Though he offered me a key to his place, I'm rarely there. My flat is closer to Bloom and Blossom anyway, and I don't like spending time at his without him. It just feels wrong to be in his space alone.

Instead, I ask him to come here, to this two-bedroom walk-up. I've taken Jack to Liam's house a few times, wanting them to build some kind of relationship. The two of them aren't exactly best of friends yet, but they are as good as they can be for now. Jack has surprised me. He isn't used to having men around, but he doesn't seem to mind the new addition to his life.

Another one of my most consistent hormone changes is how desperately horny I am. The second trimester has made Liam even more attractive, which I didn't think was humanly possible. His hair just falls so naturally sexy and when his dark eyes look into my soul, my panties are soaked through instantly. There is no doubt that Liam is hot; he is kind and gentle and fills out a suit like a god.

Whoever penned the rule that NHL players should wear suits to and from games deserves a medal. Or some kind of sainthood at least. Before every game I get the visual treat of him dressed to the nines, and I revel in it every damn time.

But it's truly a joke from the universe that I have one of the sexiest men in the NHL at my beck and call, and yet I can't sleep with him. Since the day of the twelve-week scan, my libido has been making me flirt with him, even unconsciously. Scout's honour that it isn't *my* fault, just my libido moving me like a marionette. I've done all the things that used to work back in university: biting my lip, touching his thighs, batting my eyelashes and laughing at all of his jokes even when I don't think they're funny. And still I remain untouched. Liam is staying true to his word and the boundary we set. At the very least, it means I can trust that he keeps a promise. But sometimes I wish it could be broken, just for one more night.

There is also the very real possibility that he no longer finds me attractive now that I'm pregnant. My belly has popped and I'm finally looking like a pregnant lady, but what man isn't attracted to growing boobs? I have some new stretch marks and sometimes I don't have the energy to wash my hair so the blonde strands lay flat against my head, but Liam looks at me as though he wants me. There is a heat in his gaze and every time his fingers graze my skin electricity sparks between us. But he has never leaned in for a kiss, never lets his touch linger.

If sex isn't on the cards, I was hoping to convince him to find out the gender as a distraction. But it's been to no avail. Instead I have to listen to him give valid reasons on why we shouldn't.

Every day, the sixteen-week scan grows closer, and the anticipation of knowing is eating me up. It would be so much easier if I could just tell him that if we can't find out the gender, there is another need we could both satisfy.

But I can't be the one to break the agreement. Over the past four months I have come to the realisation that I am *very* demanding. I like things done a certain way and I don't see why I should expect less than what I want. However, I am going to enter a co-parenting dynamic in the near future, so my way or the highway is no longer going to be the default. I had the great idea that I could loosen the reins and be chill about finding out the gender. Right until Liam told me he wanted it to be a surprise. Sentimental bastard.

I know I'm being selfish, about both the gender and the flirting. I think deep down the reason I want to sleep with him is because I need him to fuck me. Not want – *need*.

Is it possible to die from a lack of satisfaction? I think I will be the first documented case: killed from lack of sex. Maybe my libido will get so high that all the blood will go to between my thighs and away from my brain until I die. Dramatics aside, that is simply how turned on I am.

Take this for example: Liam is sitting in the armchair in my living room in grey sweatpants and a white T-shirt, the sluttiest outfit a man can wear, naturally. He is man spreading with his head resting against the back of the chair, his longer brown hair wet and stuck to his forehead. His face is angled up away from me but I know his eyes are closed and a small smile is gracing his face. He only came over to check on me and bump on his way back from the rink and all of a sudden he was taking everything off my plate by doing the chores I was putting off. He might be still trying to make up his indiscretion to me. To prove he is dependable.

It has been an hour since he got here and in that time he washed my dishes and cleaned my bathroom before jumping in the shower from working up a sweat. He was just a wall away from me in *my* shower, naked, and there was nothing I could do to stop my mind from imagining a million sordid things. Imagining him stroking his cock to the thought of me. Thinking about joining him and falling to my knees to get the taste of him I have been craving. Imagining him using my showerhead to get me off in record time because I already feel seconds from coming and he hasn't even touched me.

Jack is at Lyndsey's house because she wanted to give me the night off, so there isn't even anyone here to create a buffer. There's nothing for me to focus my energy on except for Liam and whether or not he has underwear on. He is here to make sure I am feeling okay. I know he wants to feel useful and deep down I am enjoying letting him wait on me. That's why I haven't asked him to leave even though we both know there isn't anything left for him to do.

I angrily eat some more crumpets, which Liam made for me, like if I chew hard enough I can wipe the thoughts of him away. It feels silly to imagine him like this when just a few months ago it was a reality: us all over each other like no time had passed. Now I'm daydreaming as though I don't know every inch of him.

It's taking a lot of my willpower not to go sit on his lap. I don't think he would push me off, judging by the way he looks at me, but that doesn't mean I should test it. God I would love to feel his thighs underneath me, to feel if he is hard at the weight of me on top of him. I wonder if I sat at the right angle would he be able to feel how wet I am at the thought of him. *Shit*, I'm doing it again. I have to stop fantasising about us—

"Do you want it to be a boy or a girl?" Liam's voice is a welcome reprieve from my runaway thoughts. I knew he wanted to talk more about what are lives are going to be like after this pregnancy, but I thought we would be talking about a schedule of when he will see the baby.

I casually shake my head and toss my hair behind me, as though I haven't just been thinking about him naked. "I think it would be easier with a boy, but I would love Jack to have a little sister."

"Why do you think raising a boy is easier?" he asks, cocking his head to look at me where I lie on the couch.

"Raising them won't be easier. But I have a bunch of Jack's old clothes they could wear, so that saves money. And I have a list of boy names I didn't use before." *Another reason we should find out the gender sooner rather than later*, I think to myself.

"Ellis, we can afford new baby clothes." He laughs.

I wave my hand dismissively. "That's not the point, reusing is good for the environment and stuff; but anyway, there are some clothes there that would be good for a girl too."

He lets a silence linger before focusing on me intently. "What names have you thought about then?"

"Well, that depends." I grimace slightly, familiar anxiety settling in my chest.

"On what?" he quizzes.

"Their surname."

"Oh."

"Yeah."

I pick at my nails, the stillness in the room enveloping me. I move to sit on the cushion closest to him, not wanting to make this conversation any more distant and awkward than it needs to be. This is Liam and I here. We shouldn't be uncomfortable.

"Is it selfish if I want them to be baby Ruinsky?" He takes my hand, squeezing it as he speaks.

"No, not selfish just… I guess it's the done thing," I say softly. "We could hyphenate, but Ainsley-Ruinsky is a bit of a mouthful."

I knew deep down he would want the baby to have his name. It was one of the first thoughts I had when I told him I was pregnant, but hearing it stings a little.

"Sunshine, if you want the baby to be an Ainsley that's fine, it's just…" He trails off, biting his lip.

"Just what?" I push.

"I guess it's just that you and Jack are both Ainsley. It's stupid really, but I guess if the baby is Ainsley too then I feel like I'm not a part of the family." When his dark eyes meet mine they are glazed over. My heart drops into my stomach at the sight.

"Liam." I wish I could be even closer to him, wish I could give him comfort, and he must agree because he pulls me even closer until I am sat on his lap.

"I know it's stupid, this baby is my family. Hell, you and Jack are part of my family too, but I guess I feel a little left out." He tightens his arms around my waist as his hand settles on my bump before he continues. "The baby will live with you and I know I am going to miss out on a lot because of hockey. I just feel like a background character in all this."

"You will never just be a background character, do you hear me? You're their dad, Liam. You always will be no matter what. Even when you annoy me you will still be their father, nothing will take that away." Shock laces my words at his revelation; it never crossed my mind that he would feel less than. I'm still a little bit mad that he told his team and mad that he is so attractive it hurts, but I know he cares about this baby. My hands come up to cradle his jaw to offer him some comfort. Liam is the more rational out of the two of us and it never occurred to me how hard this must be for him. Again, I know that's selfish, that I have spent so long thinking about all the things changing in my life that his life has barely crossed my mind.

I don't know what else to say to make him feel better so I settle for putting a hand on his shoulder, hoping it will bring comfort. If we were dating I might have stroked my fingers through his hair but that isn't my comfort to give. I have to remember that I'm the one who fought for co-parenting and nothing more.

"I have an idea," Liam says, rubbing circles on my bump. It seems like it is as calming for him as it is for me.

"Oh, do you now?" I ask with a small laugh. Liam's ideas are rarely plausible, but I will let him tell me anyway if it makes him feel better.

"Yep, and it's a pretty flawless one in my opinion." The look in his eyes has shifted from sadness to mischief.

"Hit me with it."

"You and Jack change your surname to Ruinsky and boom: we can all have the same surname," he says with a smirk. *Oh, god.* Of course, that is his idea.

I laugh at him gently. "If that's your marriage proposal, it was pretty lacklustre."

"If I asked you to marry me, would you say yes?" He quirks his eyebrows at me. A part of him must already know the answer, otherwise he wouldn't put it out there.

"No," I answer definitively. But damn, now I'm thinking about it. Liam is already a great dad based on how attentive and supportive he's been; it's a partner that I worry about. He will give the baby everything but will we butt heads constantly when it comes to how we are going to raise them. There is little I want more than to give my children a family like the ones I've seen on TV. Loved-up parents dancing in the kitchen, two kids and a dog causing mayhem, and I wish I could have that with Liam. But it's not realistic. Men like him don't have their happy endings with women like me.

He chuckles slightly. "Exactly then, I'm saving myself the heartbreak of your rejection." I can hear that he is joking by the lilt in his voice, but in his eyes there is something else: pain. Fear. Hope. Maybe he feels it too? The crushing weight of hope that we could be so much more. But I've been overthinking so much recently, I'm probably overthinking his every action and word too.

I try to keep the mood light and nudge his shoulder. "Oh, you would be broken hearted?" My breathing is more strained as I can feel the heat from his body burning me.

"Being rejected by you, yeah of course I would." His face is inches from mine and for a second his eyes drop to my lips.

There is no stopping me from leaning into him. His lips are pink and pillow soft, and the thought of them pressed against mine is too strong to ignore. I am a magnet being drawn to this man in every way. Our lips touch for a brief second before he pulls away.

No. No. No. No.

This can't be happening. I thought he wanted me. What am I missing?

"El, stop." I'm such a fool. Of course, he doesn't want to kiss me. Embarrassment flushes my cheeks.

"What? I—I thought you wanted — shit, I'm so sorry, I just—"

"No, stop," he says as I try to stand, but he holds me down, pulling my back against his chest. "Hey, stop just wait a second." His words are warm against the side of my neck where he has pulled me closer, but I need to get away from him. From all of this.

"I'm such an idiot, I shouldn't have done that, I'm sorry." My skin is red and heated from the obviously unrequited attraction.

"Ellis, listen to me." His voice is strong and I know there is no running away from this one.

"I want to kiss you," he says with a sense of passion. "I want to do a lot more than that, but not like this. Not just because your hormones are making you horny and I'm available for you. *If* I kiss you again one day, it's going to be because you are mine and it means something. It will be because you want to be with me."

"What?" I mutter. I can't seem to find any other words, my head feels completely empty.

He continues, "I am attracted to you, I wouldn't have done what we did in December had I not been. But I can't kiss you or do anything else... It wouldn't be fair on either of us." He finishes talking before releasing me.

I scramble off his lap and back to the safety of the couch. Liam stands and steps towards me, leaning down to leave a small kiss on my forehead. I'm stunned into silence from the interaction until he says, "Tea?" forcing me to glance up and nod.

I watch him walk away into the kitchen and begin pottering with the cupboards. "Oh and Ellis," he shouts from the other room, "I've been messing with you; I do want to find out the gender of the baby. I just wanted you to start asking for what you want. If you want something, I will do whatever I can to make it happen."

He says nothing else after bringing me my tea. The atmosphere shifts entirely as he goes about his day, using my home as though it's his while I am left reeling from his confession. He keeps throwing me for a loop. I think we understand each other and then he tells the team about the baby. I think there is a chance we could work together but there is always something holding one of us back.

Despite it being what I wanted, I don't even enjoy the satisfaction of knowing we are going to find out the sex of the baby. Instead, my mind is hyper-focused on everything else he just dropped on me. Never for a second did I think anything more would come from this, but his confession changes things. *If he kisses me*, he said. He needed my confirmation on how I truly feel. But yet again, I struggled to show what I actually want.

In December I said one night and he agreed, didn't he? He might have said he wanted more but I didn't think he meant it. I thought he wanted the same as me. Relive our glory days for one night. But that isn't true, I want to believe it is but I can't hide from the truth, he did want more. Liam told me that he wanted more than one night, but I thought he was just trying to woo me. Trying to get me into his bed. It never crossed my mind that he might have meant what he said. Now that I know him better I can see he wasn't just using his words to lure me in but I haven't really thought about it. I had to convince myself that he was some playboy using sweet words to get a girl in his bed. It was the only way I could get myself to leave without feeling guilty. I have been in denial, pushing myself to believe the worst in him to soften the blow when I walked away.

But his admission makes me think seriously for the first time: could it ever work? Liam and I are very different from each other for a start. He's still my ex – and do I want to get back with my ex? He also went behind my back and told the Spears about the baby. Then there is the fact that if we didn't work out it would be impossible to recover from the heartbreak. The internal debate consumes me; the constant back and forth is like emotional tennis. And then you add hormones and health complications into the mix, and suddenly I don't have a clue about anything.

But is it worth the risk? Knowing that I could lose him and still have to be in his life facing that heartbreak at every step. No. No it wouldn't be fair. Not to him and not to my heart.

Anyway, it's probably just my hormones talking for me. It has to be. I can't fall in love with him again just for my heart to get broken again. I put the limit of a year on us back then because I knew I was going to fall in love with him. But I also knew I couldn't hold him back from the draft. Instead, I set a boundary and stuck to it, even if it ripped me apart to watch him play on the other side of the country when all I wanted was for him to hold me in his arms. Now when I want to trust him he does the one thing I ask him not to. It just shows me further that I need to listen to my head. I can't listen to my heart or the sexual tension I feel. I have to protect myself even if that means stewing in my denial a little bit longer.

Chapter Fourteen

Liam

It feels like Christmas morning. That rush you get knowing when you walk down the stairs and the front room is teeming with gifts, lights are shining and the frost is crisp on the windowsill. That is the only way I can describe the feeling thumping through my veins right now. It's stupid really, I feel almost giddy just because Ellis is standing in my kitchen giving me marching orders for the day.

Finally, my team are going to meet the mother of my child. Since I told them the truth I have been pushing for Ellis to meet them. I think when she knows the type of people they are she will be a little less mad about them knowing. She can see that they will keep it a secret. Jack is stood by his mother's side looking as giddy as I feel about the idea of a big barbecue with my closest friends; it is lighting up his eyes. There is something so right about them in my space.

Images of Ellis cooking when I get home from practice or Jack sat at my dining room table doing homework flood my senses, us cuddled on the couch watching film after film while our baby is asleep upstairs. Although it's only a dream, it feels so close to reality as she tells me to get the deck ready for guests.

The springtime air is crisp but the skies are clear. I hope we get a nice summer to match my sunny disposition lately. This is the first ever barbecue I've hosted, but all my other ideas for how to introduce the guys to Ellis never felt right. Dinner party: too formal. Meal in a restaurant: too loud and not private enough. There was Ellis's plan of just never meeting them, but I'm pretty sure she was joking or that she was just still angry about them knowing. Though with her British humour, I can never quite tell.

Jack was on my side. Before me, he never really watched hockey, but I think having me in his life has brought out a love for the sport. He was most excited to meet Jackson Felix, the Spears goalie, and I had to be the one to tell him that Felix wouldn't be attending. Actually, a lot of the team still only knows the bare minimum about our situation, there is no way I am letting it slip again.

Edge was right when he said Cassie was going to kill me when I told her I was going to be a dad. The PR department were easily placated once she heard how serious I am about Ellis and my family. Still, she told me to keep everything as low key as possible right now, more so for Ellis's sake. Since she found out about Ellis's fibromyalgia, she wants to make sure Ellis has as straightforward a pregnancy as she can. Coach Mitch agreed: he was openly happy for me but he knows that it is better to keep this as close to the chest as possible to make sure Ellis's pregnancy is as stress free as we can make it.

Luckily for all of us, journalists don't care as much about me now that I'm not partying like a rookie. But if even one reporter made Ellis uncomfortable, I don't think I'd handle that well. Thankfully, there are so many more players going out drinking and getting up to mischief that it can be easy to slip under the radar. Especially now that

I am an older player. There is always someone younger, more interesting. The last time I was really in the news was when I was traded home, but even then it was a case of welcoming me back more so than anything dramatic. When there are players on the team like Anders who feature in underwear campaigns I am not the person the press wants to follow.

Keeping her and Jack out of the limelight was Cassie's advice, that was after she threw a pencil at me for not telling her as soon as it happened. Given the circumstances, I had expected her to at least throw a stapler so I will take that win.

Ellis asked if we could have a bit more time to decide how we want to tell the world and Cassie granted us that. She has a statement ready to go if it leaks before we are ready, saying we were keeping it a secret so Ellis wasn't caused any stress given her health. Cassie hopes that will garner sympathy from people who might be mad they didn't know. Only time will tell.

It's less than an hour until the guys arrive and the garden is sparkling. Back inside, the house feels like a home. Ellis is sat at the kitchen island drinking some tea while Jack is sat on the rug going through a box I haven't seen in a long time.

"He found it while polishing your trophies, I told him I'd show them to him, but he wanted to wait for you." Ellis's words are curt, still slightly stiff with me but she smiles politely, not wanting Jack to feel any tension. He runs over to grab my hand and pulls me over to the box of college pictures on the rug.

On top of the box is written "College Memories". There is another box somewhere with my first year in the

NHL but that has nothing fun for Jack in it. In this box there are a bunch of pictures of his mom and me.

Ellis leaves us to our boy time while I go through a bunch of different pictures of a younger me. I don't remember aging this much, but the boy in these pictures looks nothing like the man I see each morning in the mirror.

Jack holds every picture of his mom and I can see how much he treasures them with how delicate he is being. Most boys his age wouldn't care about any of this but Jack is not like other kids. No, Jack is quiet and introspective, so gentle just like I hope our baby will be.

"Can I keep this one?" Jack is sat close to my side, holding one picture tighter than any other. In this picture I'm sat on a couch with Ellis settled on my legs. I'm looking down at Ellis while she is laughing at whoever was behind the camera.

"Of course you can, bud, but don't you want one of just your mom?" I ask.

"No thanks, I like this one best," he says bluntly.

As Jack wonders away with the photo in tow, my doorbell rings. Ellis's eyes jump to mine, filled with anxiety. I give her a reassuring smile and sigh — all I can muster — before I swing the door open to reveal Anders. He's stood with all his Southern manners, showing up right on time with a bouquet of flowers.

"You gonna invite me in Ruin or just look at me with moon eyes?" Anders smirks, sending me a joking wink. So much for those manners I guess. Instead of replying, I move out of his way so he can waltz past me.

Ellis appears in the kitchen doorway, smiling at Anders.

"You must be Ellis! I'm sure you could have made a better bouquet than this, but I tried." He says with a Texan drawl that could win over the coldest of hearts.

Ellis's smile widens at him. "Don't be silly," she teases. "I appreciate them, thank you." She takes the flowers from him, allowing him to lean in for a peck on her cheek.

I want to listen in on the rest of their exchange, make sure there is no awkwardness between them, but the doorbell ringing again pulls me away. On the other side I can hear both Rook and Edge bickering.

"Just don't be a dick, Ellis needs to like us," I hear Edge muttering aggressively.

"Says the world's biggest asshole, don't scare the kid," Rook snaps back.

"I'm just an asshole to you," Edge spits back.

"Love you too buddy— Hey, Ruin, nice place." Rook snaps to attention when I swing the door open and I gesture towards the inside of the home. But with none of the social etiquette of Anders, he shoves past me to get inside.

I don't bother stopping him; it will be less painful to just let him introduce himself. I warned Ellis beforehand about all the boys' personalities. She refused to meet them unless she was fully prepared, not that I blame her. She was worried they were going to be the stereotypical meathead sports people that you see in teens films. I have to trust these guys every time I hit the ice and I know that they will have our back. Ellis just needs to see it for herself.

Honestly, I'm surprised she didn't start taking notes with how much information she wanted. I have known Edge for four years, Anders for two and Rook for a year; yet I still didn't have answers for everything she asked. I didn't know what any of them studied at school or how many sisters Anders has. Despite knowing Edge for the longest, it shocks me when he walks up to Ellis and smiles. Really genuinely smiles. He even has dimples, where the hell did they come from?

"Hi, I'm Jay," he introduces himself warmly, but it takes my brain a moment to adjust to what I just heard. There's no way he asked her to call him *Jay*.

"Nice to meet you, Jay." Ellis blushes. *My* Ellis blushed for Edge. Before anything else happens, Rook nudges him out of the way.

"I assume I don't need a reintroduction?" Rook says full of confidence.

"I'm sorry, have we met?" Ellis tilts her head playing the perfect role.

"Ouch, my poor heart. Don't worry Ellis, I know before Ruin stole my thunder there were sparks between us." He winks at her like he did once before. *He wishes*, I think to myself.

"Whatever helps you sleep at night." Ellis winks back at him mockingly. I can see the tension in her shoulders softening every minute.

"Hi dude, you must be Jack?" Rook asks dropping into a squat in front of Jack, lifting his hand for a high five which Jack quickly returns.

As brief introductions come to an end and the full swing of conversation fills the room, the house bursts into life. Music starts humming through the speakers as Ellis hits play on her favourite playlist and everyone is laughing as though they've known her forever. The players are waiting hand and foot on her without me having to ask, and much to her annoyance, nobody stops when she asks them to.

With the four of us she shouldn't have to do a single thing today.

-

I haven't known Jack for very long but in that time this is the happiest I've seen him. He is stood with both his hands on his hips and his brows are drawn down as he explains the rules of "football" to Rook. I keep repeatedly calling it soccer, to which both Ellis *and* Jack correct me.

Even though Rook could run circles around many professional players, he is listening with rapt attention. I think this is the longest he has ever listened to anyone that wasn't coach Mitch or Cassie. Now though, he is asking questions and asking for Jack's advice on how to kick the ball. Beside me, Ellis is hiding a smile behind a glass of juice with stars in her eyes looking at her boy.

"I like you both happy," I tell her.

"Seeing him like this, confident and open, it makes me happy. If his dad was around he wouldn't be this kid." I wish I knew more about Jack's father, but a part of me knows that if I knew how to find him I would find myself in a prison cell.

"Ellis! Help me!" Rook hollers from the ground rolling in the grass as Jack laughs above him.

"That was a red card for sure!" Anders shouts and Edge goes to join Jack above our teammate.

"Don't worry kid I'll hold him down." Edge lies on Rooks chest and Jack laughs harder, beginning to tickle him.

"Ellis! I'm a damsel, save me!" Rook is still hooting and hollering and Ellis is holding her sides from how hard she is laughing, she looks truly free and open. It's glorious to see.

Eventually Edge rolls off Rook to help him up but Rook goes limp. "I need a kiss from a princess to save me."

"If you think I'm getting down on that floor you're crazier than you look." Ellis laughs, walking away and into the house, leaving the men to fend for themselves.

I follow behind her, needing to get myself a drink too. I shake my head at her in dismay, speaking low, "If you weren't pregnant with my baby, Rook would absolutely be trying to date you."

She tuts at me. "I wouldn't date any of these idiots." She holds her pinkie finger up to promise me, but instead of linking it back, I hold her hand in mine, close to my face.

"Does that include me?" I whisper against her knuckles.

"I'm not sure. If you had asked me when you told them about the baby. There would be no way but now – I get it. They are easy to talk to. I guess I forgive you, that's what I am trying to say." Her breath is heavy and I feel the pulse in her wrist thumping against my fingers. There is barely an inch between us, but it still isn't close enough. Any distance would be too far when it comes to Ellis, so I can't help it when my body sways even closer to hers.

Every one of my prayers are answered when her body sways towards me too. She lifts her chin so her lips graze against mine. Before I close the tiny gap between us, her phone rings from the counter. Snapping out of our haze, she darts past me to grab it.

"Lyndsey is outside, I'll go let her in." Her voice is a laboured gasp, but it's enough to pull me back to the room.

After less than a minute, Ellis is ushering her friend out to the garden. The distance is a palpable thing pulling us away from each other again, but now I know she wants me too beside her hormones, I could see it in her face. Even if only for a second, she felt it. It had to mean something.

It hits me like a wave as I watch Ellis play with Jack after introducing Lyndsey to the guys. This is the life I'm lucky enough to have, and I'm going to give it my everything. After this season, I only have one more on my contract with the Spears, and I never would have thought I would be ready to retire when I signed it – but somehow I do. Plus, even if I did sign again I only have a few good years left in me. Hockey is physically demanding and soon my body is going to protest against the strain. I want to be here for Ellis and Jack and our baby, see them grow and hold them when they cry. I want to have my family. I need to figure out if now is the right time or if I am just being swept up in the emotions of becoming a parent.

Hockey was my driving force, but Ellis has given me so much more than I thought I deserved. Even if she doesn't want the same things as me, if she doesn't want to be a family, I will come to terms with that. But I don't want to miss a single moment of our future.

My life.

With Ellis.

Chapter Fifteen

Liam

Every player has a pre-game routine. Whether it's as simple as eating a specific breakfast or playing certain songs in the locker room. My routine used to be so simple: eat eggs for breakfast and not look at my phone for two hours before I hit the ice.

Simple, effective and helped me get in the zone. I don't think I have been in the zone since the day I found out I was going to be a dad. Eggs are still my pre-game breakfast, but how am I supposed to put my phone away when Ellis could need me? This morning I nearly missed the baby kicking. Again.

Ellis has been able to feel it for a little while, flutters inside her. But the last few days they've been stronger, strong enough to feel from the outside, and I kept missing it. First it was because I was at training, then yesterday I missed it again because I was at my place while Ellis was getting kicked about half an hour away.

I only managed to feel it this morning because I swung by to see if they wanted to come to the game, to which the answer was still no. I was about to walk out when Ellis called me back and I finally felt it. That feeling hitting my palm could have knocked me over and now I can't put my phone down, even though the puck drops in an hour.

"Ruinsky! My office!" I hear coach yell. He yelled at me more today during practice than ever before, and I wish I could say it is just because he's in a bad mood. In fairness, he is *always* in a bad mood, so, it must be the fact I am playing like shit that's the problem.

As I walk towards his office, Rook "oohs" and "ahs" like a child, but I don't have it in me to flip him off. Luckily, I have Edge who is more than willing to do the honour for me.

"Hey coach, what's up?" I try to avoid going in, I just lean on the side of the door frame like a scared little boy, but I don't want to be yelled at right now. Coach's thick brows are furrowed as he stares me down.

Coach Mitch is a great man. He loves the game and he loves his players. Most of the time. He knows his stuff and he is not the type of man to butt in with our personal lives unless it starts to affect the game.

"Don't play dumb, Ruin. What's gotten into you?" His voice remains stern. Giving into the tone, I sulk all the way into the room flopping onto the chair facing him.

"Just not on it today I guess," I reply limply. It's a shitty excuse but it is worth a try. This is the last game of our season, so I know he'll give me no grace.

Some would think that because this game doesn't matter in the grand scheme of the NHL he would let it go, but that is not Coach Mitch's style. He wants to win, go out on a bang, show the other teams that we are a solid team that just had bad luck this go around.

"Oh, I'm sorry, Your Highness." He is trying to get under my skin. Rile me up. "I didn't realise players got a pass because they don't want to do their job properly."

"Coach, look…" I can smooth this over. Say I have a pulled muscle or some other bullshit he might buy.

Coach's demeanour softens by only a short margin before he continues, "I know son, being *here* when you want to be *there* hurts. I know that first-hand, but you can't let everyone else down because of it."

My excuses weren't working, so I give in to his way. "What do I do?" I ask.

Coach leans forward on his desk, hands clasped together. "Your job. You get on the ice and into the zone and play your ass off until we win, and then you get to go home and be with your family." He makes it sound so simple. But getting in the zone is hard when every time I focus my mind goes back to the moment I felt that kick on my hand and it knocks me out of it all over again.

"I just wish they were here," I tell him truthfully, my voice a whisper.

I notice Coach's eyebrows are less of a frown, and his face is awash with sympathy. "I'm sorry, son. But there's nothing we can do about that." At least he genuinely looks like he feels bad for me, Coach Mitch isn't the type of man to blow up my ego just for the sake of it. "What we can do is win so you go home to a celebration. Look, this is the last game of the season and then you have months to love on your girl, just get through tonight," he urges.

"Sorry, Coach." I know he is right, each minute the puck drop gets closer.

Coach leans back in his chair again before bellowing, "Let's go play some hockey!"

–

All I can think about is skating onto the ice and seeing everyone's families smiling at them except mine. The only other person in my boat is Edge, but that's because he doesn't talk to his family much any more. Not since his dad died anyway.

I know that it's unfair to want Ellis here. She has her life to plan, and coming to a hockey game is a very large deviation from that plan. I knew when we decided to co-parent that our lives would revolve around whatever she needed because she will be the lead caregiver. She'll be there every day, doing everything, while I play hockey. I would never fault her for that.

On top of the parenting responsibilities, I think about the other challenges she faces. Ellis never chose to have fibromyalgia. Life took away that choice, so I give her as much choice as I can with how we are going to be working together going forward. Even if I wish she chooses differently sometimes.

We haven't even spoken about the near kiss last week, but I can't deny that it is another thing keeping me distracted. I wanted nothing more than to kiss her, to show her how I feel about her, but I know in my heart that she doesn't want that. Ellis is being ruled by her hormones, and I need to be the level-headed one when all I want to do is take her to bed and not let her leave until she is addicted to me.

I think Anders has picked up on my weird vibes. I expected him to come over after coach had me in his office, but he just stares at me from across the room. Anders never shies away from sharing his opinion and I know he has a bunch about the way I behaved in practice.

He was majorly biting his tongue for some reason. I guess he feels sorry for me, he doesn't want to give me a lashing when he thinks I've already had enough. A captain has to be the one to lift us up, not take a bat to our kneecaps, so he is giving me a wide birth. Even though it's probably killing him.

Even now as we line up for warm-ups, he keeps looking over his shoulder at me like he's worried I might disappear. He needn't worry though. My plan is to win this game in record time. Like, world record-breaking speed, so I can go home and feel my baby kick again before Ellis goes to sleep.

I can hear music blaring through the speakers as an omnipotent voice counts down to our entrance in the corridor leading to the ice. *Three, Two, One... Go.* In succession, we all skate on seamlessly as usual. The sight and sounds of roaring fans still hit me every time. The oppressive lighting and thundering noise from the arena flows through my bloodstream.

There is nothing else like it. It's completely electrifying. It's the thing that gets my blood pumping and my adrenalin flowing; it is the same feeling I've gotten since the first time my blades touched the ice as a child. A feeling of home, of rightness, the feeling that told me this is what I wanted to do with my life.

I once thought there was nothing better than it. That was until I held Ellis in my arms again.

Suddenly, it feels like the ice is swept out from under me. My legs feel weaker as I look beyond the glass surrounding the rink. Sat right behind the goal, are Ellis and Jack. She's wearing a large jersey adorned with my number eight. Her hair is curled and her lips are painted red to match our crimson-coloured kits.

I can't believe she's here. She must know I wouldn't be able to stay away. On shaking legs, I skate over to them while trying to ignore the lump forming in my throat.

133

The crowd is cheering so loud that I know she wouldn't hear me talking to her, instead I rip off my glove to knock on the Plexiglass in greeting. It only crosses my mind for a second that this will probably bring attention to her and our relationship; but I'm too happy to think about the consequences. For all everyone else knows, Ellis and Jack could be anyone to me. But if she's here, it must mean she's ready for Cassie to release a statement about my impending fatherhood. I can't imagine what brought about her sudden change of mind. Regardless, her presence is all the support I could need right now.

However, Jack is in my bad books. He's wearing a Felix jersey instead of one bearing what I want to be his future surname.

I will take the time to lecture him on the importance of repping the right man on the ice later though, right now I hold up my hand for him against the glass.

"You're here," I speak loudly, hoping Ellis will hear. I can't be sure she knows exactly what I said, but she nods rapidly in response, her wide smile beaming in excitement.

Jack is either hopped up on sugar or adrenalin because his eyes are wild. Still, he is looking at me with pride that nearly stops my heart. I didn't think approval from a five-year-old would mean so much to me just a few months ago.

Ice flies up next to me as Anders slides to a stop. "Surprise!" he says to me pointing at Ellis.

"You knew about this?" By the smug grin on his face, I already know the answer, but I'm still waiting for them to disappear and it all to have been some kind of hallucination caused by the amount of Axe spray Rook wears.

"I helped plan this, shit, you are a hard man to keep a secret from. You looked like a kicked pup all day." He slaps my shoulder, smiling at my still-shocked face. He skates away again, throwing a wink.

I follow behind him with a new sense of eagerness.

I know I'm going to win this game. I have some people to impress.

A shutout. 5-0. The best we have played all damn season. Shit, if we had been playing like that we might have been in with a shot of the Stanley Cup, but I'm happy with the alternative. Instead, I get a few extra weeks of break to be Liam the dad, not just Ruin the hockey player.

Felix made a point to tell me that every goal he saved was for Jack, so I think that is going to cement him as the favourite player whether I like it or not. I might just not tell him. But who am I kidding? Of course I'm going to tell him. He'll be so excited. Almost as excited as I am to get out of this arena. As soon as the final whistle blew I was all but flying down the tunnel and into the shower. The quicker I am clean and changed, the quicker I can get to Ellis and Jack.

Sliding my feet into my loafers I am near skipping every other step as I try not to run to the family room of the arena. My post-game suit jacket billows with the speed I walk down the shiny corridors towards them.

I burst through the door and my eyes find Ellis waiting for me. She's over in the corner sat in a plush-looking chair with Jack bouncing at her side talking to a few other kids. It calms me to see that she's not alone though. Cassie is sat beside her talking a mile a minute, but it seems that as soon as her eyes meet mine she loses focus.

"Liam!" Jack is quicker on his feet than his mother. He throws himself in the air at me waiting to catch him. "You were so cool! Hockey is so fast! Did you see Felix save every goal?! He's so cool, he looked at me before he skated off. I hope he thinks I'm cool, too. Do you think I'm cool? I think you're cool."

"Jack sweetheart, take a breath." Ellis interrupts the whirlwind in my arms.

I can't help but laugh at his excitement. "Felix definitely thinks you're cool, he told me that he saved every goal just for you," I tell him.

Jack's eyes widen even further. "Woahhhhhh really? I love hockey. I love you, Liam." He jumps out of my arms and runs back to join the gaggle of other children.

But I'm frozen.

Ellis is frozen.

I know it's probably just the adrenalin, but maybe he meant it. I *want* to believe he meant it.

She looks at me, slightly shell-shocked, but her eyes are still full of warmth. "Congratulations, Mr Ruinsky," she breaks the silence. I wonder if she's congratulating me on the win or receiving Jack's love.

I chuckle at her formality. "Well, thank you Ms Ainsley."

It would feel right to take Ellis into my arms to celebrate a moment like this. But I don't want to take away from Jack's admission. Instead, I let his words settle between us, and wonder if Jack can love me, could his mother ever love me the same way again?

"Jack buddy, come on," I call him over and he jumps up at me again, but this time I swing him up onto my shoulders so I can tuck Ellis into my side.

Apart from telling Jack to take a breath and congratulating me, Ellis hasn't said anything since I walked into the room. But I'm not going to push her. Being here was already more than I could have asked for.

She knows that coming here, being in this room, is a sure-fire way for our new future, her pregnancy, to hit the news. Her facing it head-on is enough to make me weak. But I'll ignore it for a few more hours, until Jack is in bed and we can make a full plan.

I don't mind waiting. Being around Ellis Ainsley is like waiting for the sun to rise, like watching the first hints of light flow over the hills and brighten everything it touches. She bursts through the darkness of the nights.

That's why I call her Sunshine.

Chapter Sixteen

Ellis

I'm on cloud nine. Coming to the game, sitting right up against the glass, was a big step. When Aiden asked if I would do it, I knew what it would mean, the public would officially link Liam and me. There was no way he would see us and be able to stay calm. I had to decide if I was ready for it.

I knew I would have to face that music sooner or later. I couldn't keep this in the shadows forever. It also wouldn't be fair of me to make Liam keep it a secret forever, nor would that be fair on our child.

So, when Aiden asked, I pulled up my big girl panties and bit the bullet. Jack has been begging to go to a game ever since he met Liam, which made the decision slightly easier. When I told him we were going he nearly rocketed through the ceiling with excitement. The team played incredibly, and Liam looked amazing on the ice. I forgot how elegant he looks out there, at one with the blades.

Then the unimaginable happened: Jack said he loves Liam. I knew he liked having him around, but I didn't know Jack had bonded in a deeper way. Of course, after the rush of adrenalin from watching the game, his emotions were heightened. Still, I could see it meant a lot to Liam judging by his reaction.

As we leave via the back entrance of the arena, there are still hordes of fans congregated outside. There are women hoping they might catch the eyes of a single player, kids hoping for an autograph, men wanting to see their heroes. Plus, there are always a few smaller news outlets who don't make it into the press room looking for a quote.

Liam takes my hand in his, to the eyes of onlookers we must look like a real family. Him with Jack on his shoulders, my growing bump stretching my jersey while we walk hand in hand through the small crowds. Liam moves to put a steady gentle hand on my back leading me towards the staff parking area until we hear something that makes us freeze. From somewhere in the crowd, someone yells my name.

"Ellis!" a male voice yells. But not just any voice – it's a voice I know. Or *used* to know.

Michael is pushing his way through the crowd until he is a few feet in front of me. Jack's dad is breathing so hard his nostrils flare with each exhale. I stand in front of Liam, my heart racing and my skin prickling with heat. Sensing that something is wrong, Liam lifts Jack from his shoulders and passes him over to Rook.

"Hey Rook, why don't you take Jack to meet Spike?" His voice is tense, he must be able to see the resemblance. Michael has the same dark hair Jack has, as well as the same eyes. Eyes I thought I loved, even when they were looking at me with hatred. Rook takes Jack's hand and leads him back into the arena to introduce him to the Spears mascot.

"What are you doing here?" As strong as I wish I could be, my voice still trembles. Today has been a long day, so high in emotion and tension. Seeing Michael was so far down on the list of things I expected today. I knew he followed hockey years ago, but the chances of him actually being here tonight were small.

"That doesn't matter, what the fuck do you think you're doing?" he spits out, his lips curling in disgust. Dark eyes glaring at me as though he caught me committing some crime.

"Excuse me?" I gasp out. It's been six years since the last time I saw him and the first thing he does is verbally attack me. Not even asking about his damn son.

"I knew you loved him. You never gave a shit about me did you? He snapped his fingers and you came running like a pathetic whore." His face was red with anger, that vein in his forehead pulsing violently. Before I have a chance to defend myself, Liam pulls me back to his side, stepping in front of me.

"That's enough." Liam's voice is low and scary. I could let him handle this. I could stand behind him and let him get rid of Michael but that's not what I want. Michael doesn't get to scare me any more.

I tug on the back of Liam's suit jacket. Facing Michael myself, I look him directly in the eyes. His six-foot-one frame is less intimidating now that I have more confidence in myself. Back when we were together, those few inches difference made me feel so small. But not now.

"Aw, can't fight your own battles Ellis? Need a knight in shining armour to save you?" He pouts mockingly, coming even closer, his scuffed shoes come to stand two feet away when he sneers.

I ignore his statements, focusing on what should matter. "Jack is great, thanks for asking." My voice is coated in sarcasm. Finally, it comes out as strong as I want it to. My gaze doesn't waiver from his.

"What?" He coughs, not expecting me to stand on my own two feet. The Ellis he knew would have backed down, submitted to him, but a lot has changed. *I* have changed.

"Your son was just here, and instead of acting like an adult, you want to throw a tantrum and swear like it will get you anywhere." My arms cross over my chest, but I'm not hiding from him. I am scolding him like a toddler.

"He is my son, I can act however I want in front of him!" He splutters his words, looking around as though he is only now remembering he is in public. He wanted to put me on the spot, make me feel small, but now that I want to dish it back he's suddenly worried about his audience.

"What's his middle name?" My voice gets louder then, every moment that I have struggled being a single mum starts to pour out of me.

"Well…" He is trying to remember, though I don't think he knows. He has never asked about Jack from the day he kicked me out. Once I got away I didn't try to reach out, worried he would claw me back to him.

"What size shoe does he wear? What is his teacher's name? What was his first word?" It seeps out of me now. My words accusatory but I won't let him get away with this behaviour. He doesn't get to corner me and act all high and mighty when he knows nothing about our life. Nothing about his own son.

"What the fuck are you talking about?" He whisper-yells now, not wanting everyone to know his pitfalls. Still, anger and resentment are prevalent in his eyes.

"You don't get to call him your son, he is a stranger to you. Did you notice the way he wasn't excited to see you, didn't run into your arms? That's because he doesn't know who the hell you are. You want to claim him, be my guest. We can go to the courthouse and start the back pay for five years of child support you owe. But there is no way in hell that you get to talk to me like that. Not any more." The anger in my voice is eerie – as though I'm listening to a stranger speak.

"I'm not paying shit," he yells, clearly shocked, "I can't even be sure he's mine."

Six years ago, that would have hurt. Not today. Michael is expecting it to hurt me, he smirks when he speaks thinking he is going to win whatever game he is playing. Instead of shrinking in on myself, begging him to believe me, I stand my ground.

"Oh for god's sake Michael, you are a pathetic excuse for a man. You are here yelling because I have a new life? You haven't been around for six years and you think you get a say? You don't get to make me feel small, I'm worthy of respect. You want to yell and swear because it makes you feel like a big man, I don't care." It feels good, regaining my power from him. Liam has given me a landing pad that I never knew I could have. I can rant and rave and yell at my ex and Liam isn't going to think any less of me.

"So, here's your choice." I steel my gaze on his. "Leave me and my family alone, disappear back into whatever hole you crawled out of or take me to court, try and see your son, but be ready for me to take you for all you are worth; not for me, I don't need anything from you, but for Jack." The whispers around us intensify but nobody moves. I watch a million emotions flit behind Michael's eyes. Shock. Anger. I wait for guilt to hit him but it doesn't, instead he smirks again.

"Fuck you Ellis. I could ruin you! You might think you're happy but he left you once, now you think he is going to stick around? You're delusional. He doesn't want you, you were just an easy piece of ass. Liam will leave you alone, you and that bastard kid." Michael all but yells that, wanting to embarrass me in front of Liam and the crowd of fans. But I don't let him.

Beside me, Liam takes a step forward. Silent, jaw clenched. A towering, intimidating athlete. Michael staggers back slightly before turning on his heels and walking away, his pace quickening.

"Goodbye, Michael!" I shout after him. "I have a life to live. I hope you grow up, but I won't hold my breath." I allow myself to inhale deeply, taking Liam's hand in mine and tugging him back into the arena to find Jack and Rook.

I just want to get to my son and get him home, where I know he will be safe.

–

By the time we pull up outside of my apartment Jack is fast asleep in the back seat of Liam's car. Liam tried to convince me to stay at his place tonight but I need Jack in his own bed, surrounded by his own things for comfort.

Liam pulls Jack from the car, carrying his sleeping body up the stairs and into his room. I follow close behind them, the glow from the dark stars on Jack's ceiling is the only light in the room apart from the light seeping in from the open bedroom door. In the low light I can see Jack snuggling up under his covers, not bothered at all by the events of tonight. I can't say the same. My skin is burning, it feels like ants are under it trying to burst out. It is a mix of the dwindling adrenalin and the mum guilt that no matter what choice I make, I always feel like I fall short.

Not letting me linger the way I want to, Liam puts a hand at the base of my spine to guide me out of Jack's room and over to the sofa. Silently, Liam potters around my kitchen making us both cups of tea. I can see that he wants to say something. Like he doesn't know where to start or he doesn't know what words to use. I could put him at ease. Break the silence for him, but I don't have the energy, I don't even know if I will have it in me to drink the tea he is making, but I will try. He is trying to help me, so I will let him. I need the support.

I need him.

Chapter Seventeen

Ellis

I never got sent to the head teacher's office in school. I just kept my head down and did what I had to do to get through the day. My peers ignored me, I wasn't part of their world, much to my mother's chagrin. She wanted me to befriend them, to worm my way into the inner circle, but I didn't. I did my school work and stayed home studying, doing my best to remain invisible, knowing that as soon as I could I wanted to get away from that life. It was so pretentious, and everyone was talking about each other behind their backs. I wanted as little attention as possible.

Now that's out of the window. Since the scene with Michael was so public, videos of our argument and Liam defending me have been making the rounds online. So here I am, effectively sat outside of the head teacher's office, except the head is Cassie, PR manager for the Seattle Spears. Last time I was here, I begged her to let us keep our relationship to ourselves. I don't owe the world anything, but now I don't have that choice. She warned me that it wouldn't last forever. It was bound to come out; that's why I was at the game in the first place. I thought I was ready for the public to know that Liam has someone in his life, but that isn't the story any more. Michael ruined that.

"Ellis, talk to me." Liam has been trying, but I just don't know what to say. He woke up after sleeping on my couch with a bunch of messages from Cassie demanding we come to her office asap. He wanted us to be able to walk in that office with our heads held high and a plan to fix the PR disaster of a pregnant woman getting into a spat with her ex in the staff parking lot. I just don't have the energy. I want to go back to sleep, for it all to have been a bad dream. It's what I get for thinking I could be happy. For being delusional enough to think the other shoe wouldn't eventually drop. I never get that lucky.

"His middle name is Thomas." Liam breaks the silence turning in his chair to face me.

"What?" My jaw is hinged open. He takes a deep breath before he speaks again.

"Jack, his middle name is Thomas." He coughs and takes both of my hands in his. "He wears size four shoes and his teacher is Mr Bowman, but I don't know his first word. I have been trying to remember if you told me, but I can't." Liam looks into my eyes and I hear everything he isn't saying. It's proof that Jack doesn't need Michael. There are people in his life who already love him, who know him. They're right under my nose.

"I'm sorry," Liam says, his voice low and dejected when I stare at him speechless.

"You have nothing to apologise for, this is on me," I tell him, my voice is steady and sure because it's the truth. My stupidity and need to seem strong against Michael is going to have a negative effect on Liam. I never wanted that. I was so busy wanting to feel strong that I let him down.

"No Ellis, I should have stepped in. Or called security, but I was so blown away watching you tear him apart." He slides over on his chair, his knees push against my thigh. There are bags under his eyes and his hair is messier than usual. "I'm supposed to protect you and I didn't do a damn thing to help."

"You can only protect me if I let you." I take his hands in mine, I need him to hear me. He did what he thought was best. "You got Jack out of there, that is more important to me. I'm sorry. This is going to mess with your job – for Christ's sake I should know better."

"You didn't know he would be there." He tries to ease my raging emotions, but it doesn't work. Even as he rubs circles on the back of my hand to calm me.

"Still, I knew showing up there would draw attention to us and I didn't think it through enough, now we are both suffering for it." I wanted to support him. I knew he wanted us there even if I hesitated. He didn't want to push, but I could see how much it would mean to him to have me and Jack there. Making him smile was all I was thinking about.

"I don't think Cassie cares about blowback on my career, I think she's mad she wasn't told you were going to be there. Like she couldn't protect you from the public the way she wanted. She knows you're important to me." Liam gives me a reassuring smile but it doesn't reach his eyes.

He hasn't let me look online, won't let me see what people are saying. Maybe it's for the best. I'm sure people told their versions of the event, captured some pictures or footage from afar. I'm already beating myself up enough for this without every Spears fan giving me hate for things that they don't understand.

I believe in Cassie. She has the guys' respect for a reason, she is dependable and a dog with a bone when someone comes for her team. To her, the Spears are her responsibility and now apparently that includes my family.

With perfect timing, a tired-looking Cassie steps into the open doorway.

"Hey guys, come on in." She smiles, it's a stiff professional one. My nerves skyrocket again as we walk in.

"Sit El, do you want something to eat?" She guides me further into the room over to a very comfortable-looking office chair, helping me sit even though it isn't necessary. "I bought some English Breakfast teabags if you want a cup?"

"That's sweet but I'm good thank you, I just want to get this over with." My muscles relax in the comfy chair.

"Can I have some water?" Liam asks taking the seat next to me, Cassie's attention flies to him when he speaks. The glare she gives him could kill. It's a mixture of anger and a bone-deep frustration. Seeing how quickly she can go from sweet little Cassie to me, to being the ball-buster I was warned she usually is, is remarkable.

"Fine," she deadpans, reaching into the mini-fridge under her desk and pulling him a bottle.

"Okay, let's get into it," Cassie says after throwing the bottle at Liam with a glare. She leans forward in her large chair, her elbows on the desk between us. "We have a couple of problems," she begins.

"First is the fact you decided to turn up at the game without giving me any warning. I would have at least expected Anders to give me a heads-up as captain. If you were ready for the public to know you should have let me release the statement pre-game and it would have solved a lot of public speculation. Obviously that's the first thing I did this morning, it has gone over as well as to be expected given the circumstances."

"That seems… easy." Liam seems unsettled when he speaks. I lean over to take his hand in mine again.

"It is, but there are some things – well, *someone* – making it more tricky." She takes a second, looking between the two of us before she speaks again. "The rumours that are flying are a little crazy. The biggest is coming from *Hot Hockey News*."

"For fuck's sake." Liam tenses at her words, his shoulders jump to his ears his muscles stiffen. I'm confused. I've never even heard of *Hot Hockey News*.

"Who?" I ask feeling out of the loop. They both look tense. I want to know who the hell we are dealing with, and what battle it's going to bring.

"It's a blog that covers the NHL, but they stretch every story – even make stories from nowhere. They aren't exactly ethical on their reporting." Cassie looks drained just talking about them. From her jaded reaction, this definitely isn't her first run-in. Liam grinds his jaw next to me.

"What are they saying?" he rumbles out. His voice is laced with a lethal anger. His nostrils are flared, a bull about to strike.

Cassie breathes in preceding her next sentence. "That you're attempting to baby-trap him." She nods to me reluctantly.

Liam rises quickly from his chair, running his fingers through his hair as he begins pacing the room behind me.

"What?" I almost ask with a laugh. I was ready for people to judge me. To say Liam could do better, or that I'm not ice hockey girlfriend material, but *baby-trapping*?

Cassie flicks her eyes between Liam and me. "They've published material stating that you both met in a bar and had a one-night stand. They claim now that Ellis is pregnant, she wants a cut of a new contract – if or when Liam signs one."

Her words hang in the air, an unwelcome presence as Liam continues to pace. My jaw open and closes, but I can't find any appropriate words. I don't know where to begin: between my anger, my shock, and my frustration, I'm completely lost.

Of course, nobody knows our history. It was such an important part of my life, but to everybody else it doesn't even exist. I was his long before he was their favourite player. We loved each other before he was number eight on the Spears. But to the fans, to the blog runners, I'm a nobody.

I might have even thought the same if I were on the outside. A woman suddenly pregnant and clinging to a hockey player. It's a fucked-up but valid theory – one we are conditioned to believe, despite whatever the reality might be.

"That's bullshit. I want a press conference now, Cassie," Liam demands. Every part of him looks ready to burst.

"Not happening," she tells him. He stops in his tracks, turning to face her directly. Seeing his anger now directed towards her, Cassie doesn't even blink. She just raises her eyebrows at him before explaining: "We aren't going to give them the satisfaction of knowing they rattled you."

"I'm not going to sit here and let them say shit like that about Ellis! No chance!" Liam is yelling now. "They think my baby is a *trap*," he emphasises painfully. I try to catch his hand when he stands beside me, but he barely notices, the hairs on his arm raised.

"Of course they are wrong, but will you let me do my job?" Cassie asks, frustration starting to edge into her tone.

"You're right Cassie. He's sorry, aren't you Liam?" I manage to grab his hand then. Pulling him back down into his chair.

He inhales deeply. "Yes – yeah, sure. Sorry." He mumbles, fumbling his fingers against mine.

"Do you have any pictures of the two of you from college?" Cassie continues, to which we both nod in unison. "Good, I want you to post one on Instagram." She instructs Liam.

"That's it?" Liam laughs, unsure. I can't say I understand either. I hate that people are thinking such despicable things of me and all she wants is a social media post.

"It will prove that you weren't strangers and end needless speculation, with a caption that says something like: 'A decade old throwback to my college days. Who would have thought we'd be starting a family after all this time?' You don't need to go into massive detail, but the cat is out the bag regarding the pregnancy, so let's at least protect the truth of your arrangement." Cassie waits for our reactions. To me, it sounds so simple yet so effective. There's just one glaring issue.

"But wouldn't that imply we're dating?" I say after a beat. And I'm not wrong. A caption referring to starting a family, with a picture from when we were dating, is going to switch from baby-trapping accusations to dating rumours. My presence at the game has already caused so many issues, if we give the wrong impression again, who knows what rumours may fly after that.

"Frankly, it doesn't matter." Cassie takes a deep sigh. "In fact, it does me a huge favour if Liam appears off the market. One less single man to worry about. We need to paint the picture that you are a happy family unit. What goes on behind closed doors isn't anyone's business, but we need to prove that you, Ellis, aren't a money hungry vulture, and that *you*—" she points at Liam, "aren't a stupid athlete who forgot to use protection."

"Done. I'll do it." Liam tells her. He sounds so sure that I don't dare contradict him, even if it scares me.

Cassie eases her back into her chair. "Now that's out of the way, there is the Michael problem." Her eyes narrow when she says his name, contempt pushing at the surface of her professional exterior. "I'm hoping Michael will be as easy to deal with. If you want to file a restraining order, we have the evidence that he was verbally abusive to you as well as videos that have been posted online. My recommendation would be to wait and see if he tries to escalate anything. Our team lawyers can send him a cease and desist which, if I know anything about men like him, will send him running with his tail between his legs. If it *does* come to him wanting to escalate, you will have full access to the Spears lawyers to fix it."

I shake my head instinctively. I know there's no point in getting a restraining order. Michael has embarrassed himself so publicly he'll go away to lick his wounds. He's always been more bark than bite, and especially after seeing Liam in the flesh – I doubt he would push his luck again. "Thank you," I say gratefully for her offers. "I think let's wait him out, but I'll let you know if I change my mind."

"Good." Cassie stands from her chair, walking around the desk to rest a hand on my shoulder. "That's all I need you for today, so take your girl home Liam, she is too pregnant for all this stress." She smiles warmly.

I wish I could force a smile back, but my mind is too busy. Whether we are in a relationship or not, the world is going to think we are. They are going to feel entitled to share their opinions about my life and I'll have no way to combat it. I'll be living a lie.

There is no way to prove to everyone what Liam and I truly are, when right now I don't know myself.

Chapter Eighteen

May

Ellis

Liam's hand slides up the outside of my thigh and his thumb rubs under the hem of my dress. The heat of his chest against mine takes my heart rate through the roof. I wonder if he can feel my heart beating against his.

Any thought is wiped from my mind when his lips drop to my throat, he nips and sucks his way up to my jaw and I feel heat flood between my legs. It still isn't enough, I need so much more. But Liam seems content with teasing me. His hands continue to run up and down my thighs before sliding around to grab my arse over my dress.

"Please Liam," I moan out and feel him smirk against my skin.

"Please what, Sunshine?" he whispers, not pulling back to look at me.

"More... Just more."

It seems he is done taking things slow, because when his hands run back down again he hooks them around my thighs and lifts me before slamming me against the wall.

Shit, that hurt.

Wait, where is Liam?

Fuck. I try to open my eyes against the bright morning light. I'm praying this is another dream, but the fact my back feels like every vertebra is fusing together tells me it's not.

Tears start to flow out of the sides of my eyes and creep towards my ears, but when I try to wipe them away my arms are like lead. A flare-up like this has not happened for a very long time. I knew stopping my meds was going to hurt, but during my last pregnancy no flare-up felt like I was undiagnosed again. Every fibre of my body feels like it is being turned inside out and ripped in half over and over.

I need to push through. I need… I need… *Jack needs me*. The pain needs to wait, I need to be a parent. What time is it? Shit, I can't get to my phone.

There are so many things I still need to do: Bloom and Blossom needs to open, and even if I could get to my phone, I can't expect Lyndsey to take the whole day by herself. No, I need to get up and push through, I can't let the pain beat me. But *fuck*, it hurts.

My tears are non-stop now because I know, I *know* the only thing that will bring me some comfort and help me move even slightly is painkillers, but I can't bring myself to take some. It would kill me for the baby to be dependent on drugs when she is born. There are painkillers that are pregnancy safe, paracetamol for one, but that wouldn't even begin to scratch the surface. I'd take codeine usually but there is a high chance the baby can become dependent on them in utero so I can't bring myself to take even one. One probably wouldn't have a big effect, but I just can't because I can't imagine having to watch my baby go through withdrawals when they are only a few hours old. That pain would out trump this by thousands.

Me and Liam are having a baby girl. When the doctor told us, my heart broke into pieces and she stole every shard. I think Liam was hoping for a girl, he has spoken non-stop about me teaching him how to do hair so he can be helpful, talking about teaching her hockey with Jack since he found out. The excitement of the news made me feel like I was floating and this is the crash back to earth. The rude reminder of my life. I know I need to do anything I can to help me get through the day and the only thing that feels like it might help is painkillers. It is either I take some or I lie here until I become one with the bedspread.

But to get the painkillers I have to move.

Shit.

There aren't many times when I wish I had a partner but now is one. If only I had a strapping hockey player sharing my bed who could help me, who would help me any way he can. I can hear Jack shuffling out of the toilet and I hate to ask him for help but I don't know what else to do. He knows that his mum has days where she isn't as strong but I try to skirt around the nitty gritty as much as I can.

"Jack, sweetie, can you come here?" *Okay game face Ellis, don't let him see how much it hurts.* Smiling wide as he walks into my room I use all my energy to roll onto my side to him.

"Morning Mum, you okay?" He rubs his eyes with his little tiny fists.

"Yeah bud, I'm okay, can you grab my phone for me? I need to call Lyndsey, I'm going to be late for work." All I need to do is get the phone and talk to Lyndsey, I might just tell her to leave the shop closed today and beg her to come look after Jack for me.

"Are you sore? You should call Liam." All hope that I was hiding my pain goes out the window. Jack is little, but not stupid.

"Yeah I am," I answer honestly. "But it's okay, can you please pass me my phone? I will talk to Liam later, don't worry." *Stay calm*, I think to myself. *Just focus on getting the phone, don't think about the pain or the nausea.* I will tell Liam when I have to but it has been a long time since he has dealt with a flare-up. Back in university I remember one time where he started questioning my use of medication. He thought he knew best and it killed me to want someone to lean on and not have them on your side.

"Ellis, you need to stop." His voice a mix of anger and defeat. His jaw clenched together so tight I worry it might crack.

"Stop what?" I am in too much pain for his riddles. He stands next to my bed holding a sheet of pills away from me.

"I know how painkillers work. You don't need more, you want more, there is a difference." Each word feels like a dagger to the heart. I've heard this all before but never from him. I thought Liam understood.

"What did you just say?" I want him to take it back and I think when he sees the rising fire in my eyes he realises his mistake too late.

"Ellis…" He tries to explain but I am revved up. I am in so much pain I think death would be kinder and he wants to accuse me of drug chasing.

"No Liam, fuck you. Get out!" I throw the pillow from next to me at him. I wish I had something more substantial to hand but it's the best I can do. Even that movement causes bile to rise in my throat.

"No, Ellis listen." Falling to his knees at my bedside, he tries to take my hands in his but I am too mad to let him.

"You have no fucking idea do you? Oh, to be so perfect."
Tears flow down my face as the anger and pain pour out of me in
tandem. "You think I want this? I thought you knew me better
than that but I am not going to let some dude without a medical
degree try to tell me what I'm feeling."

"I didn't mean it like that." He wipes the tears from my
cheeks but that act of comfort makes me madder.

"No Liam. Next time you get thrown into the boards or one
of your teammates break a bone remember that that is what I
feel every second of every day and I do it without complaint. I
get up and go to class and do what I have to do while wishing
I could scream. Now here you come making me feel worse about
something I can't change." I am full on sobbing now, my words
spoken through hiccups and laboured breaths.

"I'm sorry. I just, I hate seeing you like this." He has told me
that a million times but wishing it away doesn't work. I know
because I have tried.

"And you think I like it? Look if you're going to judge me
for taking painkillers I have been prescribed then there is no point
in you staying."

"I'm sorry, you're right. Come here." He slides himself under
the covers next to me. Part of me wants to fight him but a bigger
part just wants a hug. So I let him in; curling myself into his side
I take shallow breaths as he rubs a gentle hand up and down my
spine. "Forgive me, Sunshine?"

Safe to say he changed his opinion on medication after
that. He did what he could to help me after that but it
has been a long time. He might have gone back to his old
way of thinking for all I know. It will be better for me if I
wait until I feel good before I tell him. That way I won't
feel like a burden.

"Don't worry Mum, I got it, I can fix it." Jack grabs
my phone from the nightstand, running out of the room

with it. His face had a little flash of mischief knowing I can't chase him.

"Jack, come back!" The sound of his running footfall gets further away despite my yelling.

"JACK!" Some instinct tries to make me move and I throw my body up to a sitting position, but before I can fully make it, the pain flows through me so violently that blackness coats the edges of my vision. I fall back down onto the bed again as darkness clouds my eyes.

Knowing I can't afford to lose consciousness right now, I try to wiggle myself up again but to no avail. Each inch I move feels like molten knives are puncturing my muscles. Each joint feels fused together, clicking as I shift.

Jack doesn't come back when I yell for him, but I can hear him chatting on the phone. I don't know where my boy got his sudden heroism from, but I hope Lyndsey forgives me for letting my child call her so early.

She knows better than anyone that having a flare-up can't be scheduled. As much as I wish they could. There are things I can do to prevent them, like rest and not push myself, but that isn't realistic day to day – especially now I'm pregnant again.

Everything will be okay, I think silently to myself.

Just.

Breathe.

Chapter Nineteen

Liam

My phone is ringing in my pocket as I leave the gym. Seeing the words "Sunshine Calling" light up my screen is a good start to the day already. Perhaps a thirty-year-old man wouldn't normally admit it, but the incoming call gives me butterflies.

"Morning Sunshine, you missing me already?" I laugh.

"Liam?"

My heart skips a beat. That isn't Ellis. Jack's little voice comes through the speaker of my cell and my blood runs cold. It's not strange for me to talk to him when I'm away, but him calling me out the blue threatens to bring up my breakfast. A sense of dread instantly cloaks me.

"Jack? What's wrong, buddy? Where's your mom?" I ask, already pulling out of the car lot, indicating in the opposite direction I usually turn. I know I'm not going home now.

"She's sore, her fibre is bad." Jack's voice sounds so tiny, almost tearful.

"Her fibre? You mean her fibro, buddy?" I ask.

"That's what I said, she's sad and can't move much, and she told me to call Lyndsey... but I called you instead." A hiccup interrupts him before he continues. "You told me

160

to call you if I was scared, and it makes me scared when she cries."

I hold it together as I drive. Barely. "You did the right thing Jack, I'm on my way. Don't worry okay?" I press my foot against the accelerator, speeding through the thankfully quiet streets.

"Is the baby okay?" he asks.

"The baby will be just fine." A croak slips into my voice. "Is the front door unlocked?" I need to change the topic, if I let myself spiral down before I have even seen her, then I might crash the damn car.

"No, but I can do it with my step, are you nearly here?"

"Yes I am, bud, you are such a brave boy Jack. I'm around the corner, so unlock the door for me." On the other end of the line I hear him moving around and the scraping of his stool on the wooden floors.

"I don't feel brave," Jack admits. I want to hug him so badly that my heart aches.

"Being brave isn't about not being scared," I ramble, hoping it'll keep us both distracted. "It's about knowing when to ask for help when things get scary, okay? I'm parking now – I'm right here." I throw the car into a space outside Ellis's and dive out of it. The main door hits the wall with the force I used to push through it and if it breaks that will be something to deal with later.

"Liam!" Jack yells as I burst through the door and he jumps from his stool into my arms. It takes more strength than I thought it would to stop from hitting the floor and holding him until his tears stop.

"It's okay Jack, I'm here, I'm right here." I tell him rubbing a hand down his back as he catches his breath again.

"Liam? Is that you?" Ellis's voice is equal parts stressed, strained and a little shocked.

"Hi Sunshine, I heard you were having a flare with your fibre?" I attempt to joke as I carry Jack into her bedroom on my hip.

She looks incapable of movement, though her eyes widen at the sight of me. They are rimmed red and her already pale skin looks ashen in the dark room. She is looking from Jack to myself with doubt as though she may be hallucinating.

"Jack called you?" she realises. I see the moment her fogged brain catches up to the present.

"Yeah, El. He was scared because he didn't know how to help you." I bring Jack over to her bed where her arms are outstretched for her little boy, who looks smaller than I have ever seen him snuggled up against her.

"Baby, I'm sorry I didn't mean to scare you, come here." She nuzzles her face into his neck. Her arms don't tighten around him as hard as she usually does. Instead she kisses the top of his head.

"Have either of you eaten?" I ask the room to which I receive double head shakes. "Okay, so first thing; Jack do you wanna stay here with your mom or come help me make some pancakes?" I ask. I know Ellis might want to hold on to him for a little longer, but she deserves all the rest she can get.

"Pancakes?" His little face pops up from the bed suddenly excited and no longer tearful.

"Right, little dude, I'll meet you in the kitchen." I lift him down from the bed, watching him scuttle out of the room before turning back to Ellis.

Before I can open my mouth again, she holds one hand up weakly. "Liam, you don't have to stay. I know this looks bad, but I swear I *am* a good mum, everything is just so much worse when I'm pregnant. I swear I'd never leave him hungry. I just can't get to any painkillers and—"

"Ellis, sweetheart, it's okay." I had to interrupt her rambling. She didn't need to justify herself to me. "You couldn't be a bad mom if you tried, just let me help you. I'm not going anywhere and I am at your service, I'm done with my training for the day so I'm free to spend time with you and Jack for as long as you need." I reassure her. Without thinking too deeply, I lean forward and plant a kiss on her forehead.

For a moment I linger close to her. She doesn't speak as I hold her face in my hands, memorising her from top to bottom. I don't know if I'm the only one who feels it, but the air feels thick with unspoken words.

"Is there anything you need me to grab apart from painkillers?" I break the silence.

"No, that's fine," she replies quietly.

I head to join Jack, who waits patiently for me on a kitchen stool. Even if El doesn't think I need to stay, I can't think of where else I would go regardless. I know that I need to work out and I also need to watch game tapes from the season but I can do that tomorrow, what matters right now is making sure they are both okay.

I know me being here takes some weight from her shoulders. She might not ask for the help, but if she can just let me take a small part of that weight from her, I'll do so happily.

Unlike her, though, I am not too stubborn to ask for help.

If I am going to balance the season and having a pregnant girl and little boy looking up to me, I am going to need help. I can't imagine the fear I would have if this had happened when I was travelling. Knowing I wouldn't be here to help sends a shiver down my spine. I can't help but think about my contract ending and wondering what would be best for our collective future, I have people I need to consider now, it isn't just me.

I'm sure my team are going to jump at the chance to spend more time with Jack and Ellis. The only obstacle I can foresee is Ellis being willing to accept more of that help. She's so damn stubborn. I hope she will see it's for the best.

For the first time since she got pregnant, I question if we can really do any of this alone.

Chapter Twenty

Liam

A week has passed, but the memory isn't any less scary.

I'm man enough to admit that seeing Ellis's flare-up worried me. It wasn't just seeing her in pain, but seeing how scared Jack was, and how hard she was trying to pretend to be okay shook me.

On top of it all, I went from being this fun guy in Jack's life, a cool ice hockey player, to a man he came to for support, looking at me to help his mom. That was when I realised that I might be the first real man in Jack's life.

I may be getting a daughter in a few months' time, but that isn't the only new thing in my life. I have a son now as well. And I think Jack might be accepting me as somewhat of a dad. Surprisingly, it feels good. Better than good. It feels… fulfilling.

Ellis was a little bit slower to come around to letting me support her, but that wasn't a surprise. Still, seeing her tear-stained cheeks and ashen skin scared me. It's all I see every time I close my eyes. She looked so helpless and gaunt and I couldn't make it better. It brought back suppressed memories of similar incidents in college – ones I had perhaps pushed to the back of my mind. I remembered her as that sunshine girl, *my* sunshine. I had almost forgotten how bad it can truly get. The guilt of not knowing what to do, how to help, was and still is eating me alive.

I'm a protector; at least I believe I am. I am supposed to keep her out of harm's way. But there was no magic wand I could wave, there was nothing I could throw my money at to make it go away. All I could do was offer her water, food and a hot compress. It wasn't enough.

One good part of the day, if anything, was my alone time with Jack. Though we've had some brief time alone together, it was never to that extent. I loved every second. He is smart and thoughtful, just so much like his mom. He might look like his dad – with dark hair and blue eyes – but every time he speaks, he is his mother's son through and through.

By the end of the day, I got to read him a bedtime story. For a moment in time, I actually felt like a father. I couldn't help but feel giddy with excitement about what I have to come.

But then comes the bad part – the part where I had to leave. I thought about camping out on the sofa but it felt like an imposition to stay over without asking Ellis's permission. I didn't want her to be uncomfortable waking up with me in her space especially knowing she is going to be drained from her flare.

I left Jack and Ellis sleeping in their rooms when I let myself out and drove silently home. But every part of me wanted to crawl into bed with her. To stay close to the family we had created. To pretend, even for one night, that the fake relationship we were allowing the world to believe could be real. Every second I'm not with them, Ellis and I are texting. Little updates on the baby and whatever vegetable they are this week (turnip apparently), or what Jack did at school and if there were any fun customers at Bloom and Blossom that day. Those small, mostly insignificant details of our daily lives keep me attached to my phone.

As though she knows she's on my mind again, my phone pings in my pocket when I walk through my front door coming back from the gym.

> I know I've said it a million times but thank you for last week. <3

> Spending time with you both is never a chore.

> Still, it isn't your job.

> Why isn't it?

> Because you didn't sign up for looking after me.

> I know what I signed up for El, I want to be the person who helps you.

> I want to be a person who doesn't need help.

> Everyone needs help.

My heart sinks at her messages. Ellis isn't wrong, she has thanked me a million times. And I have responded a million times in the same way.

I plop my phone on my couch, knowing Ellis probably won't reply to my final message for a while with her busy schedule. I need a distraction from thinking about how little I can really do to help. I notice one of the many parenting books I have read is open on my coffee table, waiting for me to dive back in. Even though I've read so many, I have yet to be comforted by the words. I have found a trend; every single one of them says that there is no way to fully prepare. I can summarise all of these books in barely one page:

1. *Babies cry.*
2. *Babies shit.*
3. *Babies eat.*
4. *Have patience.*
5. *Good luck.*

So far these books have been unhelpful, and Ellis is going to have to lead the blind. I can't think too hard about that, because it reminds me how Ellis had nobody to help her with Jack, and my heart hurts for her all over again.

It's become a new pattern of mine to keep concealing my emotions for Ellis. My worries for her, my caregiving, my attachment. But over the past few weeks, I have been trying to find the confidence to tell Ellis that I want us to truly be an *us*.

Spending the day looking after her and Jack just solidified to me that they are my family. Leaving them to come back to my own empty home felt exactly like that: empty. The problem is finding a second alone. I think Ellis has been holding Jack a lot closer this week because of guilt about how her flare-up affected him. But I need Ellis alone with nothing to hide behind. No Spears team, no Cassie, no major responsibilities or distractions. I need a chance to prove that I'm in this for the long haul. Plus, if there is already speculation based on our appearances together and online posts that we are likely together, then why not actually be together.

By the time I have showered and changed out of my sweaty clothes, my phone pings again. I smile before I even pick up the phone.

> I have something else to thank you for.

> Okay I'll bite, what are you thankful for?

> Shoving me out of my comfort zone, Jack is having his first sleepover at a friend's place tonight.

> Wow. Ellis that's huge.

> Yeah, don't remind me, I might freak out.

An idea strikes me like lightning in that moment.

> How about this: I'll pick up some food and come over tonight to help your anxiety?

It takes an excruciating amount of time for Ellis to reply. I watch the three little dots bob up and down on my screen as she types.

> Yes. I can't stop pacing. I know I need to let him be a kid but it's so scary.

> Don't worry, me and Chinese food are inbound.

> I'm so grateful for you Liam Ruinsky.

Despite the circumstances, the thought of us eating alone makes me excited. I don't want to blindside her; she's twenty-two weeks pregnant and I don't want to add any stress to her life. But in my heart, it feels like something more could come. I know I could be blowing this out of proportion, but Ellis might be all in on us, too.

She was in enough to sleep with me in December and I know she doesn't regret it, so I just need to show her that I don't have one foot out the door. Trusting isn't Ellis's virtue, and I know it's because she hasn't had anyone earn it. But I have been there every step of the way since January, she trusts me with Jack, and she was willing to break her routine just to come to a game for me. I just need to focus on those positives.

Pulling up outside Ellis's apartment a few hours later, I take a second to breathe before I gather all the food I ordered. I know she is going to say I ordered too much, but this way she can have second servings later when she wakes up hungry again.

I've gotten probably fifty texts in the middle of the night over the past two months from Ellis telling me how hungry she is, but not letting me buy her anything. I supposed she just wanted to tell someone about her midnight cravings. Tonight, I have the perfect remedy: Chinese leftovers. I always get this adrenaline rush whenever I knock on her door. When she opens it, it's like sunshine pouring through an open window.

Ellis is wearing a pair of baby blue leggings and a sweatshirt covering her bump. Still my hand falls to the fabric pulled tight over her stomach.

"Hi, baby girl," I whisper to the bump before leaning down to kiss it gently. "Hi, Sunshine," I say to Ellis. When I go to stroll past her, she comes up on her tiptoes to kiss my cheek, shocking us both.

My skin heats at the contact, but Ellis just walks back into her kitchen as if she didn't just initiate physical contact between us. It might not have been romantic – it could have just been friendly – but with the way I feel about her, about what we could be, the kiss lingers on my cheek like a stain.

Once I've pulled myself together, I follow her into the kitchen and start to plate up the food for us, Ellis watching over my shoulder making sure I give her extra noodles (as if I don't already know they are her favourite). I can feel the heat of her body behind me before she drops her head to rest between my shoulder blades. I swear she might be trying to kill me.

The last time we were this close was the near kiss at the barbecue that we never discussed, and once again when I pecked her forehead a week ago. Now she is wrapping her arms around my body like it is usual between us. I feel like a teenager, my heart is thumping in my chest because of the blatant openness of her affection.

"I've missed you," Ellis admits resting her forehead against the centre of my back for a few seconds before she pulls away, picks up her plate and walks over to the table to eat.

"We've been texting every day." I pull myself a seat up facing her in time to watch her roll her eyes.

"It's not the same and you know it." She points at me with her fork.

"I know Sunshine, I missed you too." I wonder what she means when she says she missed me – in the way you miss having someone around to help you? Just for company? For friendship? Or does she miss me the way I miss her? Clearly satisfied with my answer, Ellis does a happy little food dance in her chair while she eats her first mouthful of noodles and chicken.

I take a moment to watch her and I feel nostalgic. For as long as I've known her, Ellis has done this wiggly little dance when she is enjoying her food and seeing it again now calms me. A lot has changed since then, but some things never do. In her core she is the girl she has always been. The woman I've always loved. Then she moans.

Her noise breaks my chain of thought. I feel heat rushing to my crotch as she throws her head back and moans around a mouthful of chicken satay. At first I assume it is an innocent, involuntary noise – but when she brings her head forward she locks her eyes with mine before her lips tilt into a smirk.

"Ellis?" I ask it like a question but I mean it like a warning.

"What's wrong?" she asks, trying to bite back her smile but I see it all over her face.

"Stop moaning." I don't sound convincing even to my ears, but I have to try.

"I thought you liked my moans." The innocent act might kill me, her eyes are wide and she is pouting slightly. A perfectly practised face that she knows brings me to my knees.

"Ellis," I growl. But she stands up and walks to my side of the table before nudging my legs apart to stand between them. She rests her hands around my neck, playing with my hair.

"Come on, Liam." She leans down until our faces are only a few inches apart.

"I've told you, I don't want to be the person you use to scratch an itch," I tell her. Even though I mean it, I find myself resting my hands on her hips gripping onto her with all of my strength.

"What if I want more than that?" She scratches lightly at my scalp and if my cock wasn't hard before, the pinch of her nails against my head makes it want to burst through the zipper of my jeans.

"That's your second trimester horniness talking." I am trying to put space between us and I see a flicker of something cross her face before she unloops her hands from my neck.

"If you don't want this, tell me." She sighs, and even though two seconds ago I wanted her to stop, I grip her hips tighter so she can't walk away.

"That's not fair, you know I want you Ellis," I tell her.

"So you want me, and I want you." Her hands come back up but settle on my jaw this time, scratching against my five o'clock shadow.

"I want more than just sex Ellis. I want us." This is not how I pictured doing this, I wanted her to be mine at the end of tonight but in all of my wildest dreams I didn't think Ellis would be offering herself on a silver platter, nor did I think I would be trying to deny her.

"Show me what I'm missing." My brain is telling me this is a trap but my other brain is excited to be buried inside her.

"What?" I ask with all of my remaining brain power.

"Show me how good we could be Liam. Prove it to me."

She knows she has me. I can see it in her eyes but maybe she has a point. That night in December we had been drinking. I know I can make her happy, but she needs that reassurance. Needs me to show her with my body how explosive and right we are for each other.

"You know I love a challenge. But you need to know, if we do this, you're mine. I let you put space between us after what happened with Michael at the game, but I won't be able to step back from this again." I'll give her what she needs, I'll pull out all of my best moves, but I need her to know this is not going to be one and done.

I'm going to claim her and she is going to thank me for it.

"I'm already yours," she whispers. And I snap.

Gripping the back of her neck, I pull Ellis's face down to meet mine. I waste no time parting her lips with my tongue and devour her. A moan comes from deep in her throat as I pull her down over my legs to straddle me, my cock resting at the juncture of her thighs. Ellis grinds down on me without embarrassment and I suddenly find it hard to breathe.

Pulling my lips from hers, Ellis lets out a whine that turns to a moan when my lips travel down her jaw and over the soft skin of her throat until I find the pulse point where I nibble and lick at her flushed skin. With every shift of Ellis on my thighs my cock aches. It has been nearly six months since I last had sex and every time I have masturbated since then has been to an image just like this one: Ellis warm and pliable in my arms, moaning my name.

Wrapping a hand under her thighs I stand with Ellis in my arms, she squeals lightly at the change of position but quickly fixes her legs around my waist. I've been in this apartment enough to find her bedroom without having to break our kiss, which is a good thing because Ellis seems like she would be content to kiss me like this forever.

The fire burning in me wants to throw her down onto the bed and ravish her, but this isn't just someone I want to fuck. This is Ellis Ainsley. The mother of my child. I am going to worship her until she begs for more.

Instead of throwing her down, I rest a knee on the end of her queen-sized bed and tip forward until she is settled among the pillows. Her golden hair is fanned over the baby pink bedding like a halo, a deity I am going to pray to for the rest of my days. When I try to pull away she claws at my shoulders, so I take her wrists and pin them beside her head with a tut.

"Leave 'em there." I tell her and wait for her nod before I release them.

Once my hands are free, I run them over her arms, down to the bottom of her sweatshirt and pull it up over her head until she is bare to me. My breath hitches when I find no bra hiding her stiff pink nipples from me.

"Fuck," I groan, before dropping my head to take her left nipple in my mouth. Her skin is heated and I see her hands twitch wanting to run through my hair, but my perfect girl keeps them where I want them as she squirms below me. I switch to her other breast using my hand to tweak at the one I left until she is panting.

"Liam… Please." She exhales. I ignore her, kissing back up away from her chest and over her neck where I start to suck and kiss a hickey into her pale flesh. When she wakes up tomorrow she will remember that she is mine. I am going to make her feel me everywhere.

Once I'm satisfied with her bruised skin, I pull myself off her completely to take my own clothes off. I wanted to wait, have her naked and begging below me, but I think my cock is going to have an imprint of my zipper if I leave it in there any longer.

Besides, this gives Ellis a second to breathe and to anticipate what she has coming when I strip for her. Leaving my underwear for now, I hook my fingers into the waistband of her leggings, looking at her for conformation that this is still what she wants.

"Yes, Liam. Yes." With that, I rip her leggings and panties down in one pull leaving my Sunshine naked and flushed for me. I wrench her thighs apart when she tries to relieve the pressure there, I don't waste a second before hitching her legs over my shoulders and burying my tongue in her.

I lick from her entrance up to her clit before circling it with the point of my tongue. I planned to tease her, give her little licks until she begged, but once her taste settles on my tongue I go feral.

The last five and a half months has been teasing enough for her because she is drenching my face. Her juices soak my jaw as she wiggles above me, I grip her ass cheeks in my hands and massage them as I eat her.

I can feel her getting closer and closer to coming, her legs shaking by my ears and the walls of her pussy pulsing around my tongue. I know Ellis's body like the back of my hand so I know she needs more to get her there.

Moving my hands from her ass, I take one and slide two fingers inside of her making sure to curve up and hit her G spot as I suck at her clit. I use my other hand to move back up her body and massage her tits again, I am all over her. Every part of her body is mine and she calls out for god as her body tenses in my arms.

I feel her pussy grip down on me as she goes rigid, feeling the waves of her orgasm wash over her.

"God, Ellis, you're such a fucking perfect girl for me. I love making you come all over me." I praise her while pushing my underwear down finally, kicking them off as quick as I can before crawling back over her body settling between her thighs, taking her jaw in my hand.

"You ready to be fucked El?" I ask notching my tip at her soaked entrance.

"Yes, Liam! Yes!" she begs and it's my favourite sound.

"You can touch me now, Sunshine," I tell her before I thrust in to the hilt. Her hands latch on to my shoulders and dig into my skin. I can feel the tracks she is scratching as I fuck her, but the pain just heightens the pleasure.

On every thrust I grind as deep as I can, no matter how close I get, it will never be close enough for me. Ellis moans out for me, for more, and I give her everything I have lifting her legs over my elbows to get deeper.

I can feel how warm and wet she is around me, but it feels like so much more than that too. I can feel our connection, it feels like cosmic rightness to be here with her like this. I feel us putting the last decade of wrongness right again just by being back in each other's arms.

My thrusts slow as our eyes connect through the haze and I know Ellis feels what is happening between us too as tears flood her waterline.

"Liam."

"I know Sunshine, I know."

Silence surrounds us apart from the echo of our skin connecting over and over as Ellis starts to tighten around me taking me over the edge with her. We come together; I groan into the skin of Ellis's shoulder as she wraps her arms and legs tight around my waist pulling my weight down over her.

We float back down from whatever other planet we just reached together. But neither of us talk, too scared to break the energy that we feel in the room. I'm content to just hold her though. We have to talk about what this will mean, I know that, but this isn't the time. Right now is the time for us to bask in the feelings we have for each other, while I hope she knows how important this is for me, how important she is to me.

I know when my cum starts to leak out of her, Ellis will let me know she is uncomfortable. When that comes,

I will run to grab a wash cloth for her, but for now she rests in my arms. Exactly where I hope she stays.

As we lay there, the thoughts come in hot and fast. This might have been a mistake in the long run. Sleeping with Ellis is amazing but this throws every boundary I tried to set out of the window. I gave into temptation and I fear this is going to push me back ten steps. I want this to mean something, but what if it doesn't?

Her breathing becomes deeper as her eyes are heavy and sleepy. But those thoughts are what keep me from falling into an easy sleep.

Chapter Twenty-One

June

Ellis

Finding a two-bedroom flat so close to Bloom and Blossom was the luckiest thing that happened to me. It means that I can walk there when I don't feel like driving. Besides, I just didn't have the capacity to stuff myself behind the wheel of a car this morning.

Today I decided to waddle to work with the early morning sun refreshing on my skin. My ankles protest at their use but even with their swelling, I want to keep my blood flowing. I don't want to be put down by elephantitis when I have so much to do. Plus, by the time the baby comes the weather will be cooling down so I want to make the most of the summer while we have it. The walk is also a welcome distraction from images flashing through my mind. Images of Liam and I. What we did when we were alone.

I don't have the brain power to think about it right now. About what it might mean. About whether I made a mistake. I'm simply too busy, and Liam doesn't fit into the Bloom and Blossom schedule today.

As I put the key into the front door of the florist, I try to ignore how puffy my knuckles look. I am retaining so much water, every joint feels ballooned. I am lucky to have a friend like Lyndsey. Even without asking she has started coming into work early to help me in the mornings. Obviously she will be paid for her time, but I know it isn't about the cash. She hates me straining myself, she is almost as bad as Liam. Well, maybe not quite as bad.

Lyndsey is worried. She won't say the words but I see it in her eyes. They linger on me a touch too long when I bend over. She wants to help me and I am willing to let her but I have too much to do to let her take over. This store is everything to me. It was my solace after Michael, it gave me a roof and a purpose to keep pushing post-partum. I fought for this place and it is a constant reminder of how different I am now to the kid I was when I left the UK.

When young me was scared and overwhelmed, she had no systems in place for when things went wrong, but I fought against the need to run back home. It would have been easy and Eleanor would have loved me coming back with my tail between my legs but I needed to prove to myself that I could. Even if the shop failed, I needed to try. And it didn't fail. It *bloomed* in front of my eyes.

It is only when I get to the back room that I remember I skipped breakfast again. I need to be more careful about that. It's been this way for a long time. When my pain is high it becomes almost impossible to eat. Even the thought of eating makes me nauseous. Every day this past week I have felt constantly on the verge of throwing up. Acid reflux is always there at the back of my throat; it's impossible to keep anything down. Even water seems like too much at times.

I pull a granola bar out from my desk drawer but I don't bother opening it. I slip down into my desk chair still thinking about the chair in Cassie's office. Deciding I need one, I fire off a text to her to get one for myself. Maybe if I can find a comfortable enough chair I might be able to suffer through some breakfast. I lean back breathing deep through my nose to quell the sickness and dizziness that swamps my brain.

I am pulled from my quiet moment when the bell above the door rings. I push myself up out of the chair to greet my first customer of the day to find Lyndsey here even earlier than yesterday. Through the big front windows I see Aiden Anders in his car waiting for Lyndsey to come inside.

"Well, good morning." I welcome her and I smile waving at Aiden through the windows. When Lyndsey sees she has been caught she drops her head back, dropping her handbag onto the floor.

"It's not what it looks like," she whines.

"That's what they all say." I laugh walking around the counter to meet her. She doesn't look ruffled, but it wouldn't be the first time someone has dropped her off after a wild night together. Mostly women, but sometimes men. Lyndsey wears her sexuality on her sleeve, and I have always respected that.

"No! Seriously we just bumped into each other at the coffee place that has those delicious cinnamon buns and I wanted to get some for us and he offered me a ride to work, that's all." She rambles, picking up her stuff and putting the paper bag on the desk like it's proof of her story.

"He seems like a good guy?" I shrug, pulling her closer so she is standing right in front of me. I'm willing to entertain this slightly concerning conversation a little longer if it means Lyndsey won't interject and ask about Liam. I'm not ready to admit to what we did, and I'm equally not ready to lie. She is always asking if anything has happened between us. Usually there is nothing to tell her; I am planning on pretending the same this time.

"I agree, a good guy who gave me a lift to work. Nothing more." She slices her hand through the air between us wanting to move on from this but I have one last thing I want to say before we start working.

"I don't believe you." She tries to interrupt but I talk over her. "But if there is something going on I'll let you keep it to yourself for now."

"Subject change. Cinnamon buns!" She cheers, ripping the bag open between us but the sweet smell of cinnamon and icing that would usually make my stomach rumble makes bile rise up in my throat. I try breathing through my mouth so I can't smell it, but I can taste the sweetness in the air. I cover my mouth with my hand.

"Please put them away," I mumble behind my hand. Lyndsey's eyes widen before she covers the warm gooey buns quickly.

"Are you okay?" she asks cocking her brows at me, shocked by my outburst.

"The smell." I try to sip at some water to get the taste out of my mouth but I still don't feel steady. "I can't stomach the smell of basically any food today. Even crumpets sound horrible."

"That's your biggest craving!" She sounds scandalised.

"I know, it sucks but with the pain I'm in, food just keeps slipping down my priority list." I groan, walking into the back room to sit in the office chair, popping my feet on a delivery box, hoping to help with the swelling.

"Aw I'm sorry. Are you okay to be here? You should take a half day," she tells me, fussing with the delivery sheets on my desk. She is probably right but I don't want to give in.

"Yeah, maybe. I want to be here, it's my happy place, but I do really feel shitty." It sucks to admit.

"I'm here to get everything done, just think about it?" She places a soft hand on my shoulder squeezing lightly.

"I will." I promise her, but when the phone on my desk rings I still jump right into work. Maybe if I work hard enough I will be able to push everything else out of my mind. Ignore how weak I feel. Ignore the dizziness on the edges of my consciousness and the vomit wanting to surface.

After a few hours of persisting with work, the room starts spinning.

I've spent the day ordering stock and filling out delivery schedules for the weekend so everyone gets their orders on time. Lyndsey has been working out front with the customers, she wanted me to be sat down and not running – well, waddling – around. I grip the edge of the desk until everything comes back into focus. I have been dizzy on and off for a while but after this round my pulse starts to rise. I can feel a slight throbbing in my chest, and my fingers start to tingle.

Out front I hear the doorbell ding and then everything comes back into focus. It was a strange sensation, but the dizziness dissipates and even though I can still feel my heartbeat in my head, everything else seems to go back to normal. I breathe a sigh of relief. It's okay. I will have to keep an eye on that sensation, I remind myself. But for now, it's gone. *It's okay.*

I walk out into the main store, following the sound of Lyndsey's voice. I'm greeted with the sight of her helping a customer as she flashes me an encouraging smile. The smile I return to her is anything but. If she notices she doesn't say in front of the customer, which I appreciate.

Check how many stems of roses there are, go back into the office, I think silently. Bending down to pick up a bucket of roses, I shift the one on top to pull another box out from under the shelf. When I rise up with the box in hand, I know something is wrong. The flowers are practically spinning around me.

At the edges of my vision darkness starts to seep over my gaze.

I hear a shout and something hitting the floor.

Blackness completely overtakes my vision.

—

Everything is blurry.

When my vision comes back into focus, I see Lyndsey's ginger hair falling around her face. She's leaning over me, slouched on her knees. My head is rested on her lap like a cushion, but I can't seem to speak. My throat feels scratchy as I swallow.

I can make out Lyndsey holding a phone to her ear, but I feel like I'm under water. Everything sounds far away. My eyes flutter before closing fully again. The only thing I can feel is Lyndsey's fingers brushing through my hair.

"Liam," I whisper when I come back around again.

This time it's strangers standing above me. Paramedics poke me, shining a torch in my eyes. Lyndsey gives me a cup of water to sip but it feels strange to swallow, like my throat is raw. My heartbeat is still thumping in my head, like my temples are bursting.

"I'm calling him, El, I promise." Lyndsey's voice sounds closer this time. She's above me, using my phone to call him.

"Liam," I moan again. It's all I can muster. It's all I want right now. *Liam*.

As I become more aware of my surroundings, that's when fear hits.

There's a band strapped around my belly. I'm in the back of an ambulance. My baby's heartbeat is being projected onto a monitor.

Lyndsey passes my stuff into the back of the ambulance, her words a catalogue of promises: promising that she will take care of the store and asking me to promise to give her updates. But I can't think about that now.

I need to know my baby is okay.

Chapter Twenty-Two

Liam

Even during the offseason, I try to spend as much time as I can on the ice.

Not making the playoffs this season was a blessing and a curse. No NHL player wants to get knocked out, so obviously it sucks that all the hard work the team put in wasn't enough. My contract coming to an end plus the fear of being away from Ellis if she needs me is a lot to deal with. I know that I only have a few good years left, and I want to leave on my own terms – not because my body can't handle the strain.

I'm loving having extra time with Ellis and Jack during the offseason as the pregnancy has moved past the halfway point. There's just one glaring issue: the sex. It was amazing. It was what I wanted. But it was our boundary, and we broke it. Now I have no idea where I stand. Where *we* stand.

There is only one thing that keeps me from calling Ellis and putting on the pressure about our relationship: being on the ice. I wasn't expecting anyone else to be at the rink when I got here a few hours ago, but colour me surprised, because a few minutes after I got out on the ice, Edge followed behind.

Honestly, I think he is beating himself up a little bit. No player wants to lose and I think he is trying to prove himself for next season. It's a commendable thing, but I'm not good enough at pep talks to tell him that. Instead I told him to get in goal so I could work on my slap shot.

To be candid, Edge is shit in goal. Too big to move quickly enough to block, but I figure if I was in goal he'd take his frustration out on me and that doesn't sound like fun.

"Ruin I didn't come here to be your puck boy, I want to run some drills." He finally whips his helmet off yelling at me. I nod to him and with a relieved sigh he skates to the bench for some water.

We race up and down the ice for a while until someone else joins us: Anders. He announces his presence by skating over while slow clapping.

"At least I know two of my players are working out instead of drinking all night." He drawls as he nears, and I notice the bags under his eyes.

"Shit, who's in trouble?" I ask, my chest heaving. Sweat drips from the ends of my hair.

"Got a call at two a.m. from Rook because he needed a lift home from some bar. Kid was drunker than a skunk. My car still reeks." Normally Anders would be mad, but we know why he isn't. Rook is blaming himself for us not making the playoffs. He was about to score when he got slammed into the boards, causing him to give the puck away to the Kings, which led to them going one up. We lost by one and he has been punishing himself ever since.

"Do we need to do something?" Edge asks. Under-neath his burly exterior he loves his teammates, if he can do something to help he will.

"He is just blowing off steam, I'll give him till the end of the month and if he's still wallowing then I might need all y'alls help." Edge and I just nod. There's nothing I can say right now anyway, but if the time comes when we need to show up for our teammate, we will.

Anders takes over as coach for the next hour, yelling at us like we are back in college trying to impress scouts. I don't think I have ever seen Edge this shade of red before and he has more stamina than me, god knows the state I'm in.

Eventually I look over at my friend and see the same desperation in his eyes that I feel, so without an ounce of subtlety I fall back onto the ice. Edge lays down next to me. A mixture of the body exhaustion and the feeling of being reprimanded by our captain is just funny right now and we break into hysterics. Anders doesn't share our humour if the look on his face when he stands over us is anything to go by.

"What do y'all think you're doing? I didn't tell you to stop."

"Who knew he was such a hard ass?" Edge whispers out the side of his mouth, making me laugh even harder.

"I love you, Cap, but it was either stop or pass out on the ice." I give him my best shit-eating grin and he rolls his eyes before leaving us hurting.

"I think my body is shutting down now I'm becoming a dad," I tell Edge while trying to stand back up again.

"No that's not it, you're just getting old." He laughs and smacks my ass before skating off leaving me to chase after him.

I spent more time at the rink than I planned, but it was nice to spend time with Edge. Since we traded from Vancouver I feel like we haven't spent much time together alone. For a while when we got here I clung to him, I was insecure about being home again thinking my life was going backwards and he was my tether to reality.

But now, I want to spend all my time by Ellis's side, so naturally our friendship has taken a back seat. Out there on the ice though, we are as tight as we've always been.

After jumping out of the shower I change quickly so I can get to Ellis's place in time to see her before she has to leave to get Jack. I offered to get him on my way back from the rink, but she likes their car rides together, I think she wants everything to be as normal as possible before everything changes.

My heart stops when I pull my phone out of my bag to see:

9 Missed Calls from Sunshine
5 Missed Calls from Lyndsey
2 Voicemails from Sunshine
1 Voicemail from Lyndsey
6 Texts from Sunshine

The first voicemail stops me in my tracks, "*Hi Liam it's Lyndsey, Ellis is on her way to the hospital, she will probably downplay it but she fainted and was having some cramping. I have the shop covered but someone will need to pick up Jack later. Give her my love when you see her.*"

Her words echo as the next message begins to play, this one from El:

"*Liam, don't panic but I'm on my way to the hospital.*" Her voice is shuddering and my knees nearly buckle. "*I fainted but don't worry. I'm sure everything is fine. Please call me.*"

She has been crying, I can hear it in her voice. I know she must be scared out of her mind all alone. *Fuck*, I need to get to her.

I'm running down the hallways towards Anders when the third message plays.

"*Getting checked in so they can check on the baby; they just want to make sure everything's fine. Sorry for calling so much, I just want you here.*" She needs me and I was fucking about on the ice. My heart hurts and it's hard to breathe; all I can think about is getting to her.

"Ruin? What's wrong? What happened?" Anders grips my shoulders as I try to push past him. I hear him shouting for Edge but his voice sounds like it is underwater.

"Ellis – she fainted. She's in the hospital."

"Shit, okay, let's go." Anders pulls away from me and starts to jog alongside me towards the parking lot. I don't notice when Edge joins us but my captain throws him my keys. "Edge, you're driving." I don't even remember giving him my keys.

I need my keys.

I need to get to the hospital.

"No. You'll crash and you will be no help to anyone if you're dead." Either I said it out loud or he read my mind, but I can't think past my own worry enough to question him.

"Need to see her." *I need to know my Sunshine is okay.* If I don't breathe properly soon though I'm going to need the hospital bed beside her.

When I do steadily breathe again I will probably be thankful that Anders didn't take us in his car; if it smells as badly of booze as he said then I would have thrown up. I feel on the verge of it already.

"Liam, I need you to listen to me." Anders voice starts to come into focus as we drive out of the lot, but I think it's the shock of him calling me Liam instead of Ruin.

"What?" I ask.

"If you are in this state when you see her, she is going to be scared. Do what you need to now before we get there." *What does he mean?*

"Liam if you need to shout, do it now, if you need to cry go ahead, but you need to fucking breathe." Edge's voice is calm and collected, breaking through my spiral.

"Shit, okay. FUCK! AHHHH!" I yell out until my throat is hoarse but I can also feel my heart rate starting to steady. Just in time too, because Edge has just turned into the hospital parking lot – so fast I think we go in on two wheels.

I don't care – all that matters is getting to my girls. My feet pound on the pavement and the double doors slide open for me.

"Ellis Ainsley, I need to see her." Thanks to the guys, I'm able to speak in full sentences again, but I still feel the weight of five men pressing on my chest.

My voice doesn't startle the woman behind the desk, but the footfall of three hockey players running probably gave us away. Moving too slowly for comfort she starts typing on her computer and eventually she looks up at me with boredom in her eyes.

"Are you family?" She waves her hands dismissively at me and the guys.

"I'm her fiancé." I don't think and the words are out there. There is a doctor stood holding a clipboard who I didn't notice at first, tunnel vision only letting me see one obstacle at a time. She glances over the receptionist's shoulder before smiling at me.

"You must be Liam, follow me." She points down a corridor, but before I walk down it, Anders grabs me by the elbow.

"Liam, we are going to go pick up Jack okay? Cassie is on his pick-up list right?" When I nod he continues, "We'll take him to your place and wait for y'all there," he reassures me.

"Thank you, I'll call you when I know anything."

"Go get your girl man." Edge pats me on the shoulder and I'm off. I scurry after the doctor as she leads me down corridor after corridor, it's a labyrinth that my Sunshine is waiting in the middle of, a prize that I hope is alive and healthy.

"How did you know my name?" I ask the doctor, breaking out of my fog, as she leads me onto the maternity ward.

"As soon as Miss Ainsley knew she was being admitted she was asking for her partner, when you wouldn't pick up the phone she was cursing your name." I don't think I am going to let my phone out of my sight ever again. Silence falls between us for a moment but I need to know what to expect.

"Is she going to be okay?"

"Why don't you see for yourself?" At that she stops at a door and nods towards it. I know that if something bad had happened then there would have been more questions or more waiting, but I'm still terrified of what I will find. I take two deep breaths to calm my shaking hands and reach for the handle.

Behind the door Ellis is sitting up on the bed with an IV in her arm and a grey band wrapped around her exposed bump. Now my heart is thumping for a different reason. She looks so small. I know can see she's awake, but that doesn't mean she is safe.

"Ellis! Fuck, are you okay?" I'm across the room and taking her into my arms. I need to feel her skin against

193

mine. I need to feel that she is warm and alive; her heart-beat can be heard on the monitor, but it doesn't feel like enough.

"I'm fine Liam, I promise," Ellis whispers against my shoulder as I take my time breathing her in.

"And— and the baby? Is the baby okay?"

"She's fine. Strong as hell." She starts running her fingers through my hair so I settle in beside her. I needed to know she was okay but I think she just needed *me*.

"Sunshine."

"We're okay Liam, we're okay."

"I thought… I don't even know what I thought, but god, I was so scared." On the bed I sit beside her and tuck her into my side so I can rest my head on top of hers. It will take an act of god to pull me away from her.

There was a time I lived for nobody, all I lived for was the thrill of taking to the ice with hundreds of people screaming my name. As much as I loved it, there was something missing, something empty in my heart. For a minute today, my heart stopped because I thought that the person I want to spend my life with was hurting.

My heart stopped because the idea of living without her and Jack and our baby didn't feel like a life I could live. I have missed out on a lot of things that normal people have in their lives. A nine-to-five job, a steady home that I go back to every night instead of moving around the country every few years, strong relationships built on trust and not on what I can offer.

I was never ungrateful. I have money to help people who need it. I have a job people would kill for. My family loved and supported me wholeheartedly when I was young. But I would give it all up in a second to keep Ellis safe. Forget the money and the fans screaming my name, as long as I can come home at the end of the day and lay in bed next to Ellis then it will be a damn good day. Right here, as I sit beside Ellis a stillness settles over me. I don't think I can sign another contract for the Spears. Another year away, travelling and missing everything. I don't think I can stomach it. This is where I am meant to be.

"I'm waiting for the doctor, I need to pick Jack up soon so I need the discharge papers." Ellis breaks through my thoughts when she notices the time.

"No chance. Anders and Edge have gone to get Cassie to pick up Jack. They're going to take him home and chill with him until we can leave, and we are not leaving until we know for sure that you and the baby are okay," I tell her, tipping her face up to mine with a finger under her chin. Ellis didn't fight about adding Cassie to Jack's pick-up list. It made sense, if Ellis is ever in too much pain and I am travelling with the team, it means Lyndsey doesn't have to close up the shop to get him.

"They have Jack?" Her brows furrow.

"They dropped me here and left to get him, they're his family now, too." I assure her with a small kiss, just a peck on her forehead. I can't help myself, my hands itch to rub over her skin, needing to feel her reassuring warmth against me.

"Family?" she whispers as I pull away, more to herself than to me and her eyes flood with tears.

"Fuck, why are you crying?" Her face drops to the centre of my chest and her tears soak my T-shirt.

"I miss having a family." Her words are muffled against the fabric, but they hit my heart with the strength of ten men. She has a family now and I'm not going anywhere.

"So… I'm your partner, huh?" I need to see her smile more than my next breath.

"You caught that?" Her voice is still quiet but her shoulders shake in a small laugh.

"Best thing I've heard all day," I tell her honestly, but after all the other things I've heard today it wouldn't be a task to top them.

"Ignore that." She laughs and moves to look up at me. "Apparently I fainted because I was dehydrated and under nourished."

"How did that happen? Have you not been eating?"

"See, here's the thing… No, I haven't." Before I can ask what the hell she means, she continues, "Wait, look okay, so I have been in so much pain that eating hadn't even crossed my mind. I've had a few meals here and there but on the whole, not so much. It's not like I have been doing it on purpose; I wouldn't do that."

"Ellis—"

"I know, I'm going to do better, shit you can force feed me if you have to. I never meant to put me or the baby at risk, I just wasn't thinking." She interrupts me but that's not what I am mad about, I'm angry at myself.

"I'm so sorry Sunshine."

"What are you sorry for?" Confusion laces her tone.

"I should have been paying more attention, I should have noticed you weren't eating and I should have been there when you fainted and I wasn't. I'm so sorry." I kiss her head and feel her melt into my embrace. We don't say much other than me checking she is comfortable until the door opens half an hour later.

"Hi Miss Ainsley, how are we doing in here?" The same doctor that showed me in comes back into the room with a smile.

"Ready to go home please," Ellis tells her.

"We can do that, but there are some conditions." The doctor checks over the baby's heart monitor as well as Ellis's and looks up with a smile.

"Okay…?" Ellis wants to get out of here. I can feel the need buzzing under her skin.

"There was no bleeding and the cramps were just a product of the dehydration; the baby seems strong. That being said, I think it would be best for both the baby and yourself if you go on bed rest."

"Done," I say at the same time Ellis says:

"I can't do that!"

"I'll go get the discharge papers while you guys talk it through." Her lips thin as she tries to hold back a smile, leaving us alone in the room.

I turn to her. "Ellis?"

"Liam?" She is looking at me as if I am crazy, I know why she won't want to do it, but this is for her, for our baby. I can hear her complaint before she opens her mouth. "I have a kid and a business, I can't lie around all day." *There it is.*

"You can and you will, the doctor recommends it and I'm going to implement it." She can fight me all day long. She can fight me until she is blue in the face, but her health is my top priority.

"How do you plan to do that?"

"I'll step up for Jack, we don't have any games to play until the season starts up again and I'll tell coach I need a leave of absence from training. Lyndsey can look after the shop. She has keys and has been there for as long as Jack has been alive – the place isn't going to up and run away." The more I talk, the more sense it makes, it sounds like a practised argument even if I am just spitballing.

"So, what? You'll sleep on my couch and take over as head parent while I do nothing all day?" She thinks I'm being over the top but she is underestimating the lengths I will go to for the people I love.

"No—" I start, but she interrupts.

"Exactly."

"You and Jack will move into my place, there's no way I'm sleeping on a couch when I'm six foot four," I say. Before she has a chance to shoot that down, I tell her the rest of my master plan that I am making up on the spot: "You can both have your own rooms if you aren't ready to be in mine, there are plenty of them. Edge lives two minutes away if we need him, but I know we won't because I am going to be the best nurse you could ask for."

"Th-that… actually sounds like a good idea?" she says with some disbelief in her voice. *Hell, yeah it does*, I think. It will take time, but I have four more months of pregnancy and hopefully the rest of our lives where I am going to be by her side, being her support because there is nowhere else in the world I would rather be.

Chapter Twenty-Three

Ellis

I'm not an ungrateful person. When someone holds a door open for me, I always thank them and I never take simple things for granted. But I keep thinking something super ungrateful: I hate being in Liam's house.

Don't get me wrong, the guest bedroom is beautiful and full of light and he is waiting on me hand and foot – but that's part of the problem.

My flat isn't a big posh mansion, but it is *mine*. I have my own room here at Liam's, even have an en suite bathroom. But it feels more like a hotel room than a home. I am just a visitor passing through until another guest fills the room.

I feel so out of my depth being the centre of attention. Liam checks on me every hour to see if I am comfortable or if I need anything and it should be a dream. For the first day and a half it was, but now I've been bedbound for three weeks and nobody lets me move.

I tried to do some stock ordering for Bloom and Blossom and when Lyndsey found out she told on me to Liam. When I argued that the doctors said I had to stay in bed, not that I had to stop living, I was told to "enjoy my time off and relax". I tried to throw a pillow at his head but he caught it, fluffed it, then put it behind me.

Exhausting. Kind and thoughtful and oh so loving, but *fuck*, I just want to go for a walk or take Jack to school. I'm not asking to run a marathon.

Part of the problem is how beautiful everything is, because I can almost imagine having this forever. A beautiful house with a chef preparing meals for us because Liam didn't want to poison us with his lack of kitchen skills. She made me crumpets from scratch for Christ's sake, and they are incredible and they weren't burnt on one side like they are when I make them in my toaster.

It is so easy to imagine this as my life. Liam wants this to be our life. I'm okay with that, well most of it. I want to cook my own meals and to be allowed out of bed whenever I want and in my heart I know he isn't going to change his mind and leave us like Jack's dad did, but a little part of my brain can't seem to agree. We still haven't spoken about the last time we had sex. We just keep tiptoeing around it.

I know he said he wouldn't have sex with me until I was ready to be together, and I thought I was. The way he looked after me after our run-in with Michael, the way he has handled the press asking questions so I can keep my privacy. He is a great man and a great partner. But I am still scared. I don't know why I can't trust him when he tells me he is in. I wish I could pinpoint exactly what he could do to prove his devotion but I can't. It isn't him it's me – as cliché as that sounds. I need to trust myself enough to let him in. I want to commit to him, but whenever I feel ready to say the words, a little voice in my head stops me. I wish I could prove to him that it did mean something, it does mean something, but the words just don't seem to come out.

With every little thing Liam has to do for me, that judgmental voice gets louder, tells me I'm a burden to him so it won't take long for him to get bored. He has put himself on the line by telling me what he wants and all he needs is for me to meet him halfway.

Then there is the mum guilt. Every time I think about Jack, a lump forms in my throat. He must feel like I have abandoned him just like his dad because everything that I used to do Liam is doing instead. I can't take him to school or join in at bath time – instead, I am the princess in the tower.

I don't feel like his mum, I feel like I'm just someone he knows. I know it sounds crazy but going from being a full-time single mum to only seeing him for a few hours when he comes and sits in bed with me to watch *The Great British Bake Off* is hard. Every time I try to tell him how sorry I am he just hugs me and tells me he loves me, crushing me even more.

He is so damn caring and gentle, a part of me wishes he would throw a tantrum so I would know he misses me doing stuff for him as much as I miss doing it. That must make me a terrible person, wanting my son to be sad just so I can feel vindicated.

My beautiful boy is sat with me as I remind myself to just hold him and be happy. Every day after school he comes into my bedroom and tells me about his day, sometimes the boys from the team take him skating or to the park. I guess they do so to form a stronger bond as a chosen family. It's working.

"I only fell over once today, Liam says I'm getting really good out there." He tells me full of energy. He skated for nearly two hours today and I don't know how he has any energy left. *Oh, to be a kid.*

"Well, you do have good teachers, who was with you today?" Someone always meets them at the rink and Jack finally got to meet Jackson Felix – the Spears goalkeeper – last week, he spoke about it for hours.

"It was just Liam and Rook but that was good because I think Rook might be my new favourite," he says in a whisper.

"Rook? Why not Liam?" I ask.

"I love Liam but I see him all the time so he doesn't count, he's family. Rook is cool, he is funny." Before I can say anything about that Liam walks into the bedroom, stopping short in the doorframe.

"Excuse me? I must be having a bad dream because I thought I just heard Jack say that Rook is his favourite?" Liam says dramatically and as soon as he hears his voice, Jack squeals and hurries under the covers with me.

"I don't know Liam, I think he did." I laugh.

"Mummmmm!" Jack groans as Liam comes over to the side of the bed he is hiding in and rips the covers off.

"Say I'm your favourite," Liam demands.

"Nope." Jack giggles harder.

"Oh, you're gonna regret that," Liam says before attacking Jack with tickles. Beside me on the bed, the two of them toss and wiggle but Liam doesn't relent until Jack is gasping for air. Pulling back, Liam pins Jack down on the bed.

"Say it, say I'm your favourite." When Jack doesn't answer right away because he is still catching his breath Liam pokes him in the side once more.

"You're my favourite, I promise!" Jack laughs out, smiling up at Liam like a son looks at his father and my heart stops. The whole time I have had all this mum guilt and Liam has stepped up to parent Jack. He isn't just looking after him until I'm better, he *is* being his parent.

"Good. We have an hour until dinner if you want some screen time." Liam stands back up and Jack scrambles out of the bed but before he runs from the room he turns back to give me a kiss.

"Love you, Mum!" he shouts before bolting off again.

"Love you, bud!" I yell after him.

Liam kicks off his shoes before sliding onto the bed beside me where Jack was just sitting. He fusses over me for a moment, fixing the pillows behind me, and hands me a glass of water off the bedside table.

"How are you doing?" he asks.

"Going crazy in this room," I answer, the same way I have every time he has asked today.

"I'm sorry Sunshine, but you know it's right for you and the baby," he tells me again.

"I feel so useless," I sigh.

"You are growing a whole ass baby, you're doing more work than most people just by sitting here."

I wish he was less sweet. Wish he would tell me to get over it and to stop complaining.

"When can I go back to the shop?" I ask after a while.

"When the baby is born," he reminds me, ignoring my groan of protest. "I was going to take Jack to the shop today after school but Anders volunteered to go instead."

"Okay...?" He said that like it's strange, but I thought the guys were taking turns to check in on my business to make sure it doesn't burn to the ground.

"I think something is happening with him and Lyndsey," he tells me with a sneaky smirk.

"What?" I almost yell. Remembering that he dropped her off at work the day of my accident, I snap my posture ramrod straight beside him.

"I don't know for sure but every time I even mention Bloom and Blossom he either blushes – *blushes!* – or volunteers to go and check on it for me." I can't believe this is the first I'm hearing about this after Lyndsey's protests, but I know Liam. He will have been doing his own investigating so he can give me as much information as possible.

"Sneaky sneaky." I smile.

"I know but he's not telling me anything. There's a project for you: annoy Lyndsey into telling you if there's something there." I smirk at him trying to give me something to distract my mind. He knows I love a challenge. And what a wild one it is. My Lyndsey and his Anders. Oh yes, that is something I can work with.

"You're incredible you know?" I tell him. My heart suddenly warm with everything he is doing.

"Where'd that come from?" he asks rearing back a little to look at me fully.

"I just, I'm so proud that I'm having this baby with you of all people." I shrug shyly.

"Sunshine—" he starts before I interrupt him.

"No, let me say this." I know if I stop and don't get this all out right now I never will. "Liam, you have stepped up for me and Jack more than anyone else ever has and I didn't even ask. Hell, I wouldn't have asked but you did it anyway. You are basically raising my son right now while being my nurse and still keeping in shape for next season and I just, I guess I want you to know how amazing you are."

"I'd do it a million times over if it made you smile, Sunshine," he tells me. I can hear the emotion in his voice, but I don't mention it as he pulls me into his side and kisses my forehead.

"Thank you." I will be thankful for him forever.

"You need anything?" he asks, and when he goes to pull back the covers to get out of the bed, I grab his hand before he can get too far.

"How about a cuddle?" I nibble at my bottom lip worried he will have stuff to do. Instead he crawls back into the bed and shuffles down until he is lying beside me.

"I think I can manage that." He pulls me over to him so my head is resting on his chest.

We lie in a comfortable silence, breathing in sync as I listen to his heartbeat. The feeling of his T-shirt is soft against my face and he smells like something fresh and woodsy that I can't put my finger on, but I enjoy it anyway. I also enjoy when he starts to run his fingers through my hair. It's gotten so much longer recently, but I love when he plays with it so much that I don't want to cut it anytime soon.

I stay in his arms until his phone pings on the bedside table with a text from our chef telling him the food is ready whenever he wants it. Even though I'm not ready to leave his arms yet, we untangle our limbs and he goes to fetch Jack for dinner, promising me he will bring me my plate up right away.

I think about how it might be time I ask about moving into the master suite with him.

Chapter Twenty-Four

Liam

This time last year fatherhood was not on my mind. I always hoped I would be a dad someday, but I never really thought it would happen. Now, here I am in the pick-up line at Jack's school with the windows rolled down, blasting my cheesy Nineties boyband playlist with an easy smile.

Some of the other parents give me sideways glances but I pay them no mind, it feels right being here. Sun shining down on me as I wait for Jack to come out with the rest of his class, this has been my new routine since Ellis left the hospital.

Personally, I think fatherhood looks good on me. My mom said the same when she FaceTimed me yesterday. When I told her not to come up here after Ellis was put on bed rest, the only condition she had was that I had to call her every day with updates, even when there aren't updates to give her. On those uneventful days she just wants to know about me and how I'm getting on. It's the most I've talked to her in years, and she's loving it. Even dad gets in once in a while to ask about hockey and offer random baby advice. His most recent piece was not to buy baby supplies until after the baby is born. It's an old

Russian superstition, but I had to break it to him that it's far too late for that.

On quick little feet, Jack jogs over to the car and hops into his car seat. The first time I picked him up, I offered to strap him in. He looked at me like I was stupid and told me "I think I have more practice than you."

He wasn't wrong. I forget how grown up he is. Before I met him, I thought five-year-olds where basically toddlers, but Jack is a little human with opinions and the ability to strap himself into the car.

"Hey bud, how was school?" Normally he gives me a run through of every little thing he did and every thought he had, but today he just meets my eye in the rear-view mirror and shrugs.

"You okay?" I'm trying not to worry, but if something is wrong it will be my first Jack problem to possibly solve alone.

"Yeah." Jack's little voice is quiet, I'm not even sure he heard what I said, but if he isn't ready to talk I'm not going to push him. Maybe I should wait until we get home and ask for Ellis's input.

"Liam?" Jack asks after a while of driving.

"Yeah, bud?" The atmosphere in the car feels different than usual somehow. Heavier.

"Can we stop for a bit before we go home?" At its base, that isn't a strange request. Sometimes we meet up with some of the guys to skate, but I can hear a wobble in his voice and it's putting me on edge.

"Where do you want to go?" The sun is shining down, but my sunny mood feels like it's floating away in the breeze.

"Maybe the park?" I watch in the mirror as he worries at his bottom lip while watching the world zoom by out of the window.

"You wanna play in the park for a bit?" *Please want to play, please tell me this weird mood is all in my head.*

"No, I—I want to talk to you about something." *Well shit.*

"Oh okay, yeah we can do that." I just need to pull myself together before we get there.

By the time I've pulled into a space at the park I would say I am about 30 per cent more chill. Not a lot, but Ellis's son is asking for a private chat. He could tell me he doesn't want to live in my house any more. He could tell me to leave him and his mom alone altogether.

I have my fingers crossed that maybe he just has a problem at school he wants to talk about or maybe he has his first little crush. The thing that settles me most is when I jump out of the car and I flick through my wallet polaroids. Seeing Ellis's growing bump calms my soul. Every month I look forward to adding another to my collection, since she lives in my house now, Ellis argued that she doesn't need to take them any more. Yeah, *no*, I love these little reminders of what is coming.

We walk in silence hand in hand through the winding paths for a while. Summer in this park is beautiful, but until Jack came into my life I hardly spent any time here. Even when I go for a run I tend to go around the neighbourhood or in the gym, but I've been missing out.

Tall trees edge the paths and grow far overhead, painting sprawling shadows along the walkway. In the distance I can hear the sound of children in the main section of the park. It's louder than usual, but that's not surprising given the weather. I do wish we were somewhere more private for whatever this conversation is, but there is something calming about this place. Even if it is full of children and their parents staring at me to figure out where they recognise me from, it must be something to do with having Jack by my side that makes it so enjoyable.

I notice that Jack is heading towards the lake and I can't help but smile. When I was a kid this was the same little lake my dad would take me to feed the birds. Those times were few and far between. He worked so hard to make sure I had everything I could ask for, but it just made it all the sweeter when we would get that time.

There is a small fence stopping you from getting too close to the water now, but back then I used to sit right on the water's edge, listening to my dad tell me stories of his childhood. I never thought about bringing my own son here one day, I never thought I would have the chance.

We aren't here to feed the birds or to tell stories from my past. We are here because Jack needed to get me alone. The benches on the side are not the same as when I was young, back then they were rickety wooden things held together by nothing but splinters.

The newer ones are faux wood but made from recycled plastic that was collected in the park a few years ago. It was the first community project I helped out with when I joined the Spears. All the players came out in matching shirts with litter pickers while the press snapped away and asked questions about the environment. At the time, I thought it looked like we were just doing community service, but either way we now have nice, recycled benches for Jack and I to sit on.

"Come on Jack, you're killing me. What's wrong?" I try to laugh it off, but my real feelings are starting to show.

"I don't know where to start," he tells me, finally meeting my eyes for the first time this afternoon.

"Start where you want, we can always loop back if you need to." I hope he hasn't noticed how anxious I am. Perhaps my reaction is putting him more on edge.

"It's always just been me and mum," he begins. The words sink in my stomach.

"I'm sorry." I don't even know what to say but he shakes his head lightly at me.

"No, I—I like you being around. I just, well I've never had a dad and I don't ask Mum about him because I see how sad she gets." He goes back to avoiding my eyes.

"Oh Jack, your mom would always answer your questions," I reassure him. I know Ellis. It might hurt her, but she would do it every time.

"I know, but I like it better when she's happy, like when she is with you. But it's just different than before." He is breaking my heart, I can see that he still hasn't gotten to his point though, because anxiety is still flowing off him.

"I like you being around Liam, you make Mum happy, you look after her and I think you're cool. I never had a dad but you're going to be the baby's dad forever right? You're not going to leave her?" That's when he meets my eyes again and my heart drops seeing the tears he is trying to hold back.

"Is that what's worrying you, that I'm not going to stick around?" I've spent so long trying to prove to Ellis that I'm in this for the long haul that I just assumed Jack would know too. I'm an idiot.

"It would hurt if you left me too." His voice shakes, then he bursts into tears. Heavy sobs wrack his little body, his bright blue eyes filling at the brim, unable to hold them back any longer.

"Oh Jack, come here." I pull him onto my lap and some tears leak onto my shirt. I let him cry it out and rub circles on his back. "I'm not going anywhere, I'm not just staying for your mom and the baby, I'm staying for you too, okay?"

"You and Mum and the baby will be a family without me." He sobs into my shoulders. This kid has been having some huge feelings. I never would have expected a five-year-old to even have thought about this stuff but Jack has. Then again, Jack isn't a normal kid, with his mom's illness and his dad's absence, it shouldn't be surprising that he is wise beyond his years.

"No Jack, never. You are my family," I tell him and I mean it to my core.

"I wish you were my dad." His voice is scratchy and raw but I hear him over his sobs. I wish I was his dad too. I have since I found out Ellis was pregnant with him by scrolling on social media. I thought that it should've been me all along. Now that I have had the displeasure of seeing Michael up close, I wish it even more. That man didn't deserve Ellis and he sure as shit doesn't deserve Jack.

"Then I am," I tell him.

"What?" Jack pulls his tear-stained face away from my shoulder looking at me with eyes full of confusion. I wish I could hug him hard enough to put all of his broken pieces back together.

"If you want me to be your dad then I will be your dad. I'd be lucky to have a son like you." I mean it, too. If my daughter turns out half as amazing as her brother then she will be more than I could ever have wished for. I'm staying in this boy's life for as long as he wants me: it will be me who teaches him to shave, me who helps him talk to his first crush.

It will be me who shows him how to treat the people you love and I will love him so hard that hopefully he forgets his birth father ever existed. He may not share my DNA but he owns a big part of my heart.

"You promise you're not going to leave?" His little pinkie comes between us showing me again that he is still just a child.

Without a second's hesitation I link my finger with his. I haven't made a pinkie promise in a very long time but I'm sure they are as legally binding now as they were when I was young.

"The only time I'm going anywhere is when I have to go for work but I will always come back to you guys. It's the easiest promise I've ever made." I swear to him.

"I love you, Liam." Hearing him say that again for the first time since the hockey game melts my heart in my chest. I thought it was a heat of the moment thing with the adrenalin of the game, but I guess he really meant it, or at least he means it now.

"I love you too Jack, so much." I love this kid deep in my bones, a love I never thought I would get to experience until I found out I would be a parent, but I guess I'm a parent already.

Jack knows he is my family now and I'm hoping Ellis is coming over to my side after the past few weeks. She knows that I want her to be mine and I know she wants me too, but I'm going to show up every time until the two of them know there is no chance of me leaving them.

I'm going to be the man that stays, the man that gets the honour of becoming a part of this family unit.

Ellis, Jack, baby girl and me.

It sounds perfect.

Chapter Twenty-Five

July

Ellis

Screaming. There's a baby screaming.

Where is it?

I can hear it but I can't see where it is. I have to get through that big wooden door to help the baby.

Screaming. I'm yelling out, but the sound is drowned out by the poor baby.

It needs help, let me help.

I try to get out of bed but I can't move. My wrists are bound together at the headboard and my feet are weighed down, strapped to the bed. The more I try to fight against them the tighter they bind.

Screaming. As soon as I'm free, I'll help it.

Why is nobody helping me?

The baby needs help.

I need help.

The louder I shout the tighter the binds fasten.

Screaming.

I call out for Liam, begging him to help. He doesn't come. The wooden door shakes on its hinges mocking me with how easily it should open.

Everything stops.

The baby is no longer crying and I am no longer bound.

I am in a pitch-black room. The only light is coming from a window in front of me. Through the glass I see a beautiful woman holding Jack. She is curvy and full-busted, someone out of a Sports Illustrated magazine. Jack is smiling in her arms waving at someone.

I knock on the glass but the sound is muted. I shout out for my son but he doesn't hear. Then Liam joins them.

"I'm so glad you're here." He tells her, kissing her before taking Jack from her.

"Finally Ellis is out of the way." Liam sighs. Now Jack isn't in her arms I can see her baby bump that Liam rubs.

"I could never have a child with her, she was useless." He laughs.

"Women like her shouldn't be mothers."

I'm yelling apologies and pleading for them to help me. I beg for my boys, for them to come back for me, but they don't. They just laugh.

"She is worse than Eleanor. Jack is better off without her." Pain sears my chest. I have tried to be better than my mother. It's never enough. I'm never enough. The man I love wishes I was more.

"Will you be my new mummy?" Jack asks the woman. He looks at her with stars in his eyes.

"We will be a family now Jack," Liam tells him as the strange beautiful woman nods to my son.

They start to walk away from me. The dark room around me closes in but I stay locked in place. Pleading for them to return. Jack never looks back as he walks hand in hand with his new mum. Liam glances over his shoulder though. Finally, his eyes meet mine but his gaze is not filled with love. He hates me. Still looking at me full of contempt he throws his arm over the beautiful woman he finally gets to be with.

"Please come back! Jack! Liam! Don't leave me! Please…"

—

"Ellis, wake up. You're safe, I'm here." I hear Liam's voice, but it's no longer coming from the man walking away from me. "Sunshine, you're okay. It's just a dream." He shakes me lightly but my eyes snap open at the contact. As soon as my eyes meet his I burst into tears. Sobs wrack through me when Liam pulls me into his arms. He hushes me lightly but I can't catch my breath.

It might have been a dream but it felt so real.

I can see the highlights in the woman's dark hair, the disgust in Liam's eyes when he looked over his shoulder.

I can hear the baby's screams echoing. Liam lets me cry.

He holds me to his chest and rubs calming circles onto my back as I soak his T-shirt with tears. My back is pricked with sweat but I'm unsure if it is from the warm air or the fear I feel. Even the pain was real, being strapped down reminded me so vividly of the chronic pain I feel and every little movement aches deep within. The pain of that dream was real, mentally and physically.

"I'm sorry," I sob, "I'll be better. I promise, I'll be better." My words are muffled but Liam shifts when he hears me.

"You have nothing to apologise for." I hear him but I don't believe him, every word he says is silenced by the hatred I saw in his eyes.

"Please don't hate me," I'm begging and the tears are still falling but he holds me tight and kisses my forehead.

"Never Ellis, I could never hate you," he tells me. "I heard you from the other room, what was happening?"

"You left, you walked away and took Jack with you," I tell him, leaving out the other woman. I don't think I can imagine her for another second without sobbing, and my breathing has only just started to even out.

"Me and Jack are right here, do you want to go see him?" he asks, *god, he is perfect.* I shake my head though, burrowing further into his chest.

"I don't want to scare him. He'll think I'm mad. Can you just hold me for a second?" I bury myself from the world. I never want him to let me go. Every day the baby is closer to coming into this world and the only place my anxiety can't get to me is when Liam's arms are wrapped around me. He knows exactly what to do – like he has done dozens of times before, he holds me in his arms, holding my broken pieces together because I don't have the strength to.

I savour the moment, because I know it won't last. Liam will need to rest when the season starts again, and the only way I can think of that happening is if me and Jack go back to our flat. It's what Liam will need. I'll think about that tomorrow though, because right now I just want him to hold me.

"Always," he whispers.

Chapter Twenty-Six

Ellis

I know if I get caught Liam will give me attitude, but it isn't my fault. How am I supposed to spend four months on bed rest when I can hear Liam and Jack laughing downstairs? There are only so many episodes of *The Great British Bake Off* a girl can watch before she starts to lose her mind.

Fluffy socks dull the sound enough that I can move around pretty much silently. Any noise I do make, the boys counteract by being louder. I just hate missing out. Kids don't stay kids for long, and every day I miss is precious.

Not wanting to test my luck, I stay outside the kitchen to go unnoticed. Putting my weight onto the door jamb to relieve the late-stage pregnancy pain, I glance around the room, my mouth dries at what I find: Liam is stood at the cooker flipping pancakes. Shirtless.

The man is wearing nothing but a pair of grey sweat-pants, like a *harlot*. Jack is laughing louder with every pancake Liam flips as he makes it a whole performance. He wobbles back and forth, humming a circus theme. After each perfect flip he takes a second to bow to his enraptured audience.

Who created this man? I'm behind him, so I'm unfortunately missing out on a lot of ab action. But this is enough. His back muscles ripple with every movement against his perfectly sun-kissed skin. Where has he even been where he could get such a flawless tan? The man is inside more than most people I know. Gifted genetics, clearly. Still, he must find time to work out. His shoulders are wide and so... biteable. The things he can do with that body should be illegal. Especially to a heavily pregnant woman with wild hormones.

My mind wanders to what else he must be capable of doing in bed. I wonder what he has learned over the years; his dirty talk has certainly gotten more panty melting, but there must be other stuff too. Maybe he has some handcuffs he could tie me down with. The thought alone causes my thighs to clench.

"Ellis Ainsley!" His voice shakes my mind back into the room. *Shit.* I was so wrapped up in kinky fantasies that I missed him turning around.

"Hi," I reply sheepishly.

"Don't 'Hi' me! You need to be in bed." God, he is hot when he lays down the law. His skin is flushed as he stalks towards me.

Liam scoops me into his arms, bridal style, and Jack cheers from his stool. Knowing there is no point in fighting him, I loop my arms around his neck while he heads up the stairs with me. Softly he lays me in the centre of the master bed resting his weight on his hands either side of my head.

"Stay here," he demands leaving a kiss on the tip of my nose.

"Why don't you wear me out?" I ask keeping my arms around his neck so he can't get too far away.

I see his eyes look away for a moment in contemplation. He suddenly stops, pulling away abruptly. "I'm taking Jack to school, you need to rest remember?" He tells me. Was the suggestion so wrong? Did I offend him? I flop myself back against the pillowcase with a dramatic sigh, trying to shake the feeling.

"I've missed you." I pout.

"Sorry, Sunshine," he says lightly before leaving the room.

The rejection was completely reasonable, but I can't help but feel like something is off. And I think it's starting to become obvious what that is. Liam wants more than whatever we have right now. But honestly, I'm just not ready to give into that yet. Is it what I really want? I said I was his, and part of me meant it. Part of me always will.

But despite all the green flags he shows me, I can't get rid of the idea of the red ones that might turn up in the future. When my heart tells me to *stay*, my head is telling me to *run*.

Liam and I being a family and raising our kids is apparently Liam's goal. But there are so many variables he isn't considering. There is so much more to this life than just a happy ever after, and I'm not prepared to be heartbroken again. No, I can only have him in one way – the only way to protect my feelings. We just need to fuck each other. Channel whatever chemistry and passion we have that way. Just one time.

Maybe twice.

–

I thought it would be sexy. I'm sprawled on the master bed in the only lingerie that I could get over my bump. A baby pink satin teddy with lace being the only covering on my boobs, the knickers are just as scandalous, crotchless baby pink lace with satin ties on either side.

Though he might not even see them – I can't see them over my belly – in my head this plan is fool proof: Liam walks in to check on me to see me posed and ready for him with a list of pros and cons where there are no cons to him fucking me. Perfect.

Except now I'm worried I just look like an undercooked chicken, pink fabric on my stretched pale skin.

Originally I wanted to wear my black lacy set but it was way too small on my swollen boobs, I looked like a cut of meat stuffed into lace. Pink teddy was the best option other than stark naked.

It's too late to back down now as I hear Liam's heavy footfall coming up the stairs. I scrape together as much confidence as I can when the door creaks open.

"Fuck me, Sunshine." He's stock still in the doorway, his jaw on the floor. Maybe this is going to work out after all.

"I'm hoping you'll fuck me." I try to keep my voice sultry and sexy but that's never been my forte.

"Ellis…" He's shaking his head. *No no no*.

"No wait, I have a whole thing." I hold up a hand to stop his protest and pull the slip of paper from between my boobs and begin reading my pre-prepared list: "Pros: We are really good at it; we have ten years to make up for; you are very fucking sexy; I am very horny; orgasms help relieve pain which I am in a lot of; lastly, I want you. Cons: there are none." I breathe at the end of my list.

I think I have him for a moment, but by the time I get to the cons I can see him trying to hold in a laugh.

"Stop laughing!" I yell, throwing the paper at him.

"Sunshine, there is no way you wrote a pros and cons list and hid it in your underwear." When he puts it like that, it does sound crazy. But I am so pregnant and so obsessed with being in bed with Liam that it's overwhelming me. Still, I can't help but laugh with him when he joins me on the bed.

"Ellis, I've told you that I'm not just going to fuck you because you're turned on. We've done this dance once before, and I haven't known what to think since. I won't move forward unless you're ready for a *real* us. I thought after what happened before that you were ready, but then you put up a wall again. I can't keep taking one step forward three steps back. It's not good for either of us."

I don't know how to respond. He's right. He's reasonable. But I'm hormonal and stubborn. "That's got to be… I don't know… At least extortion." I tell him scooting across the bed away from him.

"Sex-tortion, more like." He snorts.

"Maybe I should just get myself off instead," I tell him. I glance to my bedside drawer where a small vibrator waits for me. It's the least I could use.

He notices my hinting. "You think it will be as good as me?" Liam raises an eyebrow. He is so fucking cocky, yet it's so hot. Damn him.

"It will be faster." I'm lying but he doesn't need to know that.

"I don't think you have it in you." Despite trying to stick to his guns, I can see him giving in to our flirting nature. I'm not sure either of us will ever be able to help falling into this habit. His dare is the shove I need. Keeping my eyes locked on him, I lean over to the bedside cabinet and pull out the bullet vibrator.

I need him to be as desperate for me as I am for him. This is all going to be a performance, but the more real it is, the more he will want it.

I suck the bullet into my mouth until it is dripping in saliva then I turn it on and drag it down over my clavicle, over the lace covering my nipples. That's when I turn it on. The vibrations are directly on my nipples and they are already sensitive from pregnancy and the friction of the lace so the sensation just heightens everything. I take the time to circle both of my nipples feeling the intensity of Liam's stare on them making my skin flush bright red.

I'm already wet and aching. When I plant my feet onto the bed and spread my knees I hear Liam inhale sharply, I guess he hadn't noticed the barely-there underwear.

It's not easy to reach around my bump, but I need to. I manage to get the bullet to my entrance where I rub it up and down to coat it in my juices before pulling it back to my mouth to taste myself. That's when I look at Liam.

His jaw is tight and I watch his Adam's apple bob when he swallows. His skin looks as flushed as I feel and his fists are gripping the bed covers like they're his lifeline. Because of how he is sitting I can't see his crotch, but I know he is hard, there's no way his jeans aren't uncomfortable but I need more to push him over the edge.

Dragging the vibrator along my skin I take it back to my thighs to tease my legs, whimpering just for Liam's benefit. But when the vibrations hit my clit, the moans are genuine.

I've masturbated more than a few times over the past few months, but it has never felt like this. Liam's gaze on me mixed with the desperation in the air makes it too much to handle. Almost immediately my back is arching off the bed and my head is tossing back against the pillow.

I can hear how wet I am. I stretch my other hand down to slide two fingers into me, keeping the vibration on my clit. I'm pumping in and out, the sound of my pussy mixing with my moans.

"Liam," I groan out. I need more, I need his hands on me.

"Fuck it." I hear his voice come out on a desperate groan. In a blink his hand pulls mine from inside me, he takes my fingers and sucks them into his mouth. Taking each finger between his lips he runs his tongue over my knuckles gently, savouring the lingering taste. Once he's licked them clean, he pins my arms next to my head.

"I have to taste you. If you want me to fuck you, you are going to have to be ready for what comes after." His voice is rough. "I'm not letting you hide after this. Not again."

He takes the vibrator out of my hand and puts it down beside him when he settles his shoulders between my thighs. I can see him looking up at me over my bump. When he knows he has my attention he winks and buries his face into me.

His tongue drags from top to bottom before swirling around my swollen clit. I can feel him moaning against my skin, the vibrations pushing me closer to the edge so quickly after I warmed myself up. Liam is clearly not done because he slips in a finger when he sucks lightly at me. His fingers are so much larger than mine that even with just one finger I can feel the stretch more than with two of mine. He curls his finger to rub my G spot and I see stars.

My legs tighten around his head as my body nearly levitates off the bed, Liam licks me through it.

"You think you can get away with teasing me Sunshine?" He tuts, still between my legs, saying, "You can give me one more, can't you?"

"Liam, I can't…" Fuck, that orgasm was so powerful.

"Where's my big independent girl? You gotta tap out already?" His voice is full of condescension, he always knows what buttons to push.

"No." I grit my teeth preparing myself for more.

"I didn't think so." That's when buzzing fills the room. I try to wriggle away, but Liam's strong arm bands over the top of my thighs as he uses his other hand to hold the vibrator directly against my clit. I'm already building up to the edge after seconds, but Liam doesn't let up.

I can't see his face because my eyes are screwed shut, but I can imagine the grin. Sadistic and satisfied as I shake under the pressure. I can feel my insides pulsing around nothing when my toes clench and I scream out into the room.

The pleasure is so intense, I could black out, but Liam kisses lightly up my body until he has me wrapped in his arms. The safe feeling of his arms around me helps tether me back to earth.

"I'm scared." I break the comfortable silence in the room. I knew I was going to have to have this talk at some point, but I was hoping to put it off until the baby came.

"Of what?" he asks, kissing my forehead and tightening his arms around me.

"You getting sick of us." I tell him my truth. My real fear that I have never been enough for anyone. My mother never cared, Jack's dad walked away, even Liam had to leave once before.

I know that isn't fair, it was technically me who told him to leave. It was my boundary to split before he was drafted. But a part of me always wondered about what would have happened if he turned up on my doorstep one day, saying he chose our relationship over hockey, and I couldn't protest the decision.

"Ellis—" Before he can talk, I interrupt him.

"It's just been me and Jack for so long I'm scared that if I give us a chance and you get bored I will have to mend his broken heart as well as mine and I don't think I could survive it." I know I couldn't survive it.

Liam takes a second to himself before he takes a deep breath.

"I wasn't going to tell you this," he says lowly, clearly unsure about what he is going to say next.

"Tell me what?" I usher him.

"Jack asked for a talk with me a few weeks ago." My body freezes.

"When?" I choke out, Jack is so introspective for a kid that he could have told Liam anything and a million different conversations filter through my head.

"Last month, the day I took him to the park and for ice cream after school."

I remember that, I woke up from a nap and the house was eerily quiet because I was there alone. I called Liam to make sure they were okay and neither of them told me anything had happened, they just asked what flavour ice cream I wanted.

"What did he say?" I ask. I'm scared to know the answer but the morbid desire to know is seeping into my bones.

"He told me that he likes having me around because I make you happy." I look up at him and find Liam looking at me as though he sees the planets in my eyes, taking a second to admire me, he holds my jaw lightly. "He asked if I was going to abandon the baby like his dad did. He made me promise that I wasn't going anywhere."

"Liam you shouldn't have promised that." I try to keep the tears at bay. This just highlights even more of my fears; Jack would be broken if Liam goes back on his promise. Besides, I'm pregnant and that means I am allowed to be overly emotional.

"I'll tell you what I told him, it's the easiest promise I've ever made. Ellis, I love you, I love your son and I love our daughter already. You're stuck with me forever so you better start getting used to it."

Then the tears flow. I couldn't hold them back if I tried.

Communication has never been my strong suit and Liam knows I'm not ready to admit that I love him again, even if the words are on the tip of my tongue, but his willingness to tell me how he feels wrecks me. Like always, Liam holds me to his chest and lets me cry.

I wish I could say it is just pregnancy hormones but I know that isn't the truth, I've just never felt safe enough to cry. I needed to be strong, always, but now Liam has given me a place to be as vulnerable as I feel without judgment.

"Will you go easy on me?" I ask him. Tears are drying on my face, my eyes must be rimmed red but he still looks at me as if I'm beautiful.

"What do you mean?" I can see a flash of hope in his gaze that he tries to hide, not wanting to wish I could be ready. Never wanting to push me if I'm not there.

"If I say I want to try with us, will you give me grace? I can't promise you an easy forever but I want to try. I really want to try." I have more than just myself to think about, but I know I can't push Liam out of my life out of fear because not only does Jack want him in his life, I want him in our daughter's life. In mine, too.

"I'll give you anything you need Ellis Ainsley, as long as you're mine," he says.

But I'm not his. Not yet. And yet, I want to be. I want to be a family, it's something I've never had and I always promised I'd give Jack a different life than me. I have the chance to give him a dad, a man who makes his mum happy and who loves me including Jack, not in spite of him.

Liam has pushed me so far out of my comfort zone since January and now I have friends I never would have imagined – I'm in a hockey group chat for crying out loud. One where his team ask for updates. One where they send me pictures of Liam reading baby books on the plane to games. A chat where they co-ordinate who is going to check on Bloom and Blossom for me. Hell, Rook has taken the liberty of letting me know he is on food duty when the baby comes, something about a bad experience with hospital food when he had his appendix removed. I am surrounded by help and people who show me I am worth going out of their way for. I just need to open myself up enough to believe them.

I deserve happiness.

It's time I stop standing in my own way.

Chapter Twenty-Seven

August

Liam

Would it be cheesy to say my life is a dream? Yes. But it would also be true. Ellis is my soul. Jack is my inspiration. Our baby girl is my future.

Everything hasn't been sunshine and rainbows, but it has been getting better. Over the past six weeks we have celebrated Jack's birthday with cake and his school friends at the ice rink, his new favourite place. Our little guy is six years old with the mind of a fifty-year-old.

He has this ability to bury himself into you so easily that he even gets Edge to join in skating with a bunch of kids – I thought I'd see pigs fly before I saw that. Though I also enjoyed showing the kids the ropes, it was fun to go back to basics.

Ellis and I have fallen asleep and woken up in each other's arms, only separating when she gets night sweats. She even let me take her on a real adult date night when Jack had a sleepover with Rook. It felt like a huge step for us, but hilarious at the same time. I took a woman who is heavily pregnant with my baby, out on our first date… but then again, it isn't technically our first date, seeing as she's also my ex. When I think about our situation, it sounds like a sitcom.

For our first "real date" I took her for a classy meal with a chef's selection menu, which didn't go as planned. They put down a plate of salmon slices on crackers for the starter and Ellis came seconds away from vomiting. Let's just say it wasn't my best idea.

I learned from my mistakes, and the second date was much more successful. As Ellis's bump has gotten bigger, she has also been in a lot of pain. I wanted to do something where she could relax and wouldn't feel the need to dress up and make herself uncomfortable.

There isn't much I can do for her pain, but I borrowed Edge's truck and took us to a drive-in cinema. I stuffed the bed of the truck with a mattress and pillows and blankets for us to cuddle under the stars. I felt like a retro teenager in the 1950s, making out in the drive-in. It's something we would have done back in college.

It's been a month and a half since Ellis vowed to try with us, and try she has. Not only has she been openly giving me a chance, she has also been trying to communicate more, even if it still isn't her strong suit.

I've learned how much she loves my praise, both in and out of the bedroom. She loves my relationship with Jack, but there are things she doesn't like, too. She hates when I spend my money on her; something about feeling guilty about it. She also hates that I have no plans to stop spending my money on her – she will get used to it.

Probably.

Another thing I've learned is as much as my Sunshine has changed since college, there is so much that is the same. She could still commit a crime when she's too hungry and she still has this intense focus on the things she cares about. In college she cared most about her studying and where our respective futures were heading. But right now, that's changed. Her focus is her family. *Our* family.

My focus is the same. My wallet is filled with polaroids of Ellis's bump, as well as shots of her and Jack together. For a while, my favourite picture was Ellis standing with a bouquet of flowers resting on her five-month bump, but now it's a picture of Jack kissing her seven-month bump.

There are only eighteen days to go until the due date and Ellis is in full nesting mode. Every day she has a new piece of furniture delivered for me to put together. I love feeling useful. I have painted the nursery a lavender colour, then pink, then grey and back to lavender because Ellis couldn't pick which she wanted.

When she walks into the nursery to see it coming together more every day, she gets this flushed glow and a shine in her eyes that makes me weak. She has me truly wrapped around her finger and I wouldn't want it any other way.

That being said though, I can tell she is getting stir crazy. I've gotten less strict with her being bed bound and have given in to her begging to live a more normal life as long as she keeps herself safe and doesn't put strain on her body.

See? I can compromise. From spending so much time lying around and scrolling, she has become a master at finding the best online deals including a spa day she has booked for her and Lyndsey. I told her they could go to any spa she wanted because money isn't an issue. She didn't love that and booked the deal she found anyway. She's been excited for this day since she booked it, giving her something to look forward to that will make her feel more human as well as relaxing her before the baby comes.

"Liam! They're here! They're here!" Jacks hyper voice yells from the bottom of the stairs. Apparently from his squeals, the team are here. Jack wanted to go back to the rink and there was no way they were going to miss out on some ice time with their new six-year-old best friend.

It takes another ten minutes to wrangle him and Ellis and get them packed into the back of Anders's car. Ellis asked to get dropped off at Bloom and Blossom where Lyndsey is waiting so she can check that the building is still there after nearly three months away. Anders was all for popping to the shop – I wonder if a certain redhead had anything to do with that.

Speaking of Lyndsey, she is waiting against the side of her car when we pull up, and Anders and I both hop out at the same time. Me to help Ellis out and help her into Lyndsey's car and Anders for… I'm not sure what.

"Hey, cowboy." Lyndsey winks over her shoulder at him after she has hugged Ellis and rubbed the bump.

"Mornin' Darlin'." The charming mother-fucker kisses the back of her hand.

"Oy fucker, you didn't kiss my hand. I thought you were a gentleman." Ellis teases, her British twang sounding stronger in her faux offence, Lyndsey runs to put Ellis's bag in the trunk of her car trying to hide a blush.

"My mama would never forgive me, ma'am." He kisses Ellis's hand which makes her cackle and make a kissy face at him.

"Okay, now a kiss from you." She demands from me, and my heart grows at her initiating intimacy like this. Not one to look a gift horse in the mouth I pull her to my chest and kiss her, nothing inappropriate in front of

Jack, but enough to satisfy us for a few hours until I can see her again.

–

By the time we pull up to the rink, Jack is vibrating with excitement in the back and he gets even more excited when he sees Edge and Rook waiting by the door. Anders barely has time to cut the engine before Jack is out of the door.

"Do you have them? Do you have them?" Jack yells as he runs over to Rook jumping at his feet. As a belated birthday gift Rook promised he would buy Jack his own pair of skates.

I wanted to get them myself but Rook felt like it was his duty as Jack's favourite player. When I tried to tell him that Felix is his favourite again, he threw a puck at my head. I settled for getting him his own stick and I'm glad because we got to have guy time when I showed him how to tape his stick properly.

"Depends on if you've been good, eh?" Rook lifts a bag over his head so Jack can't reach, he might be tall for his age but there's no way he could get close to Rook's six-one frame.

"I've been *so* good. The goodest I promise." Jack flops his limbs around. Even Edge looks excited for Jack to get on the ice with all his own gear for the first time.

"Ruin has Jack been good enough to get his own skates?" Rook asks, but I know that even if Jack had been a terror he would get them anyway; he has us all wrapped around his finger.

"Yes, I have. I have. Tell him, Dad."

Silence falls over the parking lot.

Jack must not have heard what he said because he is still jumping up to get Rook's bag.

I'm stuck in a stunned silence.

I know Jack wanted me to be his dad, but I didn't think the day would come where he actually *called* me his dad. I mean, I guess I'm the only man who's been in his life to this degree, and I know I wish he was my son, but hearing him say the words stops me dead.

The guys must see how emotional I am because while I stand there fumbling for words, Anders slaps me on the back and Rook coughs before giving Jack his bag.

"Here you go, bud," he says not looking away from me. Edge opens the door for us and Anders all but walks me into the lobby.

"Yesssss!" Jack sings gripping the skates close to his chest with a megawatt smile on his face.

"I was going to ask if you're ready to become a dad but it looks like you already are." Anders laughs lightly, testing my mood, but my heart feels like it's outside of my chest. Jack has it in his hands.

Everyone around me is talking, asking Jack if he has all his kit and helping him get pads on, but I just watch them all.

My friends are helping my son.

My son.

We are teaching him how to play hockey, buying him skates and sticks and a top-of-the-line helmet. Not because we are trying to buy his affection but because we all want him to be safe – he is mine to keep safe. In my mental future where me and Ellis are married, I always pictured Jack and Ellis sharing my surname but until right now I didn't think Jack would see me as anything other than his stepdad at best. But in his heart, in my heart, he is already mine.

To protect, to teach, to love.

Still unused to wearing a full kit, Jack waddles more than walks to the edge of the ice. The four of us follow behind him, smiling when he tries to take off his skate guards and can't because he is unable to reach past his shin pads.

With a deep laugh Edge swings Jack into the air so I can pull off the guards for him and Edge makes sure to tickle him before putting him down.

"Jay, stop! I need to focus!" Jack chastises, he sounds just like his mom.

"Sorry, bud." Edge tries to bite back a laugh but I see it all over his face.

Before I join them on the ice for a game of freeze tag, I take a bunch of pictures for Ellis. In some you can see how hard Jack is focusing to stay on his feet and keep up with the guys. Obviously they are letting him catch them, anything to make him laugh.

My favourite picture though is one of Jack skating after the three guys. His smile is wide and just looking at the picture you can almost hear his laugh as the guys scream for my help while he chases them up and down. Edge tries to trip Rook, yelling that he is a sacrifice to help him and Anders get away, but all that does is put Rook on Jack's team.

After sending the pictures over I finally join them on the ice, taking some pucks to let Jack practise shooting with his new stick.

Knowing my plan, the guys line up for Jack while he takes some practice shots towards the goal first.

"Ice dodgeball! Jack you can use as many pucks as you like and your goal is to hit the guys and get them out." His eyes flame for a second and I see nothing but determination, the same that I see on the guys before we hit the ice for a game.

"What if I miss?" he asks as if we could be disappointed in him.

"Then you try again." I shrug setting the first puck in front of him. Jack swings his head left and right and shimmies his shoulders, relaxing his limbs the way we showed him. Edge sees how focused Jack is and holds his hands in front of his junk. When Rook laughs at him he just shrugs and says he needs to protect his jewels.

"It's not my fault your jewels are so small a puck won't hit 'em." Edge laughs causing Rook to frown and push him. Anders and Rook follow Edge's actions though, as Jack skates up and slaps the puck right at them. I mean *right* at them. The puck flies past Anders's face with about two inches to spare.

"Wait I think imma need a helmet!" Anders yells skating over to the bench as I try to stop laughing.

"Sorry!" Jack calls after him but he still holds his hand out to me for a high five.

A year ago, I never would have pictured this as my life. A six-year-old son looking at me for support and guidance, a daughter just over two weeks away from her due date and a beautiful woman waking up in my arms.

Damn I wouldn't have believed it when me and Ellis slept together in December. The pregnancy has flown by so quickly and my life has changed so much for the better that I am so thankful that Cassie made me go out with the team that night. Without her threatening me that day I wouldn't have gone and my life would be just the way it always was. Lonely and stagnant. Hanging on to hockey with all of my strength because I had nothing else to hold onto.

Now my arms are full and so is my heart.

Chapter Twenty-Eight

Ellis

All week I have been excited about the spa. It has been all I could think about. I have found that when I focus on the good I can ignore all the pain I'm in. I spend 90 per cent of my time switching between heating pads and making Liam massage my back, and feet, and legs… pretty much everywhere. The last 10 per cent is split between crying and those small moments of relief that come around once in a blue moon. I am so completely over being pregnant that it's crossed my mind to ask for an induction, I am at my wits' end.

Sometimes I need to put time aside to look after my body the best I can. I love Liam, I do, I know I haven't told him yet but I will. It's why I kissed him in front of everyone. I wanted to show him that I am serious about this. It was a strange sensation, knowing everyone was watching, but it also felt good. Natural, like I was always supposed to be kissing him and I've been holding back.

Still, I know when the baby comes he is going to live by my side so I need a little bit of me time before that. As soon as I get in Lyndsey's car though, there is something a lot more fun to think about.

"So…?" I ask as I watch in the rear-view mirror as the boys drive away for a rink day.

"So... what?" she asks watching them just as closely as me.

"You and Anders?" I nudge.

"We're just friends." Lyndsey is good at a lot of things. Lying is not one of them. Her skin flushes pink and she can't meet my eye.

"Friends my arse. You *want* him," I sing, like the mature adult I am.

"Ellis!" She slaps my leg lightly but it just makes me laugh until my sides hurt. The harder I laugh, the pinker she gets. I am seconds away from peeing myself when she switches on the ignition.

"I'm not saying anything, but he is handsome as sin," I tell her when I manage to pull myself together again.

"He doesn't want me like that," she says quietly.

"Why?" I'm not laughing any more. I don't think I've ever seen her so dejected.

"He's just being a good guy, that's all. You know how much I love the Spears, how attractive I think Anders is, but there's no way I would go there – especially now." I can clearly see this isn't the first time she's thought about this.

"Why not now?" I ask confused.

"Because you're having a baby with his teammate and we are going to be in each other's lives forever through little baby Ruin so if things didn't work out it would be way too awkward." Wait, she isn't going to go after Aiden because of me? My baby? I think the baby will bring them closer together in a good way.

"Lyndsey—" I start to argue but she interrupts me.

"Let's just have fun today okay? No boy talk." We pull up at a red light so she looks over at me for a second and

I can see that the topic alone is weighing on her so I give in.

"Fine. Just know I think you guys would be cute together." I bite my tongue even though I'm eager to tell her all the reasons she's wrong. Lyndsey moves on and asks me about what else needs to be done before the baby is born and I go off on a tangent about how unprepared I feel as we drive out of the city.

—

After about an hour, we pull into the car park and Lyndsey runs to check us in while I check my phone. I promised her I'll put it away for most of the day so we can focus on relaxing but I'm getting one last look.

I'm glad I did too because Liam has sent me a bunch of pictures of Jack skating with the guys. His smile is wider than I think I've ever seen it.

That last picture is everything, Rook sprawled on the ice with Jack standing over him laughing. I can practically hear him through my screen. I love how comfortable he is with Liam and his teammates. For a long time there were no men in his life, and now he gets to have that male influence and I couldn't have asked for better men.

The weather outside might be dark but Liam makes me feel so light that it balances perfectly. I don't know how Liam did it, but with his care and time, I'm becoming less scared of what lies ahead of us. Ever since I found out I was pregnant with Jack there has been an undercurrent of fear in my life. Scared of the pain. Scared of being a single mum. Scared of failing.

Liam makes me feel so secure that the fear doesn't take over every part of my life any more. Being a single mum was the best thing I've ever done and I think I raised the most amazing kid on my own. More than that, Liam has helped me see that failing doesn't mean you are unworthy. I might fail from time to time, but I have him in my corner either way. He's been here this whole time, always by choice – I just didn't want to believe it was possible for me.

I love that Jack feels safe with him, too. When Liam first came into my life I told him that me and Jack were a package deal but I never thought he would take it as seriously as he has. Liam loves Jack like his own and Jack loves him back.

I'm pretty sure Jack would follow Liam anywhere and I would be right there with them. Six years ago, when I was this close to labour I was riddled with panic attacks and nightmares, yet this time around I feel ready. Half because I've done it before, but also because Liam won't let anything happen to me.

Not if he can help it. This time is so different. I am so different. I feel stronger and more confident both as a mother and as a girlfriend. The rational part of me always knew I was worthy of love, I just didn't know how strong being loved would make me feel.

–

Green goo has never felt as good as it does seeping into my pores. The cool paste smells like mint and grass and it's like I can feel the toxins being sucked out. Or the moisture flowing in. Maybe both, I don't know exactly what it does – I didn't ask – but I'm enjoying it either way.

Being wrapped in the world's fluffiest robe is another plus. Lyndsey opted for a lavender mask and she lies next to me humming along to the spa music. The first thing we did after checking in was a full body massage for Lyndsey and a pregnancy specialised massage for me, and now my skin feels glossy and warm.

There was a moment on the bed where I was so comfortable I thought the baby was just going to shoot right out. Honestly I'm surprised I didn't pee myself I was that calm, my pelvic floor exercises went straight out the window.

My bones still feel like butter when the facial specialist starts to remove my refreshing detoxing goo. The water she uses is warm. As she wipes away at my skin, it's as though my worries wipe away with it. A part of me wonders what my boys are up to, but there is no anxiety about being away from Jack like there has been at other points in his life.

No, today it is just sheer curiosity because I know they will be having just as much – if not more – fun than me. Skating around, eating junk food, a day filled with fun and adventure as I enjoy the opposite. The quiet calm before the storm of having this little girl running us in circles.

"You're all done Miss Ainsley, feel free to enjoy the pool during the rest of your day." The spa woman says in the classic, soft whispered tone that feels so cliché but so right.

Taking my time to soak in the last few seconds on this shockingly comfortable wooden chair I feel the baby wiggle around, followed by a small stabbing pain. I have been getting these little pains for a while now, so I know that the baby is coming closer and closer every day. Braxton Hicks scared the life out of me the last time around – the false labour pains really know how to shock you.

When Jack was coming, every little thing scared me: every little cramp, I thought he was going to come; every little kick, I thought he might fracture a rib. Basically, I was a mess. But now I'm more relaxed. I think it's because I've had a little bit of practice but I also know as strong as Liam is, when he is faced with me actually going into labour he is going to shit himself.

All day Lyndsey has been eyeing up the Jacuzzi but won't tell me she wants to go in because she knows there's no pregnant people allowed, so I walk over. I hear the hurried slap of her slipper-clad feet scurrying after me as I settle myself on the edge, dipping my legs into the jets. The warm water pulses on my swollen ankles and it makes me feel just as good as the massage.

"El! What are you doing? You can't get in there!" There is genuine concern in her voice as though she thinks this is my first time ever hearing pregnancy Jacuzzi rules.

"I know. But you can. Anyway, this feels good as hell so good luck getting me up without a fight." And I'm not lying.

"I love you, you know that." She all but moans as she drops into the water, settling into a bench seat next to me.

"I am pretty lovable." I wink. The only thing that could make this better would be a glass of prosecco because the non-alcoholic version they gave me at check-in really sucks. Another Braxton Hicks rumbles in me but I do my best to keep my face from twinging. If Lyndsey even suspected there was a chance it was a real contraction she would have me in the car faster than lightning.

If not that, she would call Liam and he would demand we go to hospital. By now I know my own body... or at least I hope I do.

Besides, hiding pain is my superpower. I'm the queen at it. The trick is to divert and distract by talking about something that might make the other person uncomfortable so they are so worried thinking about themselves they don't even notice the twitch in my eye or sweat on my brow.

"I'm enjoying not being at the shop right now. Does that make me terrible?" Distract and divert.

"Of course it doesn't make you terrible. You worked hard to get it off the ground, now you are doing the same for your family. Balance and shit." Lyndsey coming in clutch, never mincing her words.

"But what if I never want to go back?" At the moment, I do want to go back. I love Bloom and Blossom so there is no way I could give it up, but I still want to see what she will say.

"Then you'd have to hire another person because I'm great but I'm not superwoman." She laughs but I know she's right. I have put a lot on her the last few months of this pregnancy, but there is no one I trust more with my business.

"There's no way I'd stay away, but a new hire doesn't sound too bad. Spend more time with Jack and the baby." I muse. I want to be there and at home all at once, but if Lyndsey isn't a superwoman then I guess astral projecting is out of the question.

"And your baby daddy." She laughs.

"Sure, him too." My eyes roll but she's right. I like spending time with Liam. If I'm being really honest, I love it.

After a while we fall into a comfortable silence the only sound being the ripples of the water from the jets and the repetitive spa music through the speakers. We've been sat here a while and should probably think about packing up but there is a thought I can't shake. I should have expected it really; as good as Liam is, there are always going to be things I worry about and this is one. I know it is irrational, but most anxious thoughts are irrational. That's their biggest catch.

"I don't want to be like my mother," I blurt out. The words just fell right out of my brain into the air around us like a crashing cymbal.

"Jesus! Where did that come from?" Lyndsey recoils, finally slipping out of the water and joining me on the edge.

"She never worked but also never parented. What if I think I'm doing a good thing by being at home but I'm just teaching my kids to be lazy and to expect everyone to do things for you?" Hearing the words I know it's crazy. I know that traditional work isn't right or possible for everyone. But there is still a niggle that I might be my mother's daughter at my core and there would be nothing I can do about it.

"Bullshit. Ellis, I've never had the displeasure of meeting Eleanor, but the fact you are worried about becoming her already makes you miles better. She never cared about the fact she was shitty," she says sternly.

That's true. I think even if you asked her now, Eleanor wouldn't admit to her shortcomings. Maybe she just doesn't care that she hurt me for all those years. "Ellis, you are a good mom. You are a good woman. Never doubt it." Lyndsey takes my hand and squeezes it before pulling me to my feet to take us home.

–

I can hear the guys before I even get to the door. I don't need to look at Lyndsey to feel her smile as she registers them. The pair of us pause at the door listening as they laugh and joke. Rook's voice is the loudest, it sounds like he is re-enacting some hockey game where he is every player and commentator at the same time. Too desperate to see my boys and, honestly, to see the award-winning acting from Rook, I finally open the door to the smell of pizza and joy.

As soon as he sees me, Jack jumps from his place between Liam and Jay and comes with a running leap into my arms.

"Missed you," he tells me in a whisper by my ear and god, I missed him too. A few hours is nothing, but knowing I missed a day of smiles and laughter is a little bittersweet. Laughter from him is par for the course these days.

The rest of the house is a sight to see. The guys all lounging on the couches, spilled over onto the floor, surrounded by pizza boxes and cans of soda. Normally I would care about the mess but before I can even take it in, Liam is on his feet and by my side kissing my temple with a gentle hand on my belly. Just in time for our little girl to kick the hell out of him.

"My girls' doing good?" he asks, but instead of answering I stretch up onto my toes to plant a kiss right on his lips.

After all this time, I feel like I'm starting to accept it as reality: these people are my new family. I have spent time and energy on Eleanor today, wasted it thinking she is the only family I had; she's far from it. She might have given me life but Jack and Liam and his rabble of friends have made me feel *alive*. That's what I am going to focus on from now.

Chapter Twenty-Nine

September

Ellis

Stabbing pains pull me out of the sweet lulls of sleep. Even though earlier today the contractions were there, this feels a lot more prominent. It takes a lot not to double over in pain.

Soon enough it subsides and I am left in bed next to Liam, sweating slightly from the pain, but knowing sleep isn't going to come again. Falling asleep pregnant is hard as hell anyway, no position is comfortable and the ones that are I have been advised by a doctor not to lie in. Add in my regular pain and trouble sleeping, despite the fatigue, and it equals a cluster-fuck of sleepless night and ten-minute naps during the night. I moved myself into Liam's master bedroom at the end of July, and stopped fighting the fact I wanted to be in his arms every night.

Knowing it will be a long while before I can get comfortable, I decide it's better to go to the toilet now because, knowing my luck, the minute I get comfortable again my darling daughter is going to step on my bladder.

I pad as quietly as I can across the wooden floors to the hallway before I feel a popping sensation followed by a gushing of water from between my legs.

"Shit." I guess this time it wasn't Braxton Hicks. I expect a sense of panic to fall over me but it doesn't, instead there is a wave of calm. There is no feeling of doom; this time I feel tranquil, *ready*.

Liam won't be ready. I love him but he is going to panic, everything is going to hit him at once. I don't know which would be better, to wake him now and give him the time to panic or to wait and hope he can hold it together.

It's three in the morning and if I wake him up now without getting myself together, he is going to go straight into panic mode, so I leave the puddle on the floor and strip off the bottom half of my pyjamas and take them into the laundry room. While there, I get the mop to clean up the mess. I'm lucky that both of my boys sleep like the dead. It means I can do what I need to without worrying that I might wake them. Hopefully Jack will sleep until morning, none the wiser that I have gone into labour, and by the time he is up the baby might be here. A woman can hope.

Another contraction hits another fifteen minutes later and I mentally note down the time as well as how long it lasts, still I don't panic. Maybe I panic just a little bit.

Since the last time I gave birth, I forgot how painful contractions actually are. It feels like every one of my nerve endings are screaming out as my muscles tighten.

Realising I'm stood in my underwear with no trousers (or *pants*, as Liam would say) wearing one of Liam's T-shirts, a sight like Winnie the Pooh with my large belly bump, I decide to throw some clothes on and check the hospital bag before I wake Liam. Knowing that he won't mind the inevitable bodily fluids that come with birth, I leave Liam's T-shirt on and throw on a pair of his grey sweats.

There is no point in trying to wrestle on leggings, plus I don't know when the next contraction will hit. In the walk-in dressing room I take one final breath in the silence of a house without a baby.

With the hospital bag in my hand, I take in Liam's sleeping form, the top sheet is pulled up over his chest with his arms thrown over his head. He looks so calm. The opposite of me as another contraction hits only twelve minutes after the last.

"Liam, wake up." I sit beside him on his side of the bed, running a hand through his hair to rouse him.

"Sunshine, it's the middle of the night, you okay?" His voice is sleepy but full of concern when he sees the time on his bedside clock.

"Yeah I'm good but, erm, we need to go to the hospital," I say quietly. I don't know why I didn't run through this conversation in my head when I was cleaning.

"What! What's wrong?" He pops up like a jack-in-the-box sat straight in the bed, his eyes running all over my body looking for signs of distress.

"Nothing's wrong, but my waters broke about half an hour ago and my contractions are like twelve minutes apart – so we gotta get going." I remain calm. He is clearly dumbfounded by my demeanour because his mouth opens and closes a few times as his tired brain tries to catch up.

"Half an hour?! Twelve minutes?! Ellis why didn't you wake me up?" He eventually splutters out blinking a million times as though he is going to wake up from this weird dream.

"I'm waking you up now aren't I? Come on, I'm all ready to go." I stand up hoping it will get him moving but instead he stares at me freakishly still.

"Okay, you're freaking out, aren't you?" I put my hands on either side of his jaw hoping to ground him but he just swallows blinking up at me.

"I'm not freaking out," he whispers.

"Then let's go." I laugh, rubbing his stubble under my palms.

"Can't." He is paling before my eyes, he has gone a ghostly shade of white.

"Why not?"

"I'm freaking out," he finally admits. I laugh but that is quickly interrupted by another contraction ripping through me. Each one is worse than the last; the sooner I get to the hospital the better. I clearly made the wrong choice, I should have given him time to panic but between the pain of the contractions and the spike in anxiety I put myself first.

"Look, Liam I get it. This is scary but I'm in pain. I need you to pull it together because a baby is about to come out of me. We can panic together at the hospital," I say through gritted teeth, digging my nails into my palms.

"You're right, fuck, I'm sorry. I'm here, you're going to be okay." Finally he jumps out of the bed sitting me back down before darting into the closet to get himself dressed.

"You need to call Anders to come look after Jack!" I call after him. With one sock on, he hops out of the closet to grab his phone before disappearing again.

I pad down the hallway to look into Jack's room. Just as I expected, my little guy is away with the fairies, I think a hurricane could pass through and he wouldn't wake. Once I know he is okay, I wander back to find Liam picking up my bag at the top of the stairs. Luckily Anders lives in the same community a few minutes' drive away and a few doors away from Edge's home, so I know once Liam is ready there won't be long until we can leave.

"I would like to be in hospital now please. I need drugs." Another contraction hits and I consider ordering us a taxi because I know Liam's focus is going to be on me. They are getting longer and harder: each one awakens a new level of pain that sears through each part of my body.

"Drugs, okay, let's go. Anders is at the door." Liam helps me stand and walks me down the stairs. On each step I'm worried a contraction will hit and I will fall down them, but with the grip Liam has on me I know that I wouldn't hit the floor.

He has me. Strong and solid. Safe.

I can see Anders's shadow through the frosted glass at the top of the door, but he isn't alone.

"Edge, what are you doing here?" I ask when the two giant hockey players walk into the house. It's clear they both recently woke up, hair mussed, and clothes thrown on in a hurry.

"I knew Ruin was going to be a mess; there's no way he can drive to the hospital. I'm the chauffeur, so let's get going." Something about the simple way he says it brings tears to my eyes and I wrap my arms around his thick waist trying to keep the tears at bay.

"Thank you Jay."

"Any time El, let's go have a baby," he tells me, taking the hospital bag out of Liam's hand and throwing it into the trunk of the car.

"Good luck." Anders hugs me too before Liam drags me to the car, finally catching up with the fact that time is of the essence.

Next time I walk through these doors I will be a mum to two. I am about to make Liam Ruinsky a father, and apart from the pain there is no worry. Last time every little thing scared me about giving birth. I didn't know what to expect and the fact I was so very alone only added to the torment.

This time it isn't just me – hell it isn't even just me and Liam, we have a whole support system. We have more hands than I could ever imagine.

Anders looking after Jack, Edge driving us around, Lyndsey keeping Bloom and Blossom afloat and Rook volunteering to bring food to the hospital after the birth. I'm not going to complain about some non-hospital food.

This past year has proved to me just how lucky I am. Yes, I am in constant pain and life can be difficult, but I finally have people here right alongside me. Granted, I could have had that all along. Lyndsey had been in my life for almost six years before I met Liam, and yet it took letting him back in to open me up to the idea that other people want to be around me because they want to be, not because they have to.

I'm not some big bad monster who pushes everyone away. When you find the right people you won't worry about them breaking your heart, because you know they will do anything in their power to protect it for you.

Chapter Thirty

Liam

How the fuck do women do this?

It has been two hours since we got to the hospital and every second I am being humbled. I'm not a small man, I have fought giants and had my body beaten a hundred different ways on the ice, but I have never seen anything like this. Ellis is clearly in pain and yet her determination doesn't waver.

There is sweat pouring down her face, her hair stuck to her bright red forehead and she is doing it all without murdering every person in the room.

If one more person comes and sticks their hand in her without much warning I might hit someone. She is their patient and I know that, but seeing her wince with each cervical check kills me. Knowing we are closer and closer to the big moment when she will start to push, and not being able to take the pain away, is making me feel so incredibly useless.

Still, I stand by her side, patting her face with a damp cloth and holding the mask with the gas for her while she grunts through another contraction.

Ellis is focusing so completely on breathing through the pain that she doesn't see how hard I am shaking. She is no stranger to pain, but this is more than I could imagine.

I read books and watched documentaries in preparation for this, but I think a little part of my brain thought that all the pain wouldn't happen to Ellis; that she would push once and the baby would just fly out.

I was delusional but I have my reasons. If I thought hard enough about how much pain she was going to be in I think I would have spiralled. I needed to be a wall of support for Ellis so I couldn't give in to the idea that she would be suffering and I would be as useful as a chocolate fireman.

Another contraction later they tell us it's time. Ten centimetres and on the next contraction she is being told to push. Doing what the midwife tells me to, I grip one of Ellis's thighs in my hand and hold it up against her chest for her so she can focus solely on pushing.

Her face gets even redder as she uses all her energy to bear down with as much force as she can. The pressure looks like it might burst a blood vessel, but I guess the doctors know what they are doing because nobody looks concerned. I can't help but place light kisses at her temple as she pushes again. The doctors talk about seeing a head but all I can focus on is my Sunshine.

As that contraction passes, Ellis turns her face to me, her face is full of emotion. Pain and determination but there is a softness there still, like having me here brings her comfort no matter how completely useless I feel.

"Liam, I— *fuck!*" she yells through the searing pain. "I love you." She breathes out as another contraction rips through her. Time stops for just a moment. She knows I love her; I have told her a million times in a million different ways, but now she has finally said those words herself. After ten years apart, Ellis Ainsley loves me again.

Before I can process that, the whole room splinters apart as the doctor tells us the head is out, I tell her over and over how much I love her, how proud of her I am as she prepares to push again. A mantra of affection. Ellis pushes again and the room buzzes with the first cry of our baby girl.

Just like that – I'm a dad.

The nurse welcomes her into our world and she marks the time of birth. I let out a watery chuckle. Today will be her birthday, for every year ahead. 1st September.

One of the nurses moves Ellis's gown out of the way to lay the baby down on her exposed chest. The baby is covered in blood, yet she is beautiful. The most beautiful thing I've ever seen.

Every part of her is so much smaller than I could ever imagine as she grunts and cries about being out in the world. Her scrunched face rests against Ellis's heartbeat as I look at my girls in awe.

Ellis whispers to the baby, private words for just the two of them before the nurse picks her up again, asking me if I want to cut the cord. I try to take in the instructions but all I can think about is making sure I don't hurt her as I snip it. It's tougher than I expected, then with all of the expertise that can only come from years of practice the nurse wraps a blanket around the baby before handing her to me to hold.

Everything stops.

I knew I loved her. Of course I did, from the moment I knew Ellis was pregnant I have loved the life we were bringing into the world – but this is beyond anything I could imagine. Every strand of my DNA changes to make room for the love this little girl is bringing into my world.

Knowing this baby is part of me tears part of my soul. And I give it to her willingly, it is hers to keep.

My baby, my daughter, my little girl.

I don't notice the tears until one drops onto the blanket wrapped around her and I let them fall. We cry together as she gets adjusted to the world and I get used to how much my world has grown.

Ellis lies in bed watching us with a smile as I slide onto the bed placing our daughter into her waiting arms. She must sense her mom's presence because once she settles into Ellis's arms she calms for the first time since she burst into our world. The pink bundle in her arms looks even smaller than in the nurse's somehow, each one of her features are tiny and perfect and I can't wait to show her off.

The three of us sit together basking in the light of our daughter as she falls asleep in her mother's arms. Ellis shuffles closer to me until we are fully pressed together before she rests her head on my chest, her eyes still glued to the sleeping bundle.

"I meant it, you know?" she whispers, so quietly I'm not sure if she is talking to me or the baby until she nudges my side.

"Meant what?" I ask.

"That I love you." She looks up at me, skin still shining from sweat looking radiant as ever.

"I love you, too, Ellis Ainsley." I bring my head down to kiss her lightly, my lips barely skimming hers.

"I think I love her a little bit more though," she laughs, looking back down again.

"I'm okay with being third on your list," I tell her honestly, our kids always come first.

"You're second, Jack and baby are joint first." She nudges me again harder this time, clearly putting me in my place.

"Second sounds good to me." And it really does, as long as Ellis loves me, I am on top of the world. "I'm going to ask you to marry me one day."

"I'm going to say yes." She winks. I was expecting to see shock at my words, but there isn't any. She seems settled to know she is a part of my future.

"The Ruinskys, that has a nice ring to it. I want Jack to be one, too," I tell her. He feels like mine as much as this little girl. Just because he doesn't share my DNA that does not make him any less my son.

Ellis smiles. "It makes sense," she says. "You'll need to ask him first, but I think he'd like that."

I silently hope he will. It would kill me if he doesn't feel like a part of this family just because of blood. As I wonder about Jack, now a big brother, we're interrupted by a nurse with a clipboard coming to check Ellis's vitals.

"So Mom and Dad, do we have a name?" she asks.

"Charlotte Ruinsky," we answer together.

A united front.

Chapter Thirty-One

Ellis

Deciding not to breastfeed was an easy choice for me. It not only meant I can start taking my medication again, but it also means Liam can feed the baby while I sleep. And sleep I do. Not long after Charlotte was born the adrenalin wore off and I knocked out. Liam paid extra for us to have a fully private room for my recovery; it's nice to be alone with my family and it will also mean we can have more visitors than we probably should. I tried to protest, to tell him not to throw his money around, but I know our friends – there is no way any of them would be willing to miss this.

Selfishly, I've been awake for ten minutes but I'm lying incredibly still with my eyes closed while listening to Liam talk to Charlotte. I know Jack will be coming by soon, so I will wake up for him, but right now I'm enjoying lounging. As soon as the thought materialises there is a light knock and Edge's head peeps through a crack in the door.

The room is lit up by one of his rare smiles as he meets my eyes, I nod to let him know we're ready. He has barely cracked the door open before Jack flies into the room from behind him.

"Hi buddy!" I smile at my son as he climbs onto the hospital bed carefully before snuggling into my side.

"You okay, Mum?" he asks, his big bright eyes looking between me and the pink bundle of blankets in Liam's arms.

"I'm great Jack, you ready to meet your sister?" I watch as he shakes out his little arms and sits higher on the bed so he is rested against the pillows before he nods seriously at Liam holding his arms in a clearly practised position.

Liam smiles full of contentment as he lays Charlotte in her brother's arms and we watch as Jack tries to bite back a wave of emotions as he looks at her.

"She's so little," he whispers reverently, eyes locked in with hers. They share a moment, their gaze connected before Jack whispers again, "I love you, baby." My heart turns into a puddle.

Edge walks around the bed to Liam's side before pulling him into what they would call a "bro hug", but we all know it is a real hug. A hug of congratulations, a hug of support, a hug of brotherly love between two men who know each other better than anyone else.

"You're a dad." Edge's voice is filled with hidden emotion while his hand rests high on Liam's shoulder.

"I'm a dad." Liam doesn't hide his emotions though and I watch from the bed as he wipes a stray tear.

"Wow dude, she's perfect. You did good, El." He winks at me but I notice he doesn't come any closer to the baby. He is going to need to get over that very quickly. I look at Liam and give him a subtle nod as a wide smile breaks out across his face.

"Sunshine, wasn't there something you wanted to ask Edge?" Liam would make a terrible spy, acting is not his strong suit and Edge immediately knows something is afoot.

"Oh yeah, thanks for reminding me. So, Jay, would you like to come hold your god-daughter?" He just looks at me for a beat.

"You're— are you serious?" Jay Brink, the giant enforcer of a man, is near tears as he takes small nervous steps towards the bed. I nod in response, a grin spreading across my face with watery eyes.

You would think that when the baby is out your hormones would fall back in line pretty quickly, but they don't. No, I think they might be even crazier for a while. Edge stops next to Jack, who still has his sister in his arms, and looks down at her.

"Me?" he asks, eyes locked in on Charlotte.

"You," I choke out, lifting the baby from Jack and handing her over to the hulking hockey player who has never looked so soft. Charlotte has shrunk in his arms, one of his biceps is near double her size but I know he would rather die than cause her harm.

Safe to say she is going to have a hard go of it when she wants to date one day. An older brother, a hockey dad and hockey uncles scaring off anyone who looks her way.

Liam joins me on the bed so I am surrounded by my boys as we watch Edge rock Charlotte slightly like he has fallen into a trance looking at her scrunched little face. The moment is broken by another knock on the door. Liam goes to answer, the door opening to Lyndsey and Anders. It's not lost on me that they arrived together. I raise an eyebrow at Lyndsey, but decide I'll put it in my pocket for now. She ignores my suspicious look, instead beaming at me with a wide smile.

"Oh Ellis! I'm so proud of you, look at her!" Her voice is higher than I've ever heard it. She is looking over to where Edge is cradling Charlotte.

"Edge, give me the baby and we can still be friends." Lyndsey threatens with a sugar sweet smile, but Edge is undeterred. Instead, he lifts Charlotte further up his chest shaking his head.

"I'll hand over my god-daughter when I am good and ready." If he were less mature, he would be sticking his tongue out at her. Lyndsey huffs, but goes to stand as close to him as she can, cooing up at the baby on tiptoes.

"Hey El, how you feeling?" Anders asks leaning over to kiss my cheek.

"Good, tired, but so damn happy," I tell him honestly.

"You need any snacks?" Anders offers. I shake my head and elbow Liam in the ribs, nodding at Lyndsey.

"Oh, right, okay," he says, coughing loudly to get everyone's attention. "Lyndsey, we were wondering if you would do the honour of being Charlotte's god-mother?" Liam askes, voice filled with hope. I still don't know why he doubts that she would say anything except yes.

"Yes!" Lyndsey squeals, jumping up and down on the spot. "God-parent high five!" She cheers at Edge, who humours her by slapping his hand against hers.

As we watch the god-parents celebrate to themselves, a voice rounds the corner. "Now you better not be partying without me, eh? I would have been here sooner, but I was sweet talking a nurse into letting me in." Rook bounds into the room like a bull, the only one who didn't bother to knock – but to be fair, his hands are very full. In one hand there is a huge bouquet of flowers with a Bloom and Blossom ribbon tied around them, the other hand is clutching a plush rabbit with big pink ears and the bag of food he promised me. Among the gifts he has a balloon tied somewhere as it bobs above his head.

"We have a private room, you didn't need to sweet talk anyone," Liam tells him, shaking his head.

"She was pretty, it was worth it." He laughs running his eyes over the room until they fall on Charlotte. "Welcome to the world, Baby Ruin!" He cheers. His booming voice makes Charlotte jump and begin to wail. "No, no, no, baby I'm sorry, don't cry. Look, it's Uncle Jonas." He somehow manages to wrangle the still crying baby out of Edge's arms by replacing her with the bunny.

"Damn rookie, making her cry." Edge rolls his eyes.

Rook breaks into an amazingly off-tune rendition of a medley of nursery rhymes until Charlotte settles.

Anders saunters over to check on her, and Lyndsey follows close behind, huddling over Rook, swearing that she better be next in line for a cuddle. Jack laughs at the scene of his new family fussing over Charlotte.

"They are all silly aren't they, Dad – I–I mean Liam?" His laughter dies out. All of my body tenses in the bed.

"I told you Jack, I would be honoured to be your dad if you want me to be." Liam seems completely unfazed, unlike me – I feel like I have entered the twilight zone.

I know Liam said he wants Jack to have his name, and I know Jack called Liam "Dad" once in the past in the heat of the moment, but I thought we were a long way from Jack feeling comfortable calling him "Dad" full time.

It came out so naturally, there has never been anyone for him to call his dad. I am shocked it's even part of his vocabulary.

"I'd like that, please." Jack breaks through my running mind as he smiles up at me and Liam.

"Okay son." Liam smiles.

Again, the afterbirth hormones hit me square in the chest, I feel outside of my body. A gaggle of uncles and an aunt fussing over our baby. Liam holding me from one side while Jack cuddles me from the other. My heart is full and warm as I relax in bed. I have always hated hospitals, but right now, they don't seem half bad.

This room, at least, isn't too bad. Last time the recovery room was starkly quiet and empty. The only sound was the quiet sobs I couldn't hold back as my son slept in my arms. I was completely alone and terrified of what was to come for our future. And somehow here I am again six years later, but the room is full of sound. Jack asking how long we will be in hospital. Liam whispering how much he loves me. Rook still singing no matter how much everyone tells him he is going to hurt Charlotte's ears. Lyndsey threatening to fight every hockey player if she doesn't get to hold the baby in the next twenty seconds. Just noise and laughter and happiness.

More happiness than I ever thought I deserved.

These people are here for the long haul.

For me.

For my family.

Chapter Thirty-Two

Ellis

Eventually, everyone starts to leave. I'm tired and Liam wants me to get some rest. Jack goes with Aiden for a sleepover because it was the only way we could get him to leave. My little guy wants to make sure I'm okay, and I love him for it, but there just isn't enough room for all four of us to sleep in here. Charlotte has a cot next to me and Liam is hunkering down on the sofa in the corner.

When the room has cleared, it means we have to do something I am not too excited for. FaceTiming Liam's parents. I don't know why I am dreading it. Tracy Ruinsky has checked in a lot over the past few months but now that the baby is here what if that changes? They might decide that now that my job is done they can push me aside, convince Liam that it would be better to raise Charlotte alone, kicking me and Jack to the kerb. In my heart I know he wouldn't agree, he would never do that to Jack and me, but there is niggling anxiety I can't shake.

"You ready?" If I told him right now I couldn't do this he would send them a text and we would be done until the morning, but putting it off isn't going to make this easier. So I cuddle up further into his side and nod as he pulls his phone out.

The three seconds that it takes before the Ruinskys appear on the screen feels both too long and not long enough. Some loop of never-ending anxiety and a yearning for them to be asleep and miss the call altogether. They do answer though, and are both smiling widely.

"Oh Ellis! You look amazing! I looked terrible after Liam was born!" Tracy laughs and Alek rolls his eyes at her, still smiling.

"You're sweet." I laugh, hoisting Charlotte up on my chest so they can see her. They "ooh" and "ah" at her for a moment before Alek turns his eyes on me.

"Are you okay?" he asks, his voice still has a hint of an accent from growing up in Russia. If you didn't know to listen for it you would miss it.

"Charlotte is great, she is so beautiful," I assure him with a smile.

"I'm sure she is, but are *you* okay?" he asks again and I freeze. I didn't expect them to want to know about me. I just gave birth to their granddaughter, I assumed she would be their priority. The Ruinsky men keep shocking me.

"Oh. Oh, yeah I'm–I'm good, thanks for asking." I stumble through my words. I *am* good. I have Liam keeping me warm and fed and a beautiful baby who has made my heart grow three sizes.

We talk for a while, they ask about the birth and Liam tells them everything with a reverence I don't expect. It makes me melt. If I didn't already love him I think I would swoon right here. He looks at us as though I am the moon and Charlotte is made up of stars. Alek's eyes sparkle the same shade as his son's as he watches with pride as Liam waxes poetic about how amazing I did.

"Can you send me some pictures to show to my golf guys?" Alek asks Liam and as soon as the words come through the phone Liam bursts into laughter, confusing me.

"You're playing golf? You always said it was an old man sport." His parents roll their eyes at him. Seeing how much love is between the three of them makes me smile.

"It *is* an old man sport, I am an old man. I'm a grandpa now, remember." Alek deadpans, clearly bored with his son's antics, which just makes Liam laugh more. "Anyway, there isn't much else I can do around here and if I'm at home your mom finds jobs for me." I join in their laughter then as Tracy glares at her husband.

"We will send some over for both of you." That makes Liam's mum's face split into a smile again and we both have to hold back our laughter at their antics.

When Liam and I grow old I want us to be like his parents. They obviously love each other but they are also their own people. I don't want to be like my mum, throwing myself so deep into a relationship that it drowns me. I don't want to be Liam's housewife, barefoot and pregnant. I want to be his partner. His confidant. I want us to be there for each other and our family the way his parents are. The type of love that spans time zones and generations.

"So, I have had an idea but if you hate it then we can pretend I never mentioned it." Tracy is biting her lip now. I side-eye Liam to find him looking back at me just as confused.

"What is it, Mom?" he asks finally, apprehension is clear as he tightens his arm around my shoulders.

"Well, I think it might do good for your dad and I to come up for a few weeks, be there for anything you need."

She takes a deep breath giving us a second to process before she speaks again, "We can do the housework and take Jack to school so Ellis can heal and you can both bond with Charlotte."

"Oh. Well, I…" I stumble over my words. I feel like I have to say yes. She is their granddaughter after all but I haven't seen them in person in over ten years. Spending real time with them might be terrible, we might clash about everything. I don't know if I can cope with that post-partum.

"Look don't answer me now, talk it through and get back to me." She takes the heat off. "Either way, I want to come up for a visit so it's just if I am coming for a few days or a few weeks to take a load off, okay? Now go get some sleep Ellis, you deserve to rest."

We say our goodbyes then, promising updates and more pictures to come. I have had a hectic yet fulfilling day, but I don't think I will be able to sleep right now. Tracy's offer is a really sweet one but my mind can't help but think of every way it could go wrong.

"We can tell her no," Liam says after a beat of silence. He is still sat next to me on the small hospital bed and I don't chance looking up at him yet.

"I don't know what I want to say," I whisper, looking down at the bundle in my arms.

"What's scaring you?" he asks, turning me slightly so we are looking at each other.

"Everything," I tell him honestly. Having a new baby is scary. Bringing new people around is even scarier.

"Okay, but what's scaring you most?" he tries again and I let out a deep sigh. His eyes are locked on mine and there is nowhere to hide from him or my anxieties.

"What if they come here and think I'm a terrible mum? They don't approve of me at all?" My arms tighten around my baby as if she is going to be snatched from me. My voice is shaky and I see emotions flit across Liam's face too quickly to pinpoint.

"You are an amazing mother already, Sunshine. I would never say yes to them if I thought for a second they wouldn't love you as much as me." He hooks his fingers around the back of my neck as he speaks, his thumb sliding up and down in a calming rhythm, pushing away some of the tension.

"I'm not used to having help." I laugh lightly. It's a humourless laugh but the smile Liam gives me is anything but. His eyes dance with mischief as he raises a single brow at me.

"You're getting used to it." He grins, squeezing the back of my neck again.

"What do you mean?" I ask, tiredness sweeping through my body as I relax under the touch of his hands.

"Ellis, you have me," he tells me, taking Charlotte from my arms and putting her into the cot next to us. "Jack is staying with one of my teammates tonight. Your room was filled with people who are here to help an hour ago, so what's a few more?"

"I've never had a village before." I know he knows this but I am too tired to come up with anything more profound. It's strange how big my life has become.

"You do now." He places a light kiss on my hairline to comfort me. "Look, if they come and step a toe out of line, I will put them on the first flight back to Florida. I would never let them disrespect you in your own home."

"Okay then, let's do it," I agree. I have already let so many people help I would be remiss to deny more help now. Having a new born is hard and no one can ever be completely prepared.

"Yeah?" Liam smiles widely at me. Clearly excited to have his parents here. I can't be selfish, I can't hide away from everyone because it is different to when I had Jack. Different can be good. Hell, it can be amazing, Liam is proof of that. We are a partnership. We have a village. A big village that I think will only get better as it grows.

It really is the more the merrier for us. A year ago I had a son and a really good friend, but that was my whole circle. My bubble has expanded so vastly in such a short amount of time and it has brought nothing but joy. Plus, I believe Liam when he tells me he will keep them in line if they push on our boundaries. He will keep me and our family safe even if that means keeping us safe from his parents. I just have to remember that there are people who care about us, who want us to be happy. Time isn't repeating itself.

Chapter Thirty-Three

October

Liam

I would be a liar if I said the last month has been easy. There is a screaming baby who doesn't seem to understand that night-time is for sleeping and daytime is for playing.

I would also be a liar if I said I don't love it. Yes, I want to sleep. I can't remember what having a dream is like, but then I pick Charlotte up and suddenly I don't care if I never lie down again. It's been hard, but I know it would have been near impossible if not for my parents. When they left last week I nearly locked them in. Terrified that once they left it would all fall apart. It didn't. Or it hasn't – yet.

Right now, she is sleeping. She screamed and screamed until around six a.m. and now at nine a.m. she is snoozing softly in her crib swaddled in a special Spears blanket her god-father bought for her. The leaves have fallen from the trees and I can't help but feel excited for the winter. Dressing her as a pumpkin on Halloween. Her first Christmas, my first Christmas with Ellis and Jack.

Ellis is trying that "sleep while the baby sleeps" thing, but there is so much else she thinks she has to do. She tried to do the laundry so I sent her to bed and did it instead, when I went to check on her, she was sat in the bed ordering autumn stock for the shop. Having a supportive female presence here was good for Ellis, I think it was the final nail in the coffin of her relationship with Eleanor. Ellis has a bunch of people here where she needs them and she isn't going to try and force a relationship with someone who I don't think has ever loved her the way she deserves. Still, she keeps moving, as though she is constantly unsettled by all the changes that have happened.

It's like she knows she needs to stop but can't. As though if she falls asleep she will miss something with Charlotte even though we are nowhere near any major milestones. Today, she is going through all her clothes for some unknown reason.

"El, Sunshine, can you please try getting some sleep?" I ask from the doorframe but she just rolls her eyes.

"The season starts soon so I need to figure out what I'm taking home," she says exasperated. *Wait. What did she just say?*

My ears just heard her say she needs clothes to take home... as though she isn't currently home. Does she mean her apartment? Because that's not going to work for me. I was under the impression that we are doing the family thing; loving each other and raising our kids. *Our* kids, because Jack is mine, too. I could just be sleep deprived, but if Ellis thinks I am going to let her move out of this house then I haven't been clear enough with my intentions. I love her, she loves me, I've told her I want to marry her, and she is just going to move out?

"Liammmm! Hello, is anyone in there?" Ellis's hand is waving in front of my face.

272

"Are you moving out?" My voice doesn't sound like my own, but it must have been me because Ellis cocks her head to the side with furrowed brows.

"Yeah, of course," she says casually. *Oh, of course, she says.* I'm in disbelief. Having my baby and then ditching me to live in a two-bedroom apartment was never obvious to me.

"That's not going to work for me." My voice still sounds odd, its low and crackly like I have been on the ice for hours.

"What?" Ellis laughs.

"Ellis, you can't just move out. We're a family. Don't you see this place as home?" I see something click behind her eyes when they widen a little but her face falls back to normal.

"Liam, it's not that, the season—" She tries, but I know where that is going.

"Fuck the season! I want you here with our kids, Ellis!" I don't mean to yell but my voice is rising. My heart is beating faster than I think is healthy as I imagine coming home from a game to an empty house while my entire world is somewhere else.

"Don't yell at me!" Ellis stabs a finger against my chest as her voice matches mine.

The sudden volume must wake up Charlotte because her high-pitched wails flow through the wall. Ellis's eyes fall closed and we both take deep breaths, still worked up.

"Okay stop, let's just... let me go get her back down and we will talk? Just go wait downstairs for me," Ellis says, but before I have a chance to argue she turns her back on me and stalks into the nursery talking lowly to our daughter.

I walk down the stairs in a sort of trance. My steps echo around me and I can't stand the sound of my stupid feet hitting the stupid floor so I flop down onto the sofa dropping my head in my hands.

I'm not an idiot. I know I didn't handle that conversation well.

I shouldn't have yelled, not at Ellis. She is not even who I am mad at, I'm mad that I haven't shown her how much I want her here. But I don't know what else I could have done. Still, she didn't deserve my misplaced temper. She gave birth a month ago for crying out loud! I shouldn't add to her stress with yelling, I should do whatever the hell she tells me to do.

And she is half right.

I think that's what hurts more. The season is starting and it means I'm going to be away a lot for the next few months. Even if they live here, I am still going to miss too much.

I could miss Charlotte rolling over and I will miss Ellis's birthday in January. I already know I am going to miss Jack's first day of school next week because I will be doing press for the first game of the season.

I want to be around my family as much as I can while I can, the niggling in the back of my brain is reminding me about the idea I had to quit hockey a few months ago. I knew deep down that it wasn't the right time, I would be going back on my contract which would have led to a ton of legal issues. Now though, my life is in a different place. Hockey is not my first priority any more – it's not even in the top three.

As soon as I hear Ellis's footfall on the steps I need her in my arms. So that is what I do. She has barely reached the bottom step before I hug her, my head buried in her neck, inhaling her scent. It's a good thing that she doesn't push me away. No, she holds me just as tightly as I hold her. Like if we hold each other hard enough it will rewind time and none of this would have happened. We would be smiling and I would be making her lunch and we would be okay.

"I'm sorry, Sunshine," I say into her hair and squeeze her tighter. She buries her head as close as she can to me.

Keeping her in my arms I walk us over to the sofa with her tight to my side. We sit together wrapped in each other for a few minutes. I don't know what to say, I know I am scared to upset her, I can't let what happened upstairs happen again. I need to stay calm, at least now I know she isn't planning on staying, so the surprise is gone.

"Do you want to move out?" I ask. At the end of the day, no matter how much I want her here, I won't force her to stay.

"I guess it never crossed my mind that I wouldn't go back; I only moved here because I was bed bound and now I'm not. You don't need to look after me any more." It's logical but I don't care about logic. There is nothing logical about the way I love her.

"I love you, I want you in the house, in my bed. If you don't want to live in this house we will look for somewhere else, but if you think you won't be sleeping in my bed every night then you are crazy. If I have to move into that two-bedroom place with you then that's what we'll do." I will do it, the four of us in a two-bedroom will be cramped, but I can think of it as cosy.

Though we will definitely need a bigger bed because I've tried lying in her queen before. I don't even completely fit.

"Liam, Charlotte won't stop crying, Jack starts school again next week so it's going to be hectic and you need to be able to sleep. The season is going to be busy! You need rest. Your contract is up, you need to show them you're ready to sign again." She thinks this is what I want. I can see it.

She thinks I'm putting up a fight to look like a good guy not kicking her out. I forget that Ellis is so used to men not showing her what love means. To me at least love means I want to see her as often as I can, hear about her day and help her with her troubles, knowing she will help me with mine.

"I can't rest without you! If you guys aren't here I'm just going to drive myself crazy with what I'm missing. I'm already going to miss so much when I'm travelling, don't make me miss even more." I beg, and I pout, full on puppy-dog eyes. Not very masculine but it gets Ellis to smile at me, which is always a win.

"Liam sweetheart, I love you. I will love you here and I will love you if I move out. I guess I thought you would like having your own space," she admits. I knew it! My sweet Sunshine always thinking everyone is better off if she is away from them, she couldn't be more wrong.

"I want zero space. No space." I know I sound like a toddler asking for his favourite toy but I don't care, at least I make Ellis laugh.

"Baby hormones and no sleep just make me feel like we are burdening you. I know how important hockey is to you, I just don't want to be in the way."

I hold Ellis's face in both of my hands so she knows I mean what I am about to say.

"El, look, I've been thinking, and this is going to be my last season. I'm going to miss so much over the next seven months if not more, and I don't want to miss any more than I have to. When my contract is up, I'm not signing a new one," I finally admit.

When Ellis was pregnant I thought about stepping off the ice for good. Now, it's becoming a reality. Now I can see what my life will be if I am not around for my family.

"Liam." Ellis sighs deeply but I kiss her before she can tell me I'm making a mistake by hanging up my skates.

"I've thought about it a lot, I swear, it's not some rash decision. I want to be an involved dad, maybe help coach kids who want to get into ice hockey – it'll give me time to help with science projects and bake sales and whatever else happens with the kids, I want it all." I kiss her again just because I like kissing her and she drops her forehead to mine.

"Fuck, you are so damn perfect for me Mr Ruinsky," she says throwing her leg over mine so she is straddling me before burying herself into my chest.

Before I know it my Sunshine is fast asleep in my arms, her soft snores puff against my throat. There is no way I am moving anytime soon; Charlotte is asleep, Jack is having a pre-back-to-school play date and Ellis Ainsley has finally found enough peace to nap.

I only wish I had the forethought to pee because damn, my bladder is screaming louder than Charlotte does.

Chapter Thirty-Four

Ellis

High pitched wailing wakes me, just like it has every few hours in the nights recently. My precious daughter has lungs bigger than any other baby ever: I'm thinking about contacting Guinness World Records. I think the rest of the mums of the world should give me my props for the beautifully shrill sound she makes.

Jack loves his sister, adores her. He has asked Liam to buy him earplugs for sleep. Today starts with more than just crying though, today starts with pain. To be fair, every morning after her birth was painful because, you know, birthing *is* painful and recovering is just as bad.

I have been anticipating this flare-up for days, I think we all have. Lack of sleep is cripplingly me in more ways than one, and being uncomfortable in every position, standing, sitting, laying down… nothing works. The worst part is: there is nothing I could have done to stop it.

Two days ago, my wrists were swollen. My grip was terrible and it was my first telltale sign that something was coming. The only saving grace is that I've been back on my meds since giving birth. While at the hospital, a nurse on the maternity ward was laying on the pressure to breastfeed very thick – but Liam put a stop to that. My body had sacrificed so much already during the last nine months – my ability to breathe properly, be intimate when I wished, take my medication, regulate my emotions, see my toes over my belly... Liam also thought it was time I had control over my body back.

He told her straight that I had given up my comfort without a single complaint and now I needed to do this for me. I think it's the most I've ever loved him. He looked hot as hell holding our baby while advocating for me.

The last time I had a new born, my mental health was so down in the gutter that there was no way I could have battled through my fibromyalgia to breastfeed while I was already trying to grip onto my sanity. Jack turned out amazing, and I am sure Charlotte will too. I reminded myself that fed is best, no matter how they get there.

Charlotte continues to cry so I know I need to push through until I can eat to take some painkillers. As a teen I knew I wanted kids but I was so worried that any child I had would have a lesser quality of life because there are things I can't do. But as I grew up, I thought about all the other mothers with different disabilities and decided that if they can do it, I can too. I didn't want to miss an experience just because of my condition; my fibromyalgia had already robbed me of so much, but I wasn't going to let it rob me of this too. Taking as deep of a breath as my body will allow, I push myself over to the edge of the bed.

Liam had to leave early for his morning skate, and I know my phone will be filled with texts asking how we are. I reach out to find my phone obstructed. I manage to squint my eyes open to see my amazing, beautiful boyfriend – partner, co-parent? I don't know what to call him; we seem too mature for boyfriend, partner is too formal, and co-parent doesn't really fit us any more, but regardless of our label, the angel has left me a banana, a bottle of water and my Aleve. It takes me less than ten seconds to scoff down the food and down the pills and drink as I prepare myself to get out of bed.

Parenting as someone with chronic pain is different than normal parenting. There are challenges upon challenges that the world doesn't try to fix.

Finding a disability-friendly crib is hard, and some that would be helpful are banned in the US. In other countries there are cribs that open with a latch on the side so I could get to Charlotte without having to bend over, but unfortunately that isn't approved in the USA.

Instead, Liam and I looked high and low until we found a crib that lifts on hydraulics called a PediaLift crib, so that wheelchair users can get in closer to the baby. It works for me because this way I don't have to worry about if I can bend low enough to get to her.

Liam did everything he could to make this as easy as possible, and this time around money is no object. Most of Jack's baby furniture was second-hand or what was on sale when I remembered what I would need. We managed, but Liam doesn't want us to just survive: he wants Charlotte to have the best by giving me the best.

I came home one day when I was nine months pregnant to find a mini fridge in the master bedroom, I thought Liam was going through some frat boy phase.

He bought it because after we talked about not breast-feeding he wanted to move the master suite downstairs. He said it would make sense, close to the kitchen for warming a bottle and not having to walk downstairs if I am in pain. Selfishly, I didn't want that.

This master suite is beautiful and the tub in the en suite has jets that work wonders for me. I didn't want to give that up so we compromised. The mini fridge was the start of that, we can keep a few ready-made bottles in there so neither of us have to go downstairs to mix it up during the night. He also bought a portable bottle warmer to help with not having to go downstairs whenever she is hungry.

Liam left a bottle in the warmer when he left and I will sing his praises until the cows come home because that means I can wait for my painkillers to kick in before having to get out of bed. I press the lift button on the crib and take Charlotte into my arms. In between screams her little perfect lips are smacking together searching for food.

Breathing is hard through the pain but eliminating the mum guilt of leaving her crying while my painkillers kick in has lifted a weight from me that I didn't even know was there.

While the painkillers start to take the edge off I get to look down at my amazing little girl as she guzzles her milk. I don't know how something so small can eat so much or scream so much, she really is her father's daughter.

After our postnatal appointment the nurse commented on how well Charlotte is doing despite being born a little bit early. I think she just wanted to make an entrance early enough that her dad could spend time with her without being distracted by hockey. I know Coach Mitch told Liam he could take some time off after the baby was born, but if the Spears were losing because Liam was at home I know the guilt would eat him up, especially seeing how this is his last season.

Liam has changed a million ways since college but one that stands out the most is his opinion on painkillers.

As a hockey player he has always been pro pain relief, but pain killers as a chronically ill person work differently. He had to find that out the hard way when we were younger, to give me the benefit of the doubt that I was in a lot of pain and my meds were not touching the sides, and this poor, stupid twenty-year-old complained that I must be lying about taking them because medication kills the pain.

I think a small part of why he is so adamant with finding every way to help me now stems from conversations we had all those years ago in university.

Once Charlotte is burped and fully awake I decide that a banana is not going to be enough this morning. Sometimes when I'm in pain I am so unbelievably nauseous that food is the last thing on my mind, but today I am craving something sweet.

Knowing there is no way my arms will have the strength to carry Charlotte around the house I tie her to me with one of the Moby carriers Liam bought. Not only did he buy one in every colour to match my outfits, he also bought hip carriers and back carriers of all sizes, Charlotte is going to be carried in style for a few years.

It helps me be hands-free too. Using the banister on the stairs is one of the only ways I can get down, well I could bump down the stairs on my arse, but the shock to my spine would probably not be welcomed. Having Charlotte on my chest means I can grip the banister on one side and support more weight against the wall with the other.

Having no stairs when Jack was born was super helpful, that was until I had to leave the flat and had to go down two flights of rickety steps. These solid wood stairs with a plush carpet runner are a lot less scary.

Everything about the postnatal life has been a lot less scary this time not just because of how great Liam has been but because I am a different type of parent now. I am stronger. I have a village to lean on and my past mistakes to learn from, fear just doesn't cripple me the way it did.

By the time I am plating some waffles I hear tiny footfalls behind me and turn to see Jack wiping the sleep from his eyes.

"Morning, bud."

"Morning Mum, morning Lottie." He yawns wide, clearly not ready to be up and about.

I know he will be more awake once he has eaten so I give him the first plate of waffles, making more for myself. I watch with a smile as he picks his fruit and honey as toppings while mine cook.

"How about once we've eaten we jump back in the big bed and watch the big TV?" I will get to spend time with Jack and rest my body as much as I can while Liam is training. Perfect.

"Can we watch cartoons?" he asks sceptically.

"Sure thing, bud." I laugh.

"Yesssss!" He pumps his fists in the air like he just scored the winning goal at the Stanley Cup finals.

He starts to shovel the waffle into his face while I plate my own up. I pick chocolate sauce for the top because there is a deep need for sugar in my blood today.

–

We spend the next few hours just cuddling in the master bed, watching anything Jack desires. Charlotte switches between laying between us making beautiful gargling noises and sleeping against my chest.

That is how she is when Liam gets home. He walks into the room to see the three of us cuddled together as *Scooby-Doo* plays in front of us. His eyes scan us with nothing but deep love and excitement, it's like his eyes don't know where to focus first. They eventually settle on me though. I know exactly how he feels when he smiles and shakes his head while kicking off his shoes and joining us in bed.

"Hey gorgeous," he whispers against my lips as he kisses me softly. He pulls Jack into his side and rests one hand on Charlotte's back feeling as she snores softly. "I'm going to order some pasta for dinner, what do you want?"

"Pizza!" Jack and I cheer at the same time, much to Charlotte's annoyance. She wakes slightly with a grumpy, wrinkled face before dropping right back off again. I notice when her dad gets out of bed to get his phone from his sports bag his smile never once drops.

Chapter Thirty-Five

November

Liam

I like having a pre-game routine. Every sports person has their own way to get into the zone. I don't think I have been in the zone once this season. No matter if I eat my lucky eggs or if I put my phone away it just hasn't worked.

My heart won't listen to my head and focus. It wants to be at home. The first away game of the season is in Carolina, too far away from my family. Too damn far. Instead of having my phone in my locker where it usually is, it's in my hand playing a cheesy slideshow of pictures of Charlotte, as well as pictures from Jack's birthday party at the rink back home.

My team depend on me to be on the ball, to have the puck, and right now I don't even know which end of the stick is which.

"Ruin! My office now," Coach's voice bellows. It's not a surprise that Coach Mitch wants to talk to me. I barely look up as I trudge to his makeshift office down the corridor. Despite being a grown man and father in my thirties, being screamed at by my coach renders me straight back to my teenage years.

"Have a seat, Ruin." His tone carries contempt and simmering anger. His eyes look bloodshot as they glare at me.

"Liam, I am going to talk and you're going to listen. You're a mess. I have seen better skating from damn children. You are going to get your head on the ice or you will be warming the bench," he states with conviction. Ice floods my veins at the thought of being benched. I might not be in it 100 per cent, but there is no damn way I am giving up the first away game for some new kid that's still wet behind the ears. Not a chance in hell.

"I don't know what to do Coach – my head isn't fully in it, but you know I am a damn good player," I argue. I know he knows. I am trying to remind *myself*.

Coach shakes his head. "Look, the new kid is chomping at the bit to get out there, so either you show me the Ruin I know or Michelson goes out for you."

Shit. Micah Michelson is not taking my spot. I knew I was in trouble when they signed a new forward, but knowing I was retiring soon made me feel safe, as though they wouldn't sub me knowing the number of games I have are limited.

"Thanks, Coach." There is nothing else to say and we both know it. My face must look like thunder when I walk back into the locker room. All of the boys whisper in my direction as I all but stomp to my stuff.

"Rookie you might want to do some extra stretches, Ruin might be warming the bench." Edge nudges Michelson, but his joking tone hides the question he wants to ask. He wants to know if I have been benched. Not yet I haven't, and I won't be if I have any control over it.

"Fuck you, Edge," I say as Jonas interrupts:

"Wait, but I'm the rookie, eh?"

"No Jonas, you're just Jonas now. Micah is the rookie this season." Edge delivers the bad news with a shit-eating grin, Rook just opens and closes his mouth in shock.

"No way! That's my damn nickname, eh," he protests.

"Shut up, Jonas," I tell him. I am going to get in the zone if it kills me. Or if I have to kill *him*.

I take the next half-hour to force my routine. I sit silently letting any adrenalin build. Anders keeps eyeing me from across the room, but I pretend not to see him. I'm not in the mood for his motivational crap right now. All I want is to get on the ice and feel the cheers of the crowd. At home games, it's been the only thing that has managed to calm my mind so here's hoping it will work tonight.

In the tunnel, we wait to skate out and the crowd is rowdy. I can already hear them slapping the glass and stomping their feet, I just know they are a few beers deep and the puck hasn't even dropped yet.

I need to feel that noise and atmosphere in my blood, it has always been my favourite part of playing hockey. Instead of calm focus coming over me, the crowd makes me feel feral. Like every one of their jeers seeps into me and flows down through to my skates. I feel like a rabid dog waiting for some prey as Anders skates to the centre of the ice for the face-off.

The game is carnage, I think every player is feeling as out of sorts as me, or at least I hope so. I can't be in this alone. Every nerve ending is firing on a hundred cylinders.

Not three minutes pass before my world is rocked.

A dirty check has me flying into the boards, but worse than that, he follows me over crushing me harder against the glass. Even with my helmet I feel the pressure against my skull from his weight against my back.

I snap.

The minute his weight is leveraged off me my fists are swinging. My stick lays forgotten on the ice, I throw my gloves beside it as I swing at the red shirt-wearing asshole.

This is what I have been feeling, my body knew there would be a fight, I just don't think it expected it so soon. I have his jersey bundled in one hand as the other swings at him until he falls. I can't seem to stop. I watch myself straddle him and watch his helmet fly off his head, his face is covered in blood as I feel his nose crunch under my fist.

It feels as though we fight for hours; him still getting some good hits in even from his disadvantaged position. I feel tugging on the back of my jersey as I am all but lifted off his body by Anders. The ref is sending me to the box but my adrenalin seems to evaporate all at once when I see a camera following me.

All at once I remember that Ellis and Jack will be watching at home. My sweet boy will have watched me beat a man for nothing more than a shove. It makes me sick.

His face would be looking up at me with confusion behind his eyes and I know Ellis will be disappointed that I didn't keep my cool. In the past, she rarely ever sat right at the glass because if someone got checked in front of her she would hate it.

Now, here I am breaking some guy's nose just because he is a dirty player. I have played against worse with way less reaction but tonight I let everyone I care about down. The first thing on my to-do list when I do get home is to tell Jack that violence shouldn't be the answer, the kid looks up to me and the team like idols since we came into his life, what kind of legacy am I creating for him and Charlotte?

My few minutes are over quickly and I am allowed back on the ice but by now it is already two nil to Carolina and I know my stupid playing is part of the reason why. I am going to play good clean hockey and make my family proud.

That lasts less than two minutes.

Edge gets the puck off the baby-faced Carolinian and shoots it to me, I am open and free and yet my arms are not quick enough. My skates feel like sandbags holding me back as the puck sails past. It was an easy puck, no blocking players, nobody pulling me back and I missed it.

I miss it completely, losing us our first chance at a goal. Edge looks like I pissed in his cereal and I don't blame him, Anders just looks confused as Carolina manage to make it three nil by the end of the first period.

The minute I am off the ice for a break I know I am staying off it. I was given one chance to show my coach I could get myself in check and I didn't. Coach Mitch barely even looks at me before he shakes his head and juts his chin towards the bench as he turns to Michelson.

The guys are giving me a wide birth, all scared I will go to attack mode with them but I don't even have that fight in me. Micah keeps glancing at me, I'm happy for the guy. Well, not *quite* happy, but I remember my first rookie game in New York when I wasn't really a part of the team yet: the same way he is now. Just on the outskirts waiting for your chance, but knowing someone is going to get traded or retire for that to happen.

Plus, it's my own fault. Coach told me to get my head in the game but it's my heart that isn't in it right now. My heart is at home, and I have to be across the country knowing I could miss a million things over the three days before I get home.

My priorities just don't include hockey as high as it used to. I have been a professional hockey player for a damn decade and have played for three teams that I have loved. I've done it all. Won cups and medals and admiration.

I don't need any more of them. I wanted one last season, one last blaze of glory but what if me staying here and playing this season is going to make the team worse? Could I forgive myself if the newer boys had a shitty season all because I wish I was cuddling my little girl instead of scoring goals?

The game comes to an end with us being all but obliterated out there: four one to them.

Waiting until the end of the season might not be beneficial for any of us. I guess another thing on my to-do list at home is going to be talking to Ellis about if I should hang up my skates now instead of in seven or eight months' time.

Chapter Thirty-Six

Ellis

I know it's coming. I could feel it through the screen. Every sharp turn and missed puck blared out at me. I could see him give up, down to the exact second I could feel the joy of the sport flow out of him and his shoulders slumped. His face was hidden behind a helmet but I could paint a picture of the hopelessness that I'm sure was there. All that said, the moment the front door opens a few days later I know what Liam is going to say.

"I'm retiring." I can hear the defeat in his voice.

Even though I was expecting it, I still can't believe what I'm hearing. "The fuck you are!" I yell. He doesn't answer me straight away. I hear as he slips off his suit jacket and kicks off his shoes before his sock-clad feet pad into the room.

"Why the hell not?" He is still undressing, rolling up his sleeves and unbuttoning the top of his shirt as he looks at me. His face is painted with confusion, frustration clear as day behind his eyes. No matter how long we were apart I can read this man like it's nothing.

"Liam. That game sucked, but how many bad games have you had over the years?" I urge him to think carefully. Having spent the better part of the weekend expecting this conversation I have a few techniques lined up.

"I don't want to leave because I played bad, come on El, I'm not that pathetic," he replies, disgruntled.

"So, you are breaking your contract why?" I quiz with a raised eyebrow. I need him to lay it out, because the Liam I know never backs down from a challenge.

"Because I don't care!" His words are loud and not at all what I was expecting.

"What?"

"I don't care that we didn't win." He drops down next to me on the couch and his head falls into his hands. I give him time, knowing he needs to find the words.

I rub circles onto his back until he is ready. "I didn't care when I was on that ice, I couldn't have given less fucks. I didn't want to be there. I wanted to be here."

I frown, worried about his state. "Can you really look those boys in the eye and tell them you don't care about them?" I ask.

"Of course I care about *them*. It's the game I don't care about. Those guys have been in my life for so long, but now my life has got a lot bigger than just hockey: it's you, it's Charlotte, it's Jack. I need to be here, not in that arena."

I shake my head aggressively. "Liam… you are already leaving. Cassie is ready to announce your retirement at the end of the season, don't you want to go out on a high, give the fans something to remember you by?" I know winning the cup has always been his dream – it's every hockey player's dream. This could be his final chance and I won't let him run away from that if I think he will have regrets. I could never forgive myself.

"I don't want to miss anything here. I feel like I'm letting you all down because I'm not going to be here, and—" He pours his heart out.

"Look—" I try to interrupt.

"No, Ellis, I missed enough during the pregnancy and I hate knowing there will be a million milestones that I'm going to miss because my pride and ego told me I needed one more season."

I wish I could stop him beating himself up like this, talk him down the way he has done for me many times.

"Okay, yes, you are going to miss things – but so will I. When I go back to work I might miss her first laugh, or her first steps, but you would never let me beat myself up for that, would you? So, I'm not going to let you do it either. Liam, there are going to be so many firsts that we will see and some we will miss. But that's life. We are still her parents, and nothing can take that away." I pause for breath, but when he doesn't speak, I keep rolling.

"Let's say you leave at the end of the season, you might miss her rolling over or holding her head up, but the big stuff? That's not coming for a while yet. Walking is a year away and talking properly doesn't come for even longer – plus every baby is different! Missing a few little things in the first six or seven months will not outweigh all the stuff you will be around for the rest of her life.

"Also, if you leave now there is a chance Cassie will kill you in your sleep and then you will miss it all, you sure you want to be on her bad side?" I nudge him and then hinge my arm back and forth like I'm wielding a knife, mimicking the sounds of a horror movie soundtrack.

"Okay, yes, you have a point." He laughs pulling my arm from the air and kissing the inside of my wrist.

"That's because I'm always right," I say smugly. "If you think you can't play any more, that you are going to end up getting yourself hurt, then I will stand by you. But don't leave because you think you're being a bad dad, because you aren't. There is no one else in the world I would have wanted to have a baby with," I say as I lean forward to lay a light kiss against his lips.

"I love you, Sunshine," he tells me.

"I love you, too. Now try my pie." I change the subject as I stand and walk to the kitchen pulling him behind me.

"You're going to initiate sex right now? In the kitchen? I'm down." He slides his arms around my waist and kisses along my neck, his stubble tickling the sensitive skin behind my ear.

"No, you pervert!" I say with a giggle. "I made a practice pumpkin pie for the team's Thanksgiving this year." I'd been thinking for a couple weeks about the holidays coming up – I don't feel like I ever had the traditional, huge family Thanksgiving. But for the first time in years, Anders isn't able to go home for the holidays, and I could see the opportunity for a new tradition being born.

Lyndsey stepped up to help Anders plan a family dinner for anyone on the team not going home, but no matter how many times I ask, she still says there is nothing between the two of them. *I call bullshit.*

"Anders told you not to bring anything except, I quote, 'your cute selves and those even cuter kids of yours'. You didn't have to make a pie." Liam's attempt at a southern accent is terrible, but it always makes me laugh. While I cut some pie for the two of us he grabs plates and cutlery for us.

"I am not going to his house for the first time empty-handed, that would just be breaking some cosmic law," I object to him. Maybe that is something Eleanor did give me: proper guest-host etiquette.

"Two slices please," Liam asks. I'm not a baker, and I will take it to the grave that this is actually the third pie I made today. On the first try I forgot to preheat the oven so it was cooked at the edges and liquid in the middle.

The second looked great, and I thought I had it figured out, until I had a slice and realised I forgot the sugar.

Third time's the charm though, and this one came out of the oven looking great and filled with all the requisite ingredients.

I watch Liam as he looks suspiciously at the fork full of pie in his hand. He seems to weigh up the worst-case scenarios before deciding to taste it. When he goes for another mouthful I dig into my own. I think I did a good job. Would it win awards? No, but is it tasty enough to give as a gift? Yes, it is.

We eat in silence for a moment, the only sound in the room is forks on plates and quiet cooing from the baby monitor on the countertop between us. I have barely finished my slice by the time Liam has devoured his and cuts another slice, I must have done something right for him to like it this much.

Once we are both done he puts the plates in the dishwasher before taking me in his arms and sways me to music apparently only he can hear.

"Can you believe it's nearly our anniversary?" he says against my forehead, still swaying left and right.

"Our what now?" I laugh.

"Anniversary?"

"Nope, we don't have an anniversary because we aren't married, in fact you never even asked me to be your girlfriend. I'm just a glorified roommate and baby mamma," I joke.

"You did not just say that." He pulls away from me, grabbing both my hands in his against his chest, laughing at me with a shocked face.

"You must mean our *one-night-stand-iversary*," I tell him, trying my best to keep a straight face.

"Never say that again." He tells me before moving both of my hands into one of his using the other to tickle my sides. I beg to be let go but he just tickles me harder rubbing his stubble on my neck until I squeal.

"Fine, I surrender!" I laugh catching my breath when he finally loosens his grips on me, but he doesn't let me get away. Instead he takes the hand that was buried in my ribs and moves it to my neck, pulling my face closer to his.

"Good girl," he says before kissing me deeply.

"Who knew Jonas flirting with me would be the best thing to happen to me?" Still in his arms we start to sway again, there is something so right about being in his arms swaying to our heartbeats and the soft snores of our little girl through the monitor.

Liam just hums as he rests his forehead against mine. My head comes up high enough to slip under his chin. That is something I have always loved about being tall while with Liam, he is still taller but just tall enough to hold me in his arms without having to crouch down.

Liam was always the man I was supposed to end up with, it was always right. His strength helps lift me up and my realism keeps him tethered and I meant what I said: there is no one else I would want to have kids with.

Chapter Thirty-Seven

December

Liam

Sneaking around is not one of my strengths. I can skate. I can make killer pancakes. I can make Ellis happy – in and out of bed. Sneaking, not so good. I think my face is just too guilty.

Every time my phone pings my eye twitches and I know she can tell. This is why I refuse to play poker with the guys, throwing my money away gets old. I have tried to leave the house today and each time Ellis has asked me to do something. Normally, I would do anything she asked but *I need to go out today.*

I tried getting dressed and slipping out while she slept, but apparently Charlotte is laughing at my downfall because as soon as I laced my shoes she started to wail. She was hungry and wet and wanted out of her crib. I could deal with all that, but then Ellis and Jack woke up.

Then Jack asked for pancakes. I couldn't say no to his big puppy dog eyes. He might not look like his mom, but they have me wrapped around their fingers the same way. Damn, so does Charlotte and she can't even talk.

So, pancakes were made, fruit was sliced and dishes were washed. Ellis got Charlotte ready for the day just in time for her pancakes to be done and I got side tracked with my family. Until Edge texted me again. This group chat is going to be my downfall today.

I thought I could make a breakaway after breakfast, but Ellis needed to get some orders in for when she goes back to work. I couldn't argue with that. She built that business from the ground up and I am going to support her however I can.

I needed to distract the kids for an hour while she worked. Jack played with his remote-control car, driving it into me while laughing maniacally while Charlotte had tummy time next to our Christmas tree. My little girl is enamoured with the twinkling lights. It is the first time I have ever had a tree, I am usually travelling so it felt pointless. Not this year. This year I have gone all out. Garlands and snowflakes, elf statues and reindeers. If I could fit it through the door it is here. My phone pings on and off every few minutes but I don't bother looking because I know what's there. Everyone asking what the plan is. But I just don't know.

I thought it would be easy, slip out of the house while Ellis slept, buy a ring and be home before lunch. Now lunch is slowly approaching and I am still here.

Ellis eventually comes out of the office while I am giving Charlotte her bottle and even with my simmering anxiety this is one of my favourite things about being a father. The way her lips suckle at the bottle and her eyes slip shut in contentment makes me feel like I'm holding an angel.

Her hair is coming in more every day and it wisps at my arm where I cradle her. She gripes and grumbles while I burp her.

"I'm going to put her down, being up half the night is catching up with her," I tell Ellis and she pecks my lips as we pass. "Why don't you try napping while she does, that is what all the books said to do?"

"I am sleepy… work is hard when you haven't slept." She yawns. She takes a softly snoring Charlotte from my arms and walks up the stairs while I stare after her. "Oh, and take Jack with you wherever you are trying to sneak off to," she adds.

My mouth falls open. She knows I am up to something and Jack is going to blow my cover. I love him, but that kid is not known for keeping a secret. No kid is, but he isn't exactly a prime engagement-ring shopping guest. There is nowhere else I can take him though. Maybe Rook can distract him outside whatever jewellers we end up at so he has plausible deniability.

"Jack!" I call him and straight away I hear him stampede towards me.

"Are we going out?" he asks.

"Yeah, bud, but I need you to make me a promise." I kneel down to his level keeping my voice low in case Sunshine thinks of eavesdropping.

"Okay!" he stage whispers.

"I am buying a gift for your mom but it is a secret gift so you can't tell her what we buy okay?"

"Will you buy me McDonald's?" he whispers again. The cheeky little troublemaker is blackmailing me. And it's working.

"Fine." I am resigned.

"Yesssss!" Then he's off running to put his shoes and jacket on, leaving them unlaced in his haste.

By the time I finally pull into Edge's driveway everyone is already there. I think they have been here for a few hours at this point, but Jack is not deterred. He jumps out of his car seat and bangs on the front door before I'm even out of the car. The house is capped with frost but there are no decorations here; if this is how boring my place usually looks I'm glad I made a change.

"Hey little guy." Jack walks right in and Edge just watches him shaking his head.

I follow the two of them inside and I find Jack hugging his Auntie Lyndsey and questioning the guys about where we are going; not that any of them know. I'm not even sure *where* we are going. I was too scared to google anything in case Ellis saw.

I never knew I was so paranoid. Superstitious, yes, but paranoid? No. When I walk into the room everyone turns to me expectantly. I think Anders sees on my face that I don't have a plan. He rolls his eyes before standing up and pulling his phone to his ear.

"Hey Felix, yeah man I'm good... But I have a question." At the sound of his favourite player's name, Jack sits up straight as a meerkat.

"Where did you buy your engagement ring?" Anders asks on the phone.

We all look at each other perplexed while Anders chats away in the background asking for directions. Soon enough he is herding us into cars. Apparently Felix got his wife's ring from a place downtown and he is going to call ahead and tell the head jeweller we are on our way. The last thing I expected was for Anders to be the hero of the day; if I find the ring, I might just bake him a cake myself.

Loaded into my car are Jack and Rook, who have talked the entire drive as I follow behind Lyndsey, Anders and Edge in the captain's car. I zone out the noise in the car, running through every piece of jewellery I can think that Ellis owns for clues on what kind of ring she would want.

Lyndsey was a great help in pointing me in the right direction, reminding me that Ellis wears silver. She even stole one of Ellis's rings the last time she came over so we know what size to buy. I can't exactly just ask to see every silver or white gold ring they have. I know finding the perfect ring might not happen today, but I feel it in my bones. Today is supposed to be the day, I don't want to go any longer without one hidden away for the perfect moment.

After a while, Anders pulls into a parking lot and has jumped out of the car by the time we pull into the spot next to him. He nods his head towards a row of shops before we all start off towards them. As we get closer to the bright white storefront I am almost blinded by the shimmering jewels behind the glass. Through the windows I can see case upon case of every type of jewellery I could imagine. Before we walk into the shop, aptly called Shimmering Elegance, Rook pulls us into a huddle. Before anyone speaks I drop down on to my knees in front of Jack.

"Okay bud, we're here to buy your mom a ring but I want to ask you something…?" I cough slightly, unsure of how to ask him for his blessing.

"You can marry her." He interrupts me.

"What?" I laugh. This kid shocks me at every turn.

"That's what a ring is for right? To get married? I want you to marry her because then you will be my dad for real," he tells me, my heart breaks and mends itself in one as he looks up at me with love and hope in his eyes.

"You are already my son, come here." I pull him into my arms, resting my head on top of his. Out the corner of my eye I see Lyndsey wipe a tear.

"Here's a plan: just buy her the biggest rock in there. You're rich after all, that's what I'd want." Lyndsey laughs trying to change the subject to hide her growing emotions, clearly joking about the huge diamond, but Jack misses the humour in her tone.

"No! Don't do that!" Jack yells as the door to the shop opens making everyone in the store swing their attention to him. When none of us reply he continues, "When Mum is sore her hands swell, she can't have something heavy or that would make it worse."

"Damn, I didn't even think of that, bud, it's a good job you're here." I ruffle his hair with my hand in approval as Lyndsey winks at him. And to think I wasn't planning on bringing him. I never planned on just buying her the biggest one anyway, but it didn't even cross my mind how her fibromyalgia might affect her jewellery.

"Also, you should buy two," he tells me matter of fact.

"Why?" Anders laughs but not at Jack, more at the fact a bunch of grown adults are being outsmarted by him.

"For when her hands swell, so she can still be wearing one," he says it like it is so obvious and he can't understand why we didn't all figure that out ourselves. I understand the logic; Ellis would feel guilty if she couldn't fit her ring on when her knuckles swell. She feels enough guilt as it is, all the pressure she puts herself under, and there is no way I am going to add to it.

The guys take Jack and look through every cabinet as I sit down with Lyndsey as the head jeweller Louis approaches us to introduce himself, telling him all of the new requirements I have thought of. Silver, lightweight but still dazzling, I need it in two sizes, maybe something blue because she looks so good in blue. He takes in all the information and begins gathering a selection. Lyndsey was quick to tell him the ring isn't for her, the only woman in a shop now crowded by men it would have been a realistic assumption, so I am glad she set the record straight.

I don't know how Felix found this shop, but it felt like Louis jumped right into my brain. After talking for a few minutes he gives me this smile as he hurries off to the back room and reappears with a little velvet tray in his hands.

Without saying a word, he places the cushioned tray in front of me with Ellis's engagement ring on it. I know this is it. From nowhere the guys are looking over my shoulder as I pick up the white gold band, there is an emerald cut diamond in the centre with two smaller baguette style sapphire stones on either side of the band. I look at it from every angle: it is perfect.

My mind paints a picture of Ellis's hand adorned with this ring no matter the price. Frankly this guy could take me for millions of dollars and I would still thank him for it. I watch him box up both sizes of the ring and I pay for them without question but only after Jack has given me the go ahead. I remind him once more to keep it a secret and he zips his lips before giving me a wink with both eyes.

Close enough.

Chapter Thirty-Eight

31st December

Ellis

Having time to get all dressed up is a rarity. Even before I got pregnant that night out last year was the first time I got dressed up in months. When Liam told me to lock the bathroom door and take as much time as I want to get pampered while he gets the kids ready for the team's New Year's party at first I argued, but I didn't argue hard.

When you have a baby, every moment of levity is a blessing and I am not going to look a gift horse in the mouth. So I am running myself a hot bubble bath with all the luxuries, with no distractions or interruptions.

Anders asked us to be there about eight, so I have time to soak a little before I do anything else. I went to the hairdresser earlier in the day so my hair is clipped up in pin curls ready to be taken down at the perfect moment. Even that night over a year ago I didn't take all this time. I showered and threw on the only dress I had. If I had known where the night would lead I probably would have taken more time to prepare. I'm not going to make that mistake twice, and tonight I am planning on ending the night with fireworks of my own.

I am planning on seducing my man tonight. Not that it will take much work, he has been obsessed with me since I got the okay from the doctor to have sex again. I can't lie, I was worried he wouldn't love my body after having Charlotte, but I think he is more obsessed now than before. Something about knowing I carried his child drives him wild. And everything we went through has bonded us closer together than I could have imagined.

I wouldn't have it any other way; there is nothing more I want than to enter the new year in his arms.

By the time the water is cold I am shaved and scrubbed, ready to moisturise to make me velvety smooth. My dress for tonight is a new purchase; it's a black Sixties shift dress with white feathers on the trim. Lyndsey said they highlighted my long legs and demanded I buy it or else. I wasn't going to wait around to find out what she'd do to me.

Cassie also told everyone we had to look our best tonight because she'll be sharing the New Year's pictures online leading up to midnight. I've never been on the official Spears socials, so that should be interesting. I have been on Liam's over the last few months, since the night with Michael at the arena, but this is different. Speculation over our relationship was rampant at first – or so I'm told. But like everything else, it quickly faded into the back of everyone's minds. Perhaps more events and photos like today will further cement me as part of Spears life. Just another character in the online algorithm that fans accept.

Last New Year's Eve, Liam was a single bachelor attending alone. Now he has a girl and two kids. It must feel like whiplash to those who have followed him over the years. Since the season started back up, me and the kids have tried to attend a few games, always ending up on the big screen – much to Jack's amusement. I was surprised that when our faces flashed for everyone to see, we were met with cheers.

Liam has always warned me that people online will have a lot to say whenever he posts about our family, but it seems those worries were not completely necessary. Our situation might not be adored by all, but it seems overall that we've been welcomed with open arms.

Luckily, I've built up a much thicker skin over the past year. I no longer care about what others think – the fans, my distant mother, Michael. They don't matter.

Cassie remains cautious. She cares enough for the both of us. She has let us know she has passed along strict orders to delete any unsavoury comments about me or the kids tonight. *God bless Cassie.* Not that I would see them myself anyway. It proved a lot easier to shut down my personal social media accounts. I only use the business one for Bloom and Blossom these days and as I never post pictures of myself on there, fans don't really link it to me.

I think back to the worries I had just a few months ago, and I want to laugh. I want to go back in time and shake myself. I was doing exactly what my mother wanted – living for the approval and opinions of others, rather than myself and what I really want. Now I've finally taken the plunge, shown the world who I am and what I want, and it wasn't nearly half as scary as I expected. The world continued to spin, and I continued to be happy.

Before long, I am finishing up my make-up. I'm no expert, but I know the basics. Tonight, I am pushing my skills to the limit. Red lip and winged liner to carry on the vintage feel of my dress, but I have brushed some silver glitter on my eyelids to match my silver strappy heels. I haven't worn heels in over a year so my bag is packed with plasters as well as baby wipes.

Every time I try to help with the kids I get waved away by Liam letting me know he's got it. I don't doubt it, but I still feel a little out of control and guilty. Here I am pampering myself, leaving him to get himself and two kids ready and one of them is a wiggling baby. I know it's ridiculous – I mean, if he couldn't handle it he would let me know.

I wonder if I've done too much. I don't know what I'm trying to prove. Of course I want to look good for Liam, but he loves me in the middle of the night with bedhead and baby vomit on my shirt just as much, if not more, than he loves me when I put in effort.

It still feels wrong sometimes that I get to be with a man like him. Athletic and strong, handsome as hell and I am just a mum who owns a flower shop. We shouldn't fit, we shouldn't work the way we do, but we do. My body fits right alongside his; when I need something he is willing to do whatever is needed to help and I do the same for him.

It takes a lot for me to let down my walls but when it comes to Liam I think they were less walls and are more like pieces of paper I tried to hide my heart behind. It didn't work. And I am so glad it didn't.

The street outside of Anders's house is packed full of cars. I only realise as we pull up that I have never really looked at his house: it's big. Of course it is, he is rich but it's bigger than I thought it would be. I saw it at Thanksgiving but it looks so different covered in Christmas lights and holly garlands. It basically glows tonight, looking like something from a holiday film. I think it might be bigger than our place, that's probably why he throws the team parties, well that and his captain status.

Liam has Charlotte strapped to his chest and she is napping softly against his black shirt. Jack is between us holding our hands and everyone watching can see our family unit at our strongest. Paparazzi are stood snapping pictures as people enter and Liam covers Charlotte's face so she's not blinded by the flashing lights.

Within seconds Cassie, with a newly styled black wavy bob, appears in front of us and Liam's steps falters.

"You guys look great! Good job Liam!" She nods approvingly. I was expecting her usual put-together look, but this sexy confident Cassie is different to her professional presentation. Short and curvy but clearly confident if the short red sequin dress she has on is anything to go by. My eyes drift over her head, even in high black heels she is a lot shorter than me, and my eyes just happen to slip to Edge. That man can't tear his eyes off the little vixen and when he realises he's been caught I just drop my head to one side and try to bite back my laugh as his face turns a wonderful red.

"Anyway, Ellis you are my hero, thank you for keeping this one out of trouble – I have enough to worry about with the other idiots. I could swear they want me to throw things at them." Cassie slips her arm through mine as I laugh, she tells me Rook's latest antics and this woman must have the patience of a saint.

Cassie herds us over to a gold sequin backdrop for our official pictures. Just in time for her baby debut, Charlotte wakes up and smiles up at her dad as he unstraps her. To give him credit Liam picked some cute outfits.

Jack is matching him with black pants and a black shirt and he looks so handsome, and Charlotte is pretty as a picture in a gold tulle dress with a matching headband.

The photographer takes a few of all of us and then Cassie takes Charlotte and Jack over to the side for some couple photos. Just when I think she is going to move us along for the next attendees she actually hands Charlotte to her brother for them to get some pictures and promises me she will send them over to me. I think I like that girl a whole hell of a lot.

As we join the party, I can't take my eyes off Liam and not because of the obvious. Of course he looks good enough to eat and our daughter cuddling on his chest should be illegal because of the butterflies it's giving me. That isn't it, though. I can't stop looking at him because he looks shifty.

It's like every time he looks my way his attention snaps somewhere else and he whispers something to Edge. Jack is running around with a few other kids and Lyndsey is saying something to me but I can't hear a word of it. I know he is planning something; he is no poker player, that's for sure.

There is nothing I could think of that would require all of the guys like this. Even Anders looks on edge which never happens. I feel Cassie come up on my left and her and Lyndsey start talking, I am just nodding along. I could be agreeing to anything but I can't look away from my man. That is until Jack pulls on my dress. "Mum! I want to come to this party every day!" Before I can reply though he runs off again disappearing into the crowd of children. When I look up again the guys are gone.

I don't know where but maybe this will give me a break and shut my brain up. The drink Lyndsey passes my way will help with that as well. Jack is also acting weird as the night goes on. This is explainable though; my boy has had so much sugar he is basically vibrating. Every few minutes he comes and asks me if it's time. And every time I tell him he'll know when it's time because everyone will be counting down from ten.

He does not seem satisfied with that though, still asking and asking. I think he will crash for days after this. Anders just had to have a chocolate fountain and a sweets bar for the kids.

It makes a change from every other New Year we have had though, normally he doesn't care. It's just another day for him, I do let him stay up and watch the countdown but this is the first time we have ever really celebrated, so seeing him so excited for midnight is a strange feeling. I'm actually glad he's having fun. Every person in this room seems to be his new best friend. Liam just popped upstairs to put Charlotte in a pop-up cot that Anders apparently bought just for tonight. Who knew giant hockey players could be so sweet to a random British woman and her kids. These ones are apparently sweet without even trying.

Liam is back just before midnight and is looking at me like he is going to eat me alive. I wanted to seduce him, but I was planning on waiting until we were home. I've never felt irresistible until I met Liam years ago and it worked just the same this time. Since last year, he has looked at me like I'm his tastiest snack.

When he holds out his hand to dance I think I melt a little bit. All night there have been people dancing, some slow dancing with their partners and some just bouncing around, but when Liam takes me in his arms I know which one we are about to do.

Dancing isn't exactly a strength for either of us but he is light on his feet. I trust him to lead me around the makeshift dance floor in Anders's dining room. We sway and spin together and everyone else falls away. Then he dips me and I laugh so hard I nearly fall out of his arms. I did not expect it for a second but I know he won't drop me. He holds me tight, gripping my thigh in his hand with the other hand spread over my back.

As it gets even closer to midnight everyone starts to filter out of the house and onto Anders's land. I would say garden but damn this is far beyond a garden, there are flower beds and outbuildings as well as a covered pool that I am sure Jack will ask to visit again next summer.

Liam has my hand in his until he pulls me to the middle of the gathering crowd. He locks eyes with me and doesn't break the contact while he drops down onto one knee before me.

My heart seems to stop for a moment. The crowd around me melts away. "Ellis Ainsley," he says. "This year has been crazy, but one of the best years of my life. From the moment I saw you again in that bar I knew I had found my way home. I can't wait to come home to you every day for the rest of our lives. You have already given me a family. But would you do me the honour of being my wife?" He gently opens the box to reveal the most beautiful diamond ring I could ever have dreamed of owning. "Will you marry me?"

I catch my breath as the lump in my throat grows larger. "Yes!" With perfect timing and co-ordination, the sky above lights up with fireworks as the word leaves my mouth. A thundering applause and cheering from everyone around us rips through the air. I jump into Liam's arms and kiss him hard.

When I finally pull my lips from his, he slips the ring on my finger as I nearly burst into tears. It's everything I would want – because it came from him, and I would take a piece of string if it's all he could give me.

Just like that, he is not my boyfriend, or my partner, or my co-parent – he is my fiancé. And I love him more than I could explain.

A second later, Jack is jumping at our side and climbing up me like a spider monkey until he is swinging around my neck. Maybe it isn't all chocolate that has made him this hyper, because he doesn't look the least bit as surprised by Liam's question as I am.

"Yay!" Jack cheers.

With the picturesque scene surrounding us, all I can think about is grabbing Charlotte, Jack and Liam and holding my whole family in my arms.

Chapter Thirty-Nine

Liam

"You happy?" I ask, sliding my arms around Ellis's waist as she surveys the rose petals on our bed and the chocolate-covered strawberries on the table.

"That's an understatement – Liam you didn't have to do all of this." She spins in my arms to rest her back against me.

"Yeah I did, anything for you." She slips her fingers through my hair and pulls me so my forehead is resting against hers before she kisses me lightly, turning back around.

"I love you," I growl, deepening the kiss. I need her closer. I am so glad Anders offered to have the kids for the night. It took a little convincing for Ellis, but Lyndsey promised to stay and help him.

When I move, she follows. I push my chest harder against hers, slipping my thighs between her legs to lift her against the wall. Ellis winds her creamy legs around my waist, gripping me tight. I grind against the apex of her thighs making her moan in my mouth but before she can get too loud I lift her into my arms and back us to the bed.

She bounces backwards on the bed but before I can lower myself over her she puts a heel-clad foot in the centre of my chest.

"I never thought I would be a wife," she tells me. "Never thought I would deserve being happy, like I never earned it."

"You deserve everything, Sunshine." I take her foot in my hand and slip her heel off before doing the same to the other one, massaging her feet as I go.

"I am finally starting to believe that. Because of you." Her smile is wide, making my heart stutter in my chest as my hands move further up her legs, massaging her calves to her thighs until she is writhing below me.

"I'll make you believe it every day for the rest of our lives, I just wish I found you again sooner." Her legs fall limp as I finally crawl up her body, kissing along the exposed skin of her neck.

"I wouldn't change anything, no matter how much it hurt, it makes the now so much sweeter." Ellis's hands slide into my hair pulling me to kiss her lips but I pull myself up onto my knees where I am straddling her thighs.

"Let's see just how sweet you are." I lift the feathered edge of her dress revealing a pair of black lace panties.

I don't bother wasting time pulling them off, I dive right in. I kiss and lick over the fabric tasting her. She is the sweetest dessert, I could have her for every meal, every hour, every day. Above me Ellis rips off her dress leaving her in just her matching underwear and fuck if my fiancée isn't the most beautiful sight.

I keep licking at the fabric of her panties knowing the friction will drive her crazy, just not enough to get her there. Oh no, I am not letting her come until she is wrapped around my cock.

Knowing she needs more, I pull the scrap of soaked lace down her legs throwing them over my shoulder. Before I go back to eating, I reach around her to unclasp her bra, freeing her to me.

During her pregnancy, her boobs grew to accommodate her milk and now they are back to a smaller size, just enough to fill my palm. My thumb rubs her hardening nipple as I settle back between her thighs. Now without the layer between us I can taste her completely, I love every second.

I lick and suck and nibble at her sensitive flesh until her juices are soaking my chin, dripping down to the bed sheets below. Ellis's hands grip at the back of my head riding my face unashamedly, but I don't let her get too close, pulling back again.

"Liam! I need it. I need you." She is a mumbling mess, I wish I could take a mental picture of this moment.

"I know Sunshine, I'll give you what you need."

This time when I feast again I use my hands too. My fingers curl inside her, feeling around for her G spot. I know I find it when she whines out a moan curling in on herself below me. I love every second of it, licking her clit in small circles while massaging her insides, sliding my fingers in and out until she is chanting my name like a prayer.

"Is my good girl going to come all over her fiancés hand?" I ask cocking my head to the side. I am still fully dressed above her and as powerful as it feels, I am worried my dick might rip through my slacks any second.

"Yes, yes, yes. Please don't stop." Ellis is delirious off the pleasure, but I'm still not ready for her to come.

"I think I will." I pull myself away from her completely, standing at the end of the bed while her chest heaves.

"Fuck you!" she yells but there is no anger, just sexual frustration. I take my time taking off my clothes, even if I do want to strip at full speed.

"My future wife looks so desperate for me, begging and flushed." I tease her further when I am finally naked but instead of joining her I take myself into my hand pumping my cock as I watch her writhe in the sheets.

"Fuck me, Liam. Please." As she begs, I pull out the packet of condoms I bought for tonight, I plan to use as many of them as possible in the next few hours.

"Oh, you beg so sweet." I slide a condom on and slide into her in one thrust. She is so wet that she pulls me into her. It feels so fucking good.

Warm and wet and tight as she pulses around me. I've edged her so much that as soon as I am inside, the orgasm I have been building explodes between us. Unable to move, I feel the aftershocks of her instant orgasm ripple around my cock. That's when I start pumping into her.

I hold her thighs open as I drill into her, hitting as deep as I can reach. Ellis's nails claw at my forearms leaving stark red streaks in their wake that I wish would scar forever. Her mark on my skin just turns me on even more, she has already marked my heart. A part of me wants to chase my orgasm but I fight off that selfishness. No, she is going to come again before I do if it kills me. I take one hand off her thigh to grab a pillow to stuff under her hips lifting them for a better angle. When she yells my name, I know she feels me in her lungs.

I thrust hard and fast into her as she pants against my throat, licking and kissing between her moans. When I start to circle her clit with my thumb Ellis moans that she is close and I am right there with her.

I whisper broken praise against her ear, telling her how good she feels, how good she is for me, how excited I am to make her my wife and then she is coming. We finish together in a tangle of limbs and sweat.

Well, at least we finish round one.

Epilogue

May

Ellis

One way I know I am nothing like my mother is the amount I worry. Eleanor couldn't care less if I did my homework or had hobbies as long as I was her perfectly poised daughter. Now, me? I care about everything, almost too much. Today I think all that worrying is going to give me an embolism.

That's because today is Jack's big day, his first real hockey game against a real team and not just his friends from the rink or sparring with the guys. My baby boy is going to lace blades to his feet and fight off a bunch of other kids for a little piece of rubber and I just have to watch. If someone takes the puck I can't yell at them. If he gets into a fight I can't jump the glass and fight it for him. If he loses, well there is nothing I can do to make that better, I just have to tell him that we all lose sometimes and to try again next time. And then I have to let him do it again next week. I think it might send me into an early grave.

"Jack, do you have everything?" I yell up at him but, to be fair, I have yelled basically everything today. I'm too on edge to talk at a regular volume.

"Of course I do Mum, can we go now?" For the first time I think ever he is the first one ready to leave. Liam is still getting Charlotte ready and instead of Jack lagging behind half asleep he is stood at the door with his kit bag over his shoulder.

"Don't worry bud, we're leaving," Liam says coming around the corner with Charlotte strapped to his large chest.

She is getting bigger every day and as much as I love watching her baby personality grow, I hate that she isn't my little tiny baby any more. No, she is pulling herself up and standing for a few seconds unsupported and I just know the walking is going to come in the next few weeks.

Liam says she is so strong because of his genes and she is so smart because of mine; she babbles a few words here and there but I am in denial for now.

"You need to breathe Sunshine." Liam takes me in his arms and Charlotte huffs between us. Jack is out the door and putting his bag in the back of the car, I get that he is excited but a little part of me hopes we have magically run out of fuel.

"How are you so calm?" I ask, I really mean it, too. If he has some alcohol on him I would gladly take a swig if it would calm my nerves.

"I *am* freaking out, but we need him to know he's got this, if we show him how worried we are then he will get in his head and who knows what will happen if he isn't focused?" He still has his arm over my shoulder but I look up at him with my eyes wide before slapping his shoulder.

"That isn't helping." I needed him to tell me Jack is a prodigy and that no one is going to touch him. It's not true, but I would still like to hear it. Jack is a great player but he's only been on skates for a year, and playing hockey casually for a few months he isn't exactly ready for the NHL. No matter how great his coach is.

"I'm sorry, I'll be right there if that helps." He leads me to the car and unclips Charlotte, knowing I need a little baby cuddle to calm my thumping heart.

"It will have to do. Come on sweet girl." I fasten Charlotte into her seat and leave a light kiss on her head. "Your brother and daddy are going to be the death of me. You will have contactless hobbies, won't you baby girl?" I coo at her.

The boys overhear me and laugh knowing they will be buying her skates as soon as her legs are strong enough to lift them. Damn hockey players.

Soon we are on our way and Jack insists Liam puts his pre-game playlist on, I don't think he is ready for the amount of Nineties boyband music he is about to be exposed to. Liam has a very specific taste in music: cheesy.

Jack starts singing along though, to my surprise. Hearing my two favourite guys belting out Backstreet Boys does a lot to calm me actually, seeing Jack so relaxed just enjoying the music puts me at ease. Charlotte giggles as Jack sings for her, pulling crazy faces and dancing just for her entertainment and I can't help but sing along.

By the time we pull into the rink, Backstreet Boys has switched to NSYNC as well as some One Direction, much to my shock – I didn't know Liam knew any songs recorded after the Nineties. Still we are all singing at the top of our lungs dancing in our chairs, so fair to say Jack is probably at least a little warmed up.

–

Liam is on one knee in front of Jack with one skate resting on his thigh. I can see that with every piece of kit Jack has put on he has gotten more and more in the zone and the skates seem to be the final part of that.

Everyone has looked at us since we got here – well, looked at Liam at least. He has ignored every glance though, taking time to make sure Jack is as ready as he can be. I have taken a leaf out of his book and have buried my scared emotions as far down as I can, though I still feel one misstep away from crumbling.

"I can't be the only one thinking this is unfair!" Some man from the opposing team whisper yells at his wife a few people over from us.

"John leave it!" she admonishes.

"No! That kid is being helped by a professional athlete! He shouldn't be allowed to help." Liam is doing a great job at pretending not to hear him, me not so much – I also hope Jack is too focused to listen. If I didn't have Charlotte strapped to my chest I think I would already be over there giving him a piece of my mind.

"That's his son." The man's wife tries again, and honestly I appreciate the fact it only seems to be him that has a problem.

Everyone around them takes small steps away as I glare at the man. "I don't care! I am going to talk to the referees." Then he is off towards the ice but when I go to follow him, to make sure Jack is not punished for this man's pride, Liam wraps his hand around my calf.

"Leave it Sunshine. Jack's skills will speak for themselves, he's a natural and some random man won't ruin this for him will it, bud?" I can see a vein bulging in Liam's forehead so at least I know he is as mad as me, but he is doing a lot better at keeping it under wraps.

"No way! I've got this." Jack stands up ready to go, fastening his helmet and sliding on his gloves before placing a kiss on Charlotte's head; he says it gives him luck. Hockey players and their superstitions.

Liam leads me over to where Anders, Edge and Lyndsey said they would wait for us. The rest of the team wanted to come, hell even Felix wanted to be here to support his biggest fan, but we thought it would be best to do it in shifts.

A few different people will come each game so we don't overwhelm the other kids. As we approach the seats, we see Lyndsey and Anders huddled together looking very serious. I pull Liam back so we don't interrupt them, and definitely not to eavesdrop – at least that's what I convince myself.

"I am not talking about this here." Lyndsey looks angrier than I have ever seen her, not even mean customers get her like this.

"Well darlin', we're gonna have to talk about it soon." His hand is holding her elbow but she pulls it free.

"Don't *darlin'* me! No one can know." She is shaking her head and he sighs, almost pleading.

"Lyndsey, you're my wife, people are going to find out."

I'm sorry, I think I must have misheard him.

"What!" Liam yells, alerting them to our presence.

"Nice going, Cowboy." Lyndsey huffs before walking away from us all, avoiding eye contact.

"Lyndsey, wait…" Anders yells after her. I want to follow her, but if Jack looks up and sees I'm not there he would be so disappointed, instead I give Anders my best mother stare before he nods getting ready to follow after her.

"I'm sorry, I think we might miss the game. I'll call you later," he tells us, jogging after Lyndsey. His *wife* apparently.

Silently we walk over to the stands where Edge is looking incredibly uncomfortable alone surrounded by a bunch of hockey mums. When he sees us he perks up more than I have ever seen him.

"Edge, you owe me fifty bucks!" Liam yells.

"They slept together?" Edge asks, shocked.

"More than that," Liam sounds awestruck. "They're *married*!" Liam tells him sliding into the chair next to him. I would say I'm shocked they bet money on Anders and Lyndsey, but honestly we all knew it would happen eventually.

I think a part of this might be our fault. We just had to have a joint bachelor-bachelorette event in Vegas. We should have guessed someone would end up married. I would think it would be us, not the team captain, but Vegas will be Vegas, I guess.

The kids are all stretching on the ice while Liam and Jay argue over whether the team's coach is good enough for Jack – I know Liam wants to start coaching the team but when he approached the head coach he was told there were no openings. I was shocked they shot down an ex-NHL player but I agree it would have been unfair to sack someone just because Liam turned up. He will just have to wait until next season and try his luck again then. I have heard through the grapevine (the other gossiping hockey mums) that the head coach is wanting to retire, so I'm sure Liam will be down there with them next year. I'm distracted from their argument, watching my son glide around the ice so calm and serene, it steals my breath just like it does every time I see how natural he is on the ice.

I am glad he found something he loves, even if it does mean I am constantly on edge because of it. When the ref blows his whistle they all skate into their positions. It is kind of strange to see so many tiny people just as focused as the Spears are when they are seconds away from the puck drop. Liam pulls me into his side kissing my temple as the whistle blows and they are off.

Everything might be scary, it might feel like it will never work out, but in Liam's arms I think we can deal with it. I know Lyndsey and Anders will deal with their problems too, we'll help them. Lyndsey might not have meant to marry Anders but she will learn, just like I did, that you become a part of this family whether you want to or not.

It is the best family I could have asked for.

Because it is all mine.

Acknowledgments

There are so many people I want to thank that I could fill another novel trying to fit them all. First, I want to thank Dan O'Brien and everybody at Hera Books for seeing something in me that they believe in. You have lifted me up and supported me in ways I am beyond grateful for. Thank you for giving me a guiding hand through this process and I hope I have done you all proud.

Next my family. You have always believed that I had something to give the world, and even when I doubted it you supported me anyway. My mum, Nicola, for showing me that even when life gets hard there is always a way through the storm, and there is no shame in admitting that sometimes the burdens have gotten too heavy. Thank you for lightening that load.

A special mention to my sister Rachel for being my human spellchecker and forcing me to watch TV from time to time. Each and every member of my family have given me grace when I have been at my worst, and this book is a testament to the patience you have shown me.

To my friends, Beth and Sammy, for standing by my side from cringe poetry and underdeveloped short stories to today. For standing by my side through my diagnosis and giving me room to vent when things got tough. I will be forever grateful for you. Our ten-year-old selves had no idea what was coming, but we have persisted with the support of each other. I am proud to call you both my friends.

To young me who doubted herself. You are stronger than you ever give yourself credit for. Dropping out of A level English will not ruin your life. Dropping out of university will not ruin your life. You needed to do what was best to keep you alive, and because of those tough decisions we get to stand here today proud of ourselves. A god damn author!

Finally, to the reader. Thank you for being here at my debut novel! I could never fully articulate how thankful I am for your support. Without readers there are no writers. So, this is for you.